MEGGE

of

BURY DOWN

THE GODDESS TRILOGY
Published by Rowan Moon

BOOK ONE: MEGGE OF BURY DOWN

BOOK TWO: THE LADY OF THE CLIFFS

BOOK THREE: THE SISTERS OF THE SORROWS COVE

MEGGE *of* BURY DOWN

The Bury Down Chronicles, Book One

REBECCA KIGHTLINGER

ROWAN MOON

Enhanced Edition © 2020

MEGGE OF BURY DOWN
Enhanced Edition © 2020 by Rebecca Kightlinger

Cover art and book design by Tamian Wood www.BeyondDesignInternational.com

First published in 2018 by Zumaya Publications, Austin, TX
Audiobook by Audible.com | Narrator: Jan Cramer
Second Edition (Enhanced: new cover art and supplementary material) published in 2020 by
ROWAN MOON LLC
Meadville, Pennsylvania, 16335

Printed in the United States of America

ISBN 978-1-7343168-0-3 (Soft cover)
ISBN 978-1-7343168-1-0 (E-book)
ASIN B07K7X6V2H (Audiobook)
Library of Congress Cataloging-in-Publication Data
Names: Kightlinger, Rebecca, 1957 –
Title: Megge of Bury Down
Identifier: LCCN 2019919401
Subjects:
FIC043000 FICTION | Coming of Age
YAFIC011000 YOUNG ADULT FICTION | Coming of Age
FIC008000 FICTION | Sagas
FIC014020 FICTION | Historical | Medieval
FIC061000 FICTION | Magical Realism

LC record available at https://lccn.loc.gov/2019919401

Permissions:
"Imbolc" is excerpted from "Imbolc Dance," *Spells: New and Selected Poems* by Annie Finch and used with permission. (Wesleyan University Press, 2013)

Map of Cornwall is used with permission from http://fromoldbooks.org/ GroseAntiquities/pages/Grose-map-cornwall/2340x1899-q80.html

To the Tamblyns of Botelet

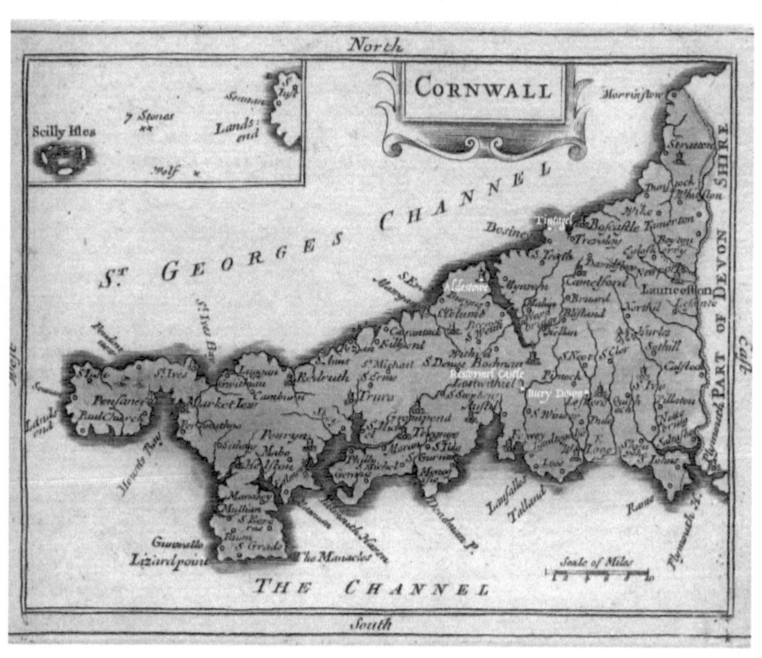

North
CORNWALL
Morrinflow
Scilly Isles
7 Stones
Seaunac
S. Tuft
Lands end
Wolf
Stratton
ST. GEORGES CHANNEL
Bosinee
Tintagel
Boscastle Kanerton
Trevalga
Wike
S. Teath
Newport
Launceston
Aldestowe
Mynny
Camelford
S. Columb
Brasant
Northil
Carantack
Kilkent
S. Weith
Wishia
Bodmin
Hurly
Anus
S. Michael
S. Denys
S. Clev
Sthill
Luggan
Redruth
S. Erme
Reswnel Castle
Pennock
S. Ives
Gwitham
Cambron
Truru
Lostwithiel
Bury Down
Tillaton
Penfance
Market Iew
Grenippord
Austol
S. Winnov
Paul Church
Pouryn
Morval
Trigony
Fowey
W. Looe
E. Looe
Sithny
Mabe
Philly
S. Michael
Helston
Genvin
Money
Longfallos
Tallant
Rame
Marazy
Mullan
S. Keans
Gunwallo
S. Grado
Lizard point
The Manacles
Scale of Miles
THE CHANNEL
South
West
East
PART OF DEVON SHIRE
Lands end
Mounts Bay

Story Locations

Aldestowe (Ăld´-stow)
> Also Aldstow: medieval name for the village of Padstow
> Situated on the estuary of the River Camel

Bury Down
> Iron Age hillfort located near Lanreath, Cornwall
> Bury: derived from burh, "a fortified place"
> Down (also don): dun or hill

Lostwithiel (Lost-with´-eel)
> Seat of governance of medieval Cornwall

Restormel Castle (Res-tor´-mel)
> Located in Lostwithiel, Cornwall

River Fowey (Foy)
> Arises on Bodmin Moor, on or near Brown Willy (The Hill of Swallows)
> Flows south to the harbor town of Fowey

Tintagel (Tin-tă´-jel)
> Village on Cornwall's north coast

IMBOLC

From the east she has gathered like wishes.
She has woven a night into dawn.

~ Annie Finch

Scientia nupta sapientia potestas est.
Knowledge wedded to wisdom is power.

PROLOGUE

KERNOW, BRITAIN
372 CE

Anwen steps into the lee of the hillfort wall, and the ripping winds go still. In the sudden quiet, she hears the thud of picks and the ring of shovels. But it's too late in the year to till, she thinks. Too hot, too dry to plant. What can they hope to reap from this parched ground?

"What one plants at daybreak," comes a cracking voice from deep in the shadows, "another harvests after dark."

Anwen swings her bow into position, nocks an arrow, and takes aim. When her vision becomes accustomed to the gloom, she sees a grey-haired little lump of a woman tilt her head and look up from her fire with her one good eye.

"Sit, Anwen." The woman pats the log she's sitting on. "I'm called Murga. And we've little time."

She knows that voice. Lowering her weapon, she draws nearer. Murga nods, and Anwen sits down beside her.

The seer takes Anwen's hand and rubs her thumb over fingertips as black and calloused as her own.

"A hunter," she muses with a glance at the bow. "Yet your inkstains and calluses tell me you etch." She fixes that eye on Anwen. "You'll do."

Anwen looks around, studying Murga's roundhouse with its roost, its grove, and its plot for growing herbs. It has fared no better than the others she has seen; the roost is silent, the ground a mosaic.

I could have stayed on the cliffs to the west, she thinks, *where the sea breeze still brings rain.*

But her dreams had called her to Murga and guided her on her journey to this dying place.

A young woman holding a bundle in her arms hails Murga from across the barren fields. Murga nods to her and beckons.

"There is hunger here," she whispers to Anwen, who already knows of the hunger. Everyone knows of the hunger in this blighted place outsiders now call Bury Down.

Murga looks over her shoulder and calls, "Bryluen!"

Cheeks flushed, a girl child emerges from the roundhouse carrying a square oak plank, its edges rounded with age and wear. With a nod, Murga takes it and jerks her head toward the door. Bryluen runs back inside the house, and Murga places the board in Anwen's lap.

"This was passed to me from a mystic called by a dream." Carved into the wood are the symbols and images Anwen has seen in her own dreams.

Bryluen returns with a tanned hide and lays it in the seer's arms.

"The meanings of the symbols are etched in this." Murga places the stiff hide on the board, then takes Anwen's hand and lays it on top. "These writings call forth the power to return to the living world." Murga's eye goes to the arrows filling Anwen's quiver. "And I've but this child to guard them when I'm gone."

Now Anwen knows why she's here.

A sound like the mewling of a cat causes Anwen and Murga to look up. The young woman from across the field stands near the fire. All bones and points, she cradles in her arms a blue-hued babe too weak to muster a proper cry. Bending close to Murga, she whispers in the seer's ear.

Murga nods as she listens and then murmurs to Anwen, "Etch what you see here today."

She gets to her feet and takes the elbow of the wasted young mother whose babe won't see another dawn.

"Come, child." Murga leads her to the grain bin and lifts the heavy lid; she scoops out a heaping cup and puts it in the young woman's hand.

Movement from across the hillfort catches Anwen's eye as a leather-aproned colossus comes out of the smithy and strides toward the seer's hut, a sledge hammer swinging from his hand. Anwen looks to see if Murga has noticed, but the seer is steadying the hand of the young mother, for she is spilling her grain.

The blacksmith stops at the young mother's back. He looks first into Murga's face and then into the dusky face of the slack-mouthed babe, and he smiles. Leaning forward, he whispers into Murga's ear. She turns her head and spits in his face.

The smith shouts, and villagers come from the direction of the burial grounds with shovels and picks. Pushing past Anwen, they circle the blacksmith and Murga, then drop their tools and take up a chant.

"Witch. Murderer."

Anwen hands Bryluen the plank and the hide then points to the grain bin.

"Take them, Bryluen. Hurry. Hide them in the grain. Then run."

She reaches for an arrow and nocks it while searching the crowd for the blacksmith. When he breaks from the mob, his long strides closing the distance between them, Anwen shuts one eye and draws back her arrow.

"Too slow, little girl." Bony fingers grab her elbow and squeeze until the arrow falls from her hand. "You think it's so easy to take down Colluen?"

The man at her side, leathery, with sparse stubble over hollow cheeks, coughs out a laugh and releases Anwen's elbow as the blacksmith wrests the bow from her hand and twists her arm behind her back, bending her wrist until she's sure it will break.

She grits her teeth to keep from screaming.

"The other one." Colluen juts his chin toward the grain bin, where Bryluen, clutching her master's writings to her chest with one hand, struggles to lift the bin's lid with the other. The old man catches her around the waist, carries her to the door of Murga's hut, and sets her down before the towering smith. Snatching the writings from Bryluen's arms, Colluen shoves her and Anwen inside the hut and closes the door.

"Keep them there," the blacksmith says.

Anwen hurls herself against the door, but it does not budge, and the man outside only laughs. Bryluen runs to the other side of the hut, stands on tiptoe, and looks out a window little larger than her head.

"They're taking her away, Anwen." Her voice quavers. "Look."

Anwen nudges her aside, bends down, and looks out.

The villagers have seized Murga. Still chanting "Witch! Murderer!", they drag her to the grove alongside her hut. Two men pin her against a sturdy rowan while others scatter branches and sticks at her feet. A woman comes running with a torch and lights it from the embers in the fire ring outside Murga's hut.

Murga says something, and the crowd goes silent. Her cracking voice repeats the words, but Anwen cannot understand them.

A chant? Anwen frowns. *A spell?*

"She's saying something, Bryluen. Something about . . . the sea? 'Sea and . . .' What is she saying? Listen."

Bryluen cocks her head, and as Murga repeats the words, the child moves her lips along with her, murmuring, "*Scientia nupta sapientia . . . Scientia nupta sapientia . . .*"

"I know those words." Anwen closes her eyes and tries to summon the words Murga had spoken in her dreams. *Knowledge wedded to wisdom. . .* There's more, Anwen is certain. She can hear the cadence, four more beats, but the final words elude her. Still, she knows this tongue. She's heard it spoken by foreign traders and tin streamers.

The language of the Romans.

She looks at Bryluen. "You know Latin?"

Staring into Anwen's eyes, the child nods.

"My master taught me."

"And you know the rest of this chant."

Bryluen tightens her lips and blinks. She's shaking.

Anwen feels the chill wind blowing through the window; but Bryluen is standing alongside the wall, out of the cold. *How much has Murga shown her of what's to come?*

"Murga taught you . . ." Anwen's voice, gentle and slow, coaxes the seer's pupil.

". . . all her secrets." Bryluen exhales slowly, her gaze steady. "She told me I'm meant to teach you—" Bryluen frowns, then lifts her face and sniffs. "I smell smoke, Anwen. My master—" She forces herself between Anwen and the window.

"Stay back." Anwen looks out again and puts up her hand to keep Bryluen from seeing her master at the stake, kindling piled at her feet and a hard-faced woman standing at her side holding a smoking torch.

The crowd parts, and Murga's voice goes silent though her lips continue to move. Colluen approaches carrying beneath his arm the plank and hide that bear Murga's writings. Bending down, he smiles at her and holds them out.

Her chant has saved her. Anwen's hands fly to her throat as Murga struggles to free her arms from the men holding her fast to the rowan.

The blacksmith leans in close to Murga's face.

"To hell with you, Witch." Then he shouts over his shoulder, "Rope."

Chapter 1

Bury Down
November 15, 1275

Mother cast a wary glance back into the cottage, hesitating at the threshold for a long moment before swinging her cape over her shoulders and stalking down the path alone, hens and chicks scattering before her ruthless step.

"Morwen?" I tugged at the old bard's woolen cloak.

Morwen knelt beside me and pulled up my hood, smiling as she tied the strings beneath my chin.

"'Tisn't every day a daughter of Bury Down turns six. Watch close tonight, Megge. Learn from your mother now, child."

We followed the path Mother had taken, and when we reached the pasture, Morwen raised her arm and swept her walking stick in a great arc as if tracing a rainbow over the herder's hill in the distance.

"Look out there, Megge, to the east. To that high, gentle slope. Can you see the sheep grazing, heads down, their white fleece tinted pink with the setting sun?"

That low voice, constant as the hum of bees in the hedges, fixed each step forever in my mind as we climbed the herder's hill. I can hear it even now, though my hair is as white as Morwen's was that day.

"Now, cast your gaze to the summit, child, to Bury Down, once a hillfort of rock and timber, now but a low stone crown set crooked upon a great green head. Can you see the last of the setting sun, blood-red upon that granite ring?"

She fell silent as we climbed, and when we reached the top, she took a deep breath, opened the neck of her cloak, and exhaled into it.

"What are you doing, Morwen?"

"I'm keeping this ember alight." Opening her cloak, she showed me a clay cup that held a chunk of turf. "The wind would blow it out, but without a breath of air it would die." She covered the cup with her cloak and held out her hand. "Come, Megge, we've fallen behind."

Mother, having gone on ahead, was out of my sight, so I held tight to Morwen as the rising breeze became blustery and the sky and the stones went grey. Walking just outside the wide stone ring, we finally came to rocks no higher than Morwen's knee.

"Come, Megge." She helped me step over the wall and, for the first time, into Bury Down circle.

A hillfort, she had said. *Rock and timber.*

But this was no fort. The hilltop was wild, one side covered with grasses laid flat by the constant wind and the other taken up with oaks.

"This, once, was Murga's grove," Morwen whispered, pointing to the copse with her staff. "She was the first of us. The first seer of Bury Down."

I was about to ask why Mother always called it the healer's grove when my eye was caught by a lone rowan standing just outside the grove, all its branches flung to one side as if it were trying to flee, its hands thrust out before it.

"Morwen . . ." I could barely breathe. "This tree . . ."

Morwen glanced at the rowan.

"There's always been a rowan here, Megge. Ever since Murga's day, nearly a thousand years ago. One tree dies, and another springs up to take its place, all its branches blown sideways by the ceaseless wind." She squeezed my hand and led me past the sentry tree and into the oaks. "Come along now, lass, the others are waiting."

Deeper and deeper we trudged until the forest floor, spongy with fallen leaves, began to smell of truffles and rot. Morwen took a deep breath.

"Can you taste the sweet night air? Can you feel the soft earth give beneath your feet?" When the sky had gone dark and the air cold and damp, she squeezed my hand. "Your aunts will have made everything ready. Tell me, Megge, are you very brave?"

I was not. I was dumbstruck with fear. Fear of the dark. Fear of the smell. Fear of that frightful rowan. Even Mother, a healer unafraid of anything at all, had appeared frightened as she prepared to come here.

Why? Why had she stalked off without me? And why had Morwen sent the others—Great-aunt Aleydis, Aunt Claris, and my younger cousin, Brighida—ahead of us to this lonely place? What were they making ready?

Morwen finally stopped walking and pointed to the sky.

"Look above you, child, to the gibbous moon dozing in the oaks. And, now, to your feet, where the fire's been laid."

In the scant moonlight that reached the ground through the skeletal oaks, I could see we were standing in a glade, within a circle of logs. When my eyes had grown used to the dim light, I saw at my feet a fire pit with split logs arranged on the ground like the spokes of a cartwheel. At the wheel's center, atop a deep nest of tinder, lay a stack of kindling. Nearby stood a green branch half again as tall as Morwen, its foot plunged into the ground and its head covered with a tightly bound rag that smelled of rendered fat.

A chill shook me, and I expected Morwen to laugh and say, "Someone's just walked over your grave," as she did whenever anyone shivered. But Morwen had not noticed, bent over as she was, drawing the cup from beneath her cloak.

From somewhere behind me, leaves crackled and twigs snapped. Heart pounding, I moved closer to Morwen and stood behind her until I saw Aunt Claris, my mother's twin sister, step from the woods, one hand clutching a bundle of branches and the other holding Brighida's hand.

Aunt Claris, seeming not to have seen me, called softly to Morwen, "All is ready." She looked around. "And my sister? Where is she?"

"I hear her." Great-aunt Aleydis, coming out of the woods behind Claris, lifted her ax and in one smooth movement pointed with it to a path I had not seen. "She's coming just now."

"Come here, Megge." Aunt Claris's voice was gentle as she laid the branches on the ground and took my hand. Aunt Aleydis propped her axe against a tree trunk and took my other hand. We gathered beside the spokes of firewood, and when we had stilled, Mother walked into the clearing.

She wore over her tunic a gauzy, hooded cape the color of that night's sunset, a crimson garment that covered her from the crown of her head to the heels of her boots. Her eyes steady upon Morwen, who held out the cup containing the ember, Mother pulled the torch from the ground and lowered it to the cup. The rag at the top flared.

Mother handed Morwen the torch then turned her back as Morwen lowered it to the tinder and the firewood burst into flame. Mother did not look into the blaze but stood with her back to it and her arms crossed as Morwen sang tales of wisdom, of courage, of fate—Mother's and mine—and of Mother's sole charge in this life.

When she had finished, Morwen nodded to Mother, who drew back her hood. Though only the side of her face was lit by the flames, I could read both fear and resolve in the muscles bunched at the corner of her jaw.

Mother turned and faced the fire, took a breath, and spoke the words Morwen gave her to say, Celtic words whose meaning I did not know. They left Mother's lips like plumes in the clear night air; and when they had dispersed, Mother knelt before me, took my hands in fingers as cold and damp as old poultices, and squeezed them tight.

"Now, Margaret, it is for you to take up your book."

My book? What was she saying?

"But I have no book, Mother." I looked to Morwen and whispered, "Have I a book, Morwen?"

"Aye, child," Morwen said. "You have."

Mother said no more, but drew that crimson cape about her shoulders and linked arms with Claris. Heads together, murmuring and nodding, they circled to the other side of the fire, where a kettle sat warming. Flames lit their faces from below as they bent to decant mulled wine into four pewter cups, gifts from a grateful earl.

Claris carried a cup to Great-aunt Aleydis and put it into her hand with a smile and a gentle embrace. Aleydis held a sleeping Brighida in an arm still strong despite the years that had grayed her hair and thinned her eyelids—so delicate were they that a fine web of blue showed when she blinked.

She closed her eyes for a moment, took a sip, then sat down on a log as thick as a blacksmith's waist. Laid end-to-end with so many others, it formed one link in the ancient oak-and-rowan ring that encircled that wheel of fire.

Mother put a cup into Morwen's hand and then joined Aleydis and Claris, settling in beneath wool blankets and tanned sheepskin hides to wait for the moon to lose herself to the dawn.

Tiny Aunt Morwen—an elderly cherub, a rheumatic imp—gave me a sip from her cup, then winked and emptied it in one long, gulping draught. She wiped her mouth with the back of her hand, leaned on my shoulder, and lowered herself onto a felled oak on the other side of the fire, away from the others. Drawing me to her and wrapping me in her old wool cloak, she sang a tale of destiny, keeping her voice low as the moon made her leisurely way across the sky.

⁓

I must have fallen asleep, for when Morwen squeezed me, I opened my eyes to the dying fire and the dawn—a single brushstroke of pink. Her voice went low.

"Now 'tis your turn, my Megge."

My turn?

Mother came over from the other side of the ring and helped Morwen up, and together we descended the long, gentle slope, the sky before us still gray, the dawn creeping up our backs.

As we gathered in the cookroom of our thatch-and-shingle cottage, whose window soon would frame the rising sun, Mother's hands began to tremble and her eye to dart, again and again, to her cupboard high overhead.

"Niece," Morwen whispered to Mother, though she was not truly our kinswoman. *Aunt* was simply a term of endearment my great-grandmother Gytha had bestowed upon Morwen for rescuing Mother and Claris when they were newly born. Still, though I knew she was not a great-aunt, like Aleydis, nor even kin, I loved her as if *she* were my mother.

Morwen tipped her head back to look up at Mother and whispered once again, "Niece."

Mother, startled, looked down, and Morwen dropped her gaze to the bare tabletop, knocked on it twice with the knuckle of her forefinger, and raised an eyebrow.

Mother drew from the sideboard a soft, tanned hide. She spread it over the table and smoothed out its folds, the purposeful motion stilling her shaking hands.

"Claris," she said. "The tapers."

Aunt Claris unrolled her soft leather pouch and took out four long, slim candles the cloudy green of the River Fowey a-churn with silt. She lit them from embers that smoldered in the grate and set them into tiny cups carved from rowan.

"Gytha's," Morwen whispered.

The flames faltered and smoked, smelling of tallow and holly. When finally they stood straight and glowing, they revealed Claris's sweet, fair face, her mild grey eyes, her smile for her gentle aunt, and her graceful hand, which beckoned Morwen sit. She drew up Morwen's chair, and the tiny bard sat down with a grunt and pulled me onto her lap whilst Claris laid peeling, silvered logs onto the grate and worked the bellows to bring up the fire. Never before had we burned but peat.

"Morwen?" I whispered.

"'Tis oak, Megge, and rowan. From Murga's grove."

Mother wrapped a warm hide around Morwen and me, and there we huddled, our backs to the hearth, Morwen singing the story of my grandmother Natalje's sixth natal day—the day she first opened *The Book of Time* and became apprenticed to her own mother, the great seer, Gytha—and I shivered, more from excitement than from cold.

Claris squeezed the bellows, blowing new life into the hearth fire. It sparked and snapped, the flames now pixies dancing over walls and floor and about the herbs drying in the racks overhead. Morwen pulled me tight to her soft belly and bosom so my head rested in the scoop of her shoulder as she sang. I reached back and stroked her sparse hair. White as our sheep, it was soft as carded fleece.

Warm now on her lap and soothed by her soft, lilting tune, I closed my eyes. Brighida—younger but already taller than me, lithe rather than pudgy, long of limb rather than squat, golden-haired and grey-eyed like her mother—pulled a chair up beside me and dozed.

Aunt Aleydis came over and knelt beside us, the candlelight shining on silver hair and deep blue eyes, irises ringed with white. She whispered something to Morwen and then stood up, her wiry hair mingling with the crisp herbs and flowers that dangled from above.

Morwen touched Brighida's shoulder, waking her, and Aleydis bent down and whispered in her ear.

"When spring arrives, you, too, shall turn six, Brighida. Learn from your cousin now, child."

"In but a moment," Morwen said, looking at my cousin, "our Megge shall take up *The Book of Seasons*, her mother's ancient book of knowledge of the physical world. And in the spring, you, Brighida, shall take up *The Book of Time*, your mother's great book of celestial wisdom. To one of you . . ." She looked from Brighida to me. ". . . shall pass much more than ever has passed to any other heir to the books.

"For to one of you, the daughters of the twin caulbearers, shall fall the duty to protect the books and to guide them from one life to the next. From one healer, one seer, to the next, each heir inscribing into the book on the last day of life a truth upon which the next will build, each then passing into eternity to serve as an immortal Mentor to those to come.

"And it will be for this chosen one to protect for the Mentors the power that preserves their spirits forever within the books." She paused and glanced at my mother. "To each of your mothers has fallen but one charge in this life—to ensure that her daughter takes up her book."

Morwen whispered now, looking only at me.

"And so, on this morning not yet dawned, this long, cold night in the dark of the year, a girl shall open her mother's great book and speak the words that shall make her a woman of Bury Down and fulfill her—and her mother's—destiny."

But I knew naught of destiny that night. I knew naught of the fears that had set Mother's hands a-tremble—that she would fail, that I would fail her, that we both would fail the Mentors. Nor of her grit—her vow to face flames rather than fail. No, I knew naught of the import of that night. That night, for me, was simply a lark and all that I ever craved—a sleepy, dreamy moment awake with the women and a part of their world.

Morwen pointed. "Megge, look."

Mother was wresting from her high shelf a weighty block as thick as her fist and as long as her arm from elbow to thumb. She carried it to the table and laid it before me with a great blow of dust. Musty and acrid, it smelled of the ages, of old, dead times. And yet, it whispered of mystery, of memory. Of belonging.

My breath quieted as I looked upon its heavy leather bindings, its oak cover deeply etched with symbols that spoke a name I knew was mine. This, once, had been mine. Had long been mine. *And for so long*, it seemed to whisper, *we have been lost to one another*.

I longed to touch it, as once, wandering lost in the woods, I had longed to touch Mother's hand.

I reached for the book.

"Courage, child," Morwen whispered.

I can still see my outstretched hand, poised for a moment over the ancient wood, over dull brass hinges that would fold back upon themselves to reveal the vast knowledge within.

Morwen drew a breath and held it. Mother leaned toward me, urging me with her stare. Aunt Claris drew her daughter near, bowed her head over Brighida's silky hair, and whispered, swaying, forward, back, forward and back.

And then they all whispered sibilant, hypnotic words I seemed to know. "*Scientia nupta sapientia potestas est.*"

My eyes drifted shut, and I could sense the book beneath my hovering fingertips, could taste dry, musty vellum, could see oak-gall ink upon curling parchment, red-berry words upon tanned leaves. I could feel the pulse of each Mentor's life and witness trusting hands etch the ancient symbols known only to the heirs to the books. All would be revealed, every spirit preserved, and Mother's destiny fulfilled, once I spoke my oath and took my place amongst the women of Bury Down, one with the heirs to the books.

Morwen touched my shoulder. My fingertips paused above the beloved book a moment longer and then lay themselves down upon it.

Something within it began to writhe. Something hot, coming to life. It called my name. It drew me in, beckoned me *come*. And then it whispered *Murderer*.

"Morwen!" I tore my fingers from the book and flung myself back into her arms.

"No, Megge!" Mother hurled herself toward me.

Morwen dropped her head to rest on mine and held me close, her lips on my hair, murmuring my name.

"There, there, Megge. There, there, little one."

It had lied. The book had lied. It told me it was mine, but it wanted only to steal me. And something fiery writhed within it.

"I won't go!" I looked from Morwen's kind face to Mother's anxious one, her traitor's eyes trying to hold mine. "You can't make me go!"

Mother knelt at my side and took my hand. She tried to draw it back to the book, but I held tight to Morwen. She whispered, "It is your birthright."

I shook my head.

She looked into my eyes. "You'll be one of us."

I buried my face in Morwen's cloak.

Mother slapped her palms on the table.

"All will be lost, Megge. We will have failed the Mentors."

I clenched my fists and hid them beneath my chin. Never again would I touch the accursed *Book of Seasons*.

Chapter 2

MAY 1, 1280

I woke early on Brighida's tenth natal day and slid from under the hides without waking her. Pulling a fleece off our pallet, I drew it over me and carried my boots past Morwen and Aleydis, asleep on the pallet next to ours, and Mother and Aunt Claris, asleep on one nearest the door of the cool, deep cave we called "the sleeping lodge."

The hills to the west were black against the bluing sky, but the stars were dark and no moon showed. *Perhaps this year will be different*, I thought. *Perhaps this year, Brighida's natal day will pass as mine always does, unheralded, all of Cornwall hunkered down beneath grey skies.*

I sat down on a rock beside the cave opening to pull on my boots and dropped the hide from my shoulders. The breeze was warm upon my neck. Winter had lost its grip.

"Spring's here, Megge. A beautiful first day of May." Aunt Aleydis leaned out the door and mussed my hair, then called into the lodge, "It's a glorious morning, Brighida. Come, your cousin is already up."

Mother came to the door, her cooking apron already tied over her best tunic, and looked out as she braided her hair. A tiny silver rose dangled from a thin chain around her neck.

"Mother." I pointed to the charm. "Who gave you that rose?"

"The Lady Margaret," Mother said as she wound the thick braid around her head and fastened her cap over it. "She's finally conceived. When she came to us in the grove last night, she brought one rose for each of her healers. Now, we must to see to it she doesn't lose this child." She threw her cloak over her shoulders and tied it at the neck. "Come, Claris," she called over her shoulder. "Work to do."

Aunt Claris, her plain tunic covered with an apron embroidered with vines and studded with colorful seeds and pods strung on fine wool thread, picked up her vial of scented water. She sprinkled a few drops onto her brush and drew it through her hair in strokes so long they stretched her arm all the way out. When she had finished, she fished two thin braids from beneath her hair and untangled them from the chain holding a delicate silver rose that matched Mother's. She crossed the braids over her head and tied them together behind her neck, leaving her hair loose and the rose in full view at the base of her throat. The village women in their caps and coifs and veils would whisper.

I went back inside. Brighida, awake now and shining with excitement, was holding her new white wool tunic before her. This one, with saffron-dyed lacings up the bodice, would cover her ankles as her old one no longer did. She slipped it over her head and pulled her necklace out, so her own silver rose showed. Then she stepped into new shoes. Even her feet had grown over the winter; and today she wore soft, low shoes, once her mother's, the handy Aleydis had cut down and cobbled to fit.

My old boots, though snug, still fit me, even after the long winter. And my dress, a yellowed wool tunic with no lacings front or back, a child's gown that nearly covered my ankles but not my boots, "would do for now," Mother had said.

"Come along quickly now." Aunt Claris kissed Brighida's forehead. "Lovely." And she slipped out the door behind Mother.

Aunt Aleydis, holding out my old dress, admired my cousin.

"Getting so tall."

I took the dress from her and pulled it over my head, then began to brush my hair as Morwen snugged Brighida's bodice lacings and tied the sash at the back of her dress.

"There." She patted Brighida's shoulder and sent her off to comb her silken hair. Taking the brush from my hand, she took a good look at me—at coarse brown hair she always had to fight to untangle, unlike Brighida's, which always lay smooth and neat. Even in the morning, Brighida's part ran straight down the middle while mine wandered over my scalp like an old country road.

Morwen gathered and combed my hair, having to work so hard at the snarls my eyes watered. Soon, my nose was running, and the tears I had been holding back all morning dripped onto the front of my dress.

"What's this now? Tears on such a festive day?" Morwen lifted my hair and her fingers closed on a wad of matted hair at the nape of my neck. "Oh, this'll take some time. Close your eyes, child, and I'll spin you a tale while I work."

"But Mother bade us hurry."

"Nonsense, Megge. Close your eyes now. There's always time for a tale."

I closed my eyes and waited for the bard's voice to take me away from this hyacinth-scented chamber where my cousin preened.

"Very well, then." Her voice went low . . .

Look out before you, Megge—out over the sea to the very edge of the world and a time long past. Can you see the sun glowing red and setting the sky aflame? Watch closely as that red, red ball falls toward the sea. Can you see it? Keep watching. Lower, lower, and . . . there.

Two masts. Two tall masts have pierced the horizon, their sails crimson with the setting sun.

On that evening, long ago, your own great-grandmother Gytha, regal, with the face of a goddess, faced the wind and the setting sun, her daughter Natalje in her arms and her serving girl at her side.

Gytha's young servant, the daughter of a traveling bard, had once stumbled, lost and hungry, upon the doorstep of Gytha's cottage. There she stayed with the seer, singing to her, serving her, and learning by heart the tales of Gytha's people—the healers and seers of Bury Down, the heirs to *The Book of Time*. Now, standing upon the quay, Gytha and her serving girl raised a hand to shade their eyes as they watched *The Navigator*, a great seagoing vessel, divide the setting sun and cut through the choppy green waters of the River Fowey to draw up alongside the quay at Lostwithiel.

When his ship had landed, Captain Adaem of Aldestowe, a giant of a man with hair yellow as the sun, a face as smooth as moonstone, and eyes as blue as the wide Welsh sky I was born under, strode onto the deck. Still exhilarated by the winds and the treacherous seas, he boomed, as though through a gale, "Lower the plank!"

And, slam! Down came the ship's plank. Adaem stormed down that creaking wooden bridge and onto the quay in three long strides. He drew his wife to him, and Gytha accepted a kiss that must have tasted of the sea.

"The lands to the east are splendid, wife!" He scooped the child out of Gytha's arms and tossed her into the air until the sky rang with her laughter. "They must be seen, daughter! And one day, Natalje, I shall show them to you. I shall show you the world!" That great mountain swung the laughing child around in a circle. "The world, Natalje!"

Gytha—seer, wisewoman, some said sorceress—reached out a hand, and as she took her husband's arm beheld a vision of Adaem racing the wind in search of the woman their Natalje would one day become.

The family returned to the great round fortress where they served the Earl of Cornwall—Gytha his counselor and Adaem his explorer—and there they stayed until the days grew cold, for Adaem sailed in the warm of the year, his ship at the service of the earl. But the dark months belonged to Gytha, so when the days grew short they returned to her ancestral home, the ancient tract of hallowed land that lay in the shadow of the ringed stones of Bury Down.

Through the dark months they lived in peace and happiness, raising Natalje. As the winds and rains raged against the cottage, Adaem taught Natalje the stars that made up the constellations of the winter sky.

"Capella. Castor. Aldebaran, the eye of Taurus. Sirius, the Dog Star of Canis Major," he said pointing into the night.

But when the breezes warmed and the seas had thawed, *The Navigator* departed upon the spring tide, Adaem at its helm.

"Wife!" he shouted over the rising wind. "Perseus!"

Gytha smiled and waved, knowing she would teach Natalje of Perseus and Aquila, of runes and symbols. She would teach their daughter the seer's arts. For that night Natalje would turn six.

In a quiet cottage warmed by peat, with tapers aglow and her servant at her side, Gytha spoke her oath and placed before Natalje an ancient tome.

"Open it, daughter," she said.

Natalje ran her fingers over tough, tanned hide and then opened the book. Then, like all who had come before and had left their mark in *The Book of Time*, she spoke her oath and became one of the seers of Bury Down.

Morwen tugged on the long braid that now lay on my back. "There."

"*The Book of Time* didn't burn Natalje's fingers?" I asked as she settled a stiff cap on my head.

She stepped back and looked at me. "Burn her fingers? No, lass. *The Book of Time* didn't burn Natalje."

"And it didn't burn Brighida when it passed to her." It wasn't fair. "Why, then, did Mother's book burn me?"

"'Twasn't *The Book of Seasons* that burned you, child."

"Then what *did* burn me?"

"I can't say, Megge. 'Twas a long time ago, now, wasn't it? It's all over." She lifted my hands and touched my fingertips to her lips.

I whispered into her ear, "Must we go to the village today, Morwen?" I held my breath as I waited for the answer.

Morwen stepped back and tilted her head.

"Why, to be sure we'll go. Whyever wouldn't we?"

Brighida whirled around.

"Not go? Whyever wouldn't we, Megge?"

I blew out my breath. Taking up my herding stick, I ran from the lodge toward the cottage, going straight up the hill and across the field. Glancing behind me, I saw Brighida close on my heels.

Across the wet field we raced, I in my boots and Brighida in her slippers; and because she was careful to stay out of puddles, I touched the door first. I leaned on it as I caught my breath, studying the milky pink sky behind Bury Down.

When my breathing had slowed, we went inside and sat down at the table. Aunt Claris set before each of us a bowl of porridge and placed a ball of hard cheese in the center of the table. She poured cold ale into tin mugs and set them alongside our bowls. Morwen and Aleydis arrived a few minutes later, took out their knives, sliced the cheese, and broke their fast with us.

"Your mother is tending the sheep." Claris laid a slender hand on my shoulder. "As soon as she returns, we will set out. Hurry, now. We want to be ready." She kissed Brighida on the head and smoothed her hair back from her brow. "Lovely," she said, tucking fine, pale tendrils up under her cap.

A glorious day, Brighida. Why, to be sure we must attend. A lovely day. Such a lovely girl. And it's her natal day. We must all celebrate Brighida's natal day. Whyever wouldn't we? Whyever wouldn't we, Megge?

I got up as soon as I had finished eating and went outside to gather eggs and rake the chicken yard. When I was through, I scooped a handful of grain from the barrel, relishing the feel of the grains passing between my fingers, and scattered it on the ground for the chickens.

"And there'll be dancing and singing and feasting," Morwen was saying as I came back inside. She picked up our bowls and took them out to the well to wash them.

"And a procession," Brighida said as she swept the floor.

Claris wiped out the pot while Brighida swept the old rushes out the door. Aleydis was scattering fresh ones when Mother came in smelling of the sheep pen.

"A shame we can't put them out to graze on a day like this." Mother took off her cloak and hung it on the peg. "I won't need this today."

"I'll stay and tend them," Aunt Aleydis said. "It's a fine day, too, for game."

I ran to her. "I'll stay with Aunt Aleydis."

"It's but one day." Claris touched Aleydis's spotted hand. "Come." Then she squeezed my hand. "You, too."

"And who's to say we wouldn't?" Morwen set the clean bowls on the sideboard, dried her hands, and picked up her stick.

Mother turned to Claris and raised her voice, putting an end to the argument.

"I've just spoken with the sickly young bride who came to us in the grove last week. It seems the spearmint I gave her hasn't stopped her vomiting."

Claris nodded, her eyes closed.

"No, I feared it would not. Spearmint calms the stomach, but she needs lavender as well, for lavender calms the mind and will assuage her fears."

"What fear has she, Mother?" Brighida asked.

"Her husband has gone off with the earl's men, and she fears he will not return," Claris said. "Many do not, it's true." Reaching to take down a bunch of lavender from the drying racks, she snapped off the tops, wrapped them in a piece of cloth, and handed the little bundle to Mother. "Tell her to steep a palmful in hot water with plenty of honey. If she drinks one cup this morning and one before the moon reaches her zenith tonight, the sickness will ease, as will her fear."

"A palmful. How much water?" Mother frowned.

"Let me go to her, Sister. She's in the grove?"

"No, she's out at the pen. She was waiting for me when I got there. Hadn't slept all night."

Brighida followed her mother to the door.

"Might we offer to make a healing image for her if she doesn't soon feel better?"

"What metal would we use?" Claris asked, now master to pupil.

"Tin, for courage," Brighida recited by heart from her mother's great book, "creating the image when the moon is in the tenth house, Venus ascending."

Claris stopped walking. "And Mercury?"

"Not asking the malefics," I called out from the cookroom.

Claris, eyes wide, turned to me. "Megge?"

"Is that right?" I did not know what the words meant but had heard them over and over as Brighida took her lessons.

"You have been listening." Claris smiled at Mother. "You see, Sister?"

Mother snorted.

"*Aspecting*," Brighida said. "Not *asking*. It means *looking toward*, or *facing*. And it—"

"Pride, Brighida." Claris held up a finger, and Brighida said no more. Smiling at me, she took Brighida's arm, and together they crossed the field toward the pen.

Morwen looked up at me and winked.

Mother, Aunt Aleydis, Morwen, and I set out across the pasture at Morwen's pace, each of the women carrying a jug of Morwen's mead. We joined Claris and Brighida behind the sheep pen, near the woods. Claris took Morwen's jug, and I walked behind them, watching the sun dapple all those white caps. Claris's unbound hair, though, seemed to catch that light and throw it all about her so she appeared an apparition. It was no wonder the church women whispered.

At the edge of the pasture, we crossed the footbridge over Fowey Creek, and I spotted on the bank a small green turtle someone could have stepped on. When I picked it up, it pulled its head into its shell. I tried to look inside, but when I brought it to my face, I sneezed hard. I lifted my arm to wipe my nose, and—

"Margaret!" Mother hollered and gave me a look that made me drop the turtle. It rolled down the front of my dress leaving a trail of muck. When Mother turned away, I wiped my nose with the back of my hand and brushed the dirt off my dress, smearing what had been a fine line into a wide green-and-black blur.

The path took us to a field of rye, and we skirted it, walking along the curving hedge that separated it from a field of oats. Just around the bend something big rooted around in the leaves.

"Boar," Mother said. "They have young right now. Stay close."

A squirrel skittered past, and I jumped. Claris took Brighida's hand. Mother put her hand in her pocket.

"Just stay on the path and you'll be fine."

We crossed into the priory fields, and Morwen bent to smell the blooms on a honeysuckle hedge.

"Careful, Morwen." I pulled her back. "It's full of bees." In and out of the hedge they went, hovering close, moving from flower to flower.

"And where do you think all the honey comes from that I use to make my mead? The good brothers have beehives just over there." She pointed to a distant field just as the tower bell sounded.

"The tolling for morning prayers." Morwen nodded toward the monks laying down their rakes and shovels and bowing their heads. "Respect, girls," she said.

We slowed as we passed the monks, then hurried past the church Morwen insisted we attend on the great feast days.

"And you'll tithe," she always reminded us. "'Twas Gytha's command. 'Though we're not of them, we dwell amongst them, and we serve them. We shall abide by their rules, even as we live by our own.' Just be thankful for these monks, girls, that they're not zealots like the friars in the abbey."

I shuddered as we neared the church's grey stone walls. The high bell tower. The wide stone steps three old women always stared and whispered from.

But today the church was empty, and the road was crowded with villagers. Hanging from each doorway were brightly colored banners embroidered with pictures of shoes, cloth, candles, and loaves of bread. Merchants and their wives called out their wares. We crossed the busy road and, passing all the shops, made our way to the green. People streamed past us in pairs and groups, the girls dancing and the boys kicking each other.

"We will be near the cooking fires. Are you listening, Margaret?" Mother put my hand into Morwen's and took Aleydis's jug of mead. "Be good, wise girls and mind your aunts." She squinted at me. Setting down her jugs, she spat on her thumb and scrubbed my cheek. Then she took a square of cloth from her apron pocket and put it in my hand. "Blow your nose," she said. "With the cloth." She noticed the black smudge on my dress and shook her head. "Ruined."

She walked away to the fires with Claris, shaking her head.

"Can this truly be my daughter?"

The breath left me.

Chapter 3

I walked backwards, watching Mother walk away with Aunt Claris. I could almost see her lips pull themselves in tight at the corners. After a moment, Morwen gave my hand another gentle squeeze.

I turned around and finally noticed that the village green, a wide, emerald meadow, had been transformed into a faerie land of flowers and ribbons. Girls dressed in white summer shifts filled the gazebo. Others danced over Fowey Creek's tidy crossing stones then stepped barefoot through the grass. The lawn was dotted with still more village girls—girls with embroidered sashes and colorful laces—picking delicate stems of stitchwort, charlock, buttercup, and lady's smock that they wove into wreaths and set upon each other's hair.

Brighida ran to the gazebo and stroked one of the ribbons.

"Vivienne," a high voice called from within.

Vivienne Penneck, who lived on a farm not far from ours but who never spoke to us, had grown up over the long winter, just as Brighida had. Lovely in her white smock and blue sash, she looked up from the bluebell posy she was tying onto her wrist and caught the eye of the girl who had called her name. The girl inside the gazebo pointed her finger at Brighida, and Vivienne looked over at my cousin. Smiling, she whispered something to the other girls on the lawn. They all swarmed Brighida.

They were going to put her out! I raised my stick and was just about to run at them when they took her hands, led her into the square, and laid a wreath on her head. A piper, resplendent in purple, lifted his flute. When he began to play, all the girls joined hands and skipped with my cousin around the maypole, a tree trunk that had no branches but was festooned with embroidered streamers.

My breastbone pricked each time Brighida skipped past me. She held out her hand to me, but I folded my arms over my chest. None of those village girls—those daughters of merchants, with their posies and their blue sashes and their soft slippers—none of them wanted me, in my ankle-high boots and dirty dress, to dance with them.

I huddled at the edge of the gazebo, my heart as tough as a chicken gizzard. Then the piper announced his final tune, and Vivienne ran to me.

"Come dance," she said and took my hand.

Now that I was so close to her, I noticed her golden hair and grey eyes. Why, she looked so like Brighida, they might have been sisters!

When the tune ended, all the girls scattered to the feast tables. Daisy garlands hung from the trestle tables on which village women were setting out wide bowls heaped with cakes. Children dipped dirty fingers into clay jars decorated with flowers and filled with butter and preserves. Leather-aproned men turned spits and heaped roasted venison and boar onto platters as long as their arms. The aroma of meat and dripping fat made my stomach grind.

One of the men sliced a piece of charred meat and held it out on the end of a fork. I took it from him, savoring the greasy, salty flavor.

"What is this?"

"Boar," he said.

Boar. I had never tasted it before. Who knew it would taste so good?

At a table alongside the spits, Mother set out pitchers of ale, and Claris poured mead into cups. One of the aproned men walked over from his spit and reached for the cup Claris was filling. His hand joined hers on the cup as he spoke to her; and for a moment, I could not tear my gaze from those two hands. *This means something*, I thought, although I knew not what.

"Megge," Brighida called. "Megge, look out!"

A tumbler careened toward me, walking on his hands with a bowl of fruit balanced atop bent knees. He kicked his legs straight up, tossing his bowl high into the air, then flipped onto his feet, colliding with me and sending fruit flying and rolling on the ground.

Vivienne ran to me. "Are you hurt?"

I shook my head and bent to pick up the fruit.

Vivienne and Brighida helped me, and when the tumbler had gone on his way, Vivienne smiled at my cousin.

"Come, Brighida, it's almost time!"

"Time?" she asked, "For what?"

"For the procession!" Vivienne took her arm. Laughing and skipping, they joined all the other girls in the white dresses, who seemed to be forming a line. Brighida looked back at me, but I ran to the edge of the square, where the festival musicians were tuning their instruments, and huddled against a fence post. Aleydis found me there a moment later. She bent down and leaned her head so close to mine that her wiry hair tickled my cheek.

"Let us go somewhere quieter, Megge, where we can sit and listen awhile."

We wound around the press of merrymakers and climbed to the top of a hillock.

"You see those flat little drums they're tapping?" Aleydis pointed. "Why, when I was a little girl in Aldestowe, my father—"

"What makes Brighida so special, Aunt?" I had to know. "Why does no one lead *me* into the dance?" I waved my arm before us. "Why do all the girls make merry for Brighida?"

Aunt Aleydis, stroking her throat, folding and smoothing her wattle, looked into the sky. After a moment, she frowned. Her hand paused.

"Megge, are you jealous because Brighida is favored on her natal day?"

It all rushed out. "Everybody loves her *every* day. Everyone thinks Brighida is special, especially today."

I wiped my tears with the hem of my dress. I had had only one special natal day, and it had ended in seared fingertips and tears. The day Brighida turned six had finished with rejoicing, with her becoming her mother's true apprentice and being called a woman of Bury Down. And now, this.

Aleydis leaned close to me, speaking each word with great care.

"Megge, surely you know that today is May Day. The village is celebrating the coming of summer. The new life it brings. They do this every year. We have simply never come to the May Day Fair before." She brushed back my hair. "People everywhere celebrate the First of May. It just happens that Brighida was born on this day."

"But no one ever celebrates *my* natal day, Aunt. No one even speaks of it. I know only that it comes in the dead of winter."

"Don't be silly, Margaret. We always celebrate the sixteenth of November. Why, Morwen even takes you to church every year on that day. It's the feast day of St. Margaret. But you were named for another Margaret—Earl Edmund's wife, *Lady* Margaret." She looked around and lowered her voice. "And for a great seer—"

"Aleydis!" Morwen shouted from the hill, interrupting her. Then she held out a hand to me. "Megge. Come, lass, and give me your hand."

I ran to help her. When I reached her, she handed me her cup of ale—nearly empty—and slipped an arm over my shoulder, rubbing a cheek as soft as pudding against mine. She dropped her stick next to Aleydis, gave Aleydis a frown, and lowered herself to the grass with a grunt.

Aleydis looked away and pointed to a flock of girls gathered at the center of the green, crowning an older girl with a daisy wreath bedecked with white and yellow streamers. A pretty young woman was helping the younger girls line up two-by-two behind her.

"Look there, Megge." Aleydis said, "Can you see what the children are doing?"

"Why, that's our Brighida!" Morwen waved and pointed to my cousin. "Right behind the Queen of the May! Oh, I hope your mothers can see her." She squinted and looked closer. "And look who's helping the girls, Aleydis. It's Jenifer Penneck!" She nudged Aleydis and pointed, lowering her voice. "Do you see the girl standing next to Brighida?"

"The girl in the blue sash?" Aleydis squinted.

Morwen dropped her voice. "Aye. That's Jenifer's daughter. The very one—"

"The one who could be Brighida's twin sister?" I jumped up and pointed, too.

"That's nonsense, Megge." Aleydis said. She reached over and pulled Morwen's hand down. "Hush now, Morwen."

At the foot of the hill, standing between the tables and the spits, Claris clapped her hands and tossed flowers into the air as the girls passed, while Mother poured ale into flagons for aproned men, who seized them the moment they were full. Aleydis offered me a sip from her mug and pulled me closer to her.

The wreathed girls paraded onto the green, led by their queen. Just behind her, Brighida took careful steps over grass flattened by hooves and steaming with manure. The girls must have released her plaits, for her hair hung in golden ripples down her back, just like her mother's. As the parade passed below, she looked for us. Before I could stop myself, I jumped up and waved. She did not see me, but Aleydis patted my other hand.

Behind the royal retinue, a girl my size rode atop a dappled horse the size of a bullock, its mane and tail plaited with ribbons and field flowers. Behind her, a man in a crimson cape flicked a whip over the hindquarters of a chained bear, spurring the beast into pawing, roaring pirouettes. When he had passed, boys raced each other into the square, set up targets, and competed at marksmanship with

longbows and spinning axes. When they were through, men cor-
ralled sheep into makeshift enclosures and sheared them so fast the
fleece appeared to simply fall off.

I tugged on Morwen's sleeve.

"That's what *I* want to do."

My hands had been too clumsy and the shears too large the summer
before, and Morwen had told me I was too young.

"Can I shear this year? You promised."

Morwen held her hand up to mine.

"They're nearly the same size," I said.

"Aye. They might do." She squeezed mine.

I looked at her closely. She was short and squat, like me. Her hands
were small, like mine. Studying her, I thought of Brighida's lithe form and
long fingers—so like our mothers'—and I heard again the words I
could not stop hearing.

Can this truly be my daughter?

Wreath gone but tiny white petals still clinging to her hair,
Brighida ran up the hill calling, "Come, Megge, they're about to
begin the egg dance."

She held out her hand. I took it and ran with her down the hill to
the green, where the girls were dancing barefoot in the grass. Brighida
slipped off her shoes, and I sat down and took off my boots. When I got
up, Vivienne took one of my hands and one of Brighida's and brought
us into the circle. Laughing and singing, we stepped lightly, careful
not to break any of the eggs hidden in the grass.

When the tune ended, Vivienne called out, "Another!"

But before the piper could begin, a grey-haired woman in a heavy
black dress broke the circle and yanked Vivienne's hand from Brighida's.
She pulled Vivienne away by the arm and bent down to speak into
her ear.

"You're hurting me!" Vivienne tried to pull away, but the old
woman hung on, pinching her arm and growling into her ear. Although
she was chastising Vivienne, she stared at Brighida and me.

She finished her tirade with words that made Vivienne gasp. Vivienne came back to the dance circle, but she walked past Brighida and me without a word or a look and took the hands of two other girls. The piper raised his flute, and the egg dance resumed. I looked for the woman who had pinched Vivienne's arm, but she was gone.

Chapter 4

"Girls, are you ready to go home?" Morwen pointed toward the road. "Mister Trelawney has his cart and is going past the cottage." She lowered her voice. "His cart's nearly full of his pots and jars, but he's offered to carry Aleydis and me home, and I believe there's room for the two of you."

I looked back at the trestle tables, where Mother and Claris were still at work.

"Can we stay and walk home with Mother and Aunt Claris?" I was still thinking about that boar meat and all those cakes.

Aleydis raised an arm and waved to catch Mother's and Claris's attention. Claris waved back and then motioned for Brighida and me to come over. She pointed to a brightly painted wagon that had just drawn up alongside the feast tables. Minstrels were jumping out of the back and straightening their long, wide sleeves. As they strolled among the tables, they pulled flutes from their sacks and blew high, clear notes into a sky already ringing with shouts and whistles. Brighida and I raced to the wagon and joined in the singing and feasting.

We were still singing "Sumer Is Icumin In" as we entered the churchyard on the way home. I lifted my face to sing out the last few words, and a flash of white in the cloudless blue sky caught my eye. Brighida, Claris, and Mother kept walking past the tilted old headstones on their way to the monks' orchard, but I stood transfixed. A gull gliding in from the river circled the bell tower, its belly and wings aglow in the late-afternoon sun, and landed on a ledge just above the church window. I searched for a nest, but could see none.

Stepping closer, my eyes still fastened on the high ledge, I tripped in the bushes alongside the church and landed on something soft. It moaned.

I jumped up as if struck by lightning and rolled off a woman lying in the weeds, her face to the stone wall, a pool of blood forming around her skirts. I would have screamed, but my throat had slammed shut.

I heard Brighida's and Mother's voices coming from the rear of the churchyard. They were nearly at the fence that separated the cemetery from the priory's orchard. I started to run to them but stopped after a few steps and turned back to the woman lying on the ground. How could I leave her? She would die.

I bent down to see if she was breathing and realized it was Mother's sweet friend, Dora Tucker, the weaver's wife.

"Mother!" I ran as fast as I could and finally caught sight of Mother searching for me, one hand on the latch of the churchyard gate, clearly vexed.

"Margaret," she said. "Where did you go?"

I grabbed her sleeve, unable to speak for lack of breath.

Mother glowered at me, but Claris encouraged me with a smile. "What is it, niece?"

"It's Mistress Tucker," I managed to say. "I think she's dying."

I ran back to the church, looking behind me once to make sure they were coming. Aunt Claris held Brighida's hand, and the three of them, skirts hitched up to their knees, were right behind me.

"There." I pointed. "She's bleeding. She's going to die."

"Hush, Margaret." Mother knelt and lifted Dora's shredded skirt. Feet, ankles, and calves—such white skin—covered with blood. Mother lifted the skirt higher. The back of Mistress Tucker's left thigh was ripped open, blood pumping from a long, jagged tear.

"She's been gored." Mother began to pull grass and bits of cloth out of the wound. "Brighida, watch for a boar. It might still be close by. Megge, get my pouch."

I ran behind her and untied the leather thong that held her pouch beneath her apron. As long as my forearm, it had enough pockets to hold all her healer's instruments. She pulled it free, unrolled it, and took out a long white cloth.

Mistress Tucker moaned and rolled onto her stomach.

"Good," Mother said. "Claris, pick up that leg."

Claris lifted the stout leg a few inches so it was out of the pool of blood. Brighida and I helped by holding the torn, bloody skirt away from the gash. Mother reached under from the far side, grasped the cloth and slipped it beneath Mistress Tucker's leg, and pulled the ends up and over, twisting them tight.

"Set it down. Carefully, now . . . Wait a minute." Her eye settled on me. "Your apron."

I tore it off, and she spread it on the ground over the blood. "Now."

Claris lowered Mistress Tucker's leg onto my apron.

"My stick," Mother said to Brighida.

Looking confused, Brighida picked up Mother's walking stick. "This?"

"My *stick*. Now!"

I grabbed Mother's pouch, pulled out a smooth, pale-yellow stick as long as my hand and gave it to her. She wrapped the ends of the cloth around it and twisted it so tight the blood stopped flowing. She held it there while her own breathing slowed.

Mistress Tucker began to moan and then to writhe.

"Steady her," Mother said.

"Get it off!" Mistress Tucker thrashed, her voice muffled by the weeds.

I began to cry.

"Stop it, Margaret. A healer does not cry. Take this and hold it."

I held the stick while Mother moved up closer to her friend's head and took her hand.

"It's stopping the blood, Dora. Lie still. It won't be on for long." Without looking up, she said, "Claris, go for her husband."

Claris's apron, so lovely that morning, was now smeared with blood. Her hands were covered with it. She ran along the side of the church, stopping only for a moment at the edge of the road to wait as a cart passed, then ran across the road and pounded on the Tuckers' door.

"Gus!" She pounded harder. "Mister Tucker!"

The door flew open.

"What do you—" Mister Tucker's shout died as his eyes moved from Claris's face to her blood-smeared dress.

Claris grabbed his hand and pulled him to the road, speaking so fast I could understand nothing. She waved toward the church. Mister Tucker slammed his door and ran down the market road.

"I'll get my cart," he shouted.

"And bring help," Claris hollered after him. "A strong man. Get Robert Angwin!" She ran back across the road to the church, shouting to us, "He's coming. He's bringing the cart."

When Claris had caught her breath, she knelt beside Mother.

"After he sees to his customers and collects their money, you mean." Mother spoke through tight lips. "My apron, Megge. Untie it and help me take it off."

I pulled it over her head, knocking off her cap. I tried to put the cap back on over her braids, but she slapped my hands away.

"Never mind that. Here." She took her knife from the pocket of her skirt. "Hold up the edge."

I picked up the apron and held up the hem. She sliced it.

"Tear it in two." She motioned for Brighida to sit down next to Dora's head. "Keep Mistress Tucker talking." She folded the pieces of her apron and laid them over the gash. "Hold this." She put my hands on the cloth. "Gently now." She pressed on the backs of my hands. "Like so. Press."

"Well, will you look at this," Mother said only minutes later. She pointed at a cart carrying Mister Tucker and the enormous Robert Angwin.

"Faster!" A frantic Mister Tucker whipped the galloping horse. The cart bumped and rattled down the narrow path and stopped alongside us. Mister Angwin, the stonemason whose shop was just down the market road, clambered out of the cart and helped Mister Tucker pull a wide plank from the back.

Mister Tucker ran to his wife, bent down so his face was practically in the dirt next to hers, and shouted, "Dora, can you hear me? Turn over so we can pick you up."

"She can't move, Gus. Can't you see she's hurt?" Mother tightened the alder stick. "We have to keep her on her stomach so I can hold this."

The men lifted Mistress Tucker carefully onto the board and slid it into the cart.

"Gently, now," Mother cautioned the men as she climbed in alongside her friend and then pulled me up. Brighida had moved away from us and was picking wild marigolds for a healing infusion while Claris scraped willow bark into her doubled-up apron to brew into a pain-killing tea.

Mother slowly released the stick again.

"Almost done," she told me. "Just press down for another moment."

Mistress Tucker moaned, but I flattened my hands over the swaddled leg and leaned on it till my arms began to tremble and I felt faint.

"Relax, Megge. Breathe," Mother said. And then a rare thing happened—she looked into my eyes and nodded with approval. "You've done well, Daughter."

Daughter.

I sat back on my heels and took a long, deep breath. For as long as I could remember, I had stood alongside Mother as she saw babies into the world, set bones, and dabbed ointment on stinking, draining sores. But never before had I truly helped her heal.

Maybe I can become her apprentice without opening that book, I thought. *Maybe, now that I've proved myself, I too can become a woman of Bury Down. Maybe now she'll make me her—*

Mother looked up from Mistress Tucker's dressing.

"If you want to be a woman of Bury Down and a healer's apprentice, you've but to take up your book."

Had she heard my thoughts? Did she always know what I was thinking? My thumb began to track back and forth over my fingertips. Catching the motion, Mother pulled in the corners of her mouth and drew away from me.

The cart stopped. Mister Tucker and Mister Angwin slid Dora's makeshift litter out of the back and carried her into the Tuckers' smoke-blackened cottage, one of so many along the crowded market road. Claris and Brighida had already put water to boil on the cooking fire in the middle of the room, and smoke rolled out the door when we opened it.

Mother and I settled Mistress Tucker on her pallet; then, Mother showed Mister Tucker how to cleanse the wound and change the dressing.

"Once a week?" Gus grimaced and looked away from his wife's injury.

"Once a *day*, Gus. Without fail," Mother said, her raised eyebrow scolding Mister Tucker.

"Come, Sister," Aunt Claris said, "it'll soon be dusk."

Mister Tucker raised a hand and shook his head at her.

"It's late. I'll carry you home in the cart."

Claris said goodbye to Dora, her voice low and soothing, then thanked Mister Angwin.

"What would we have done without you?" She laid a hand on his muscled arm, and a flush crept up his neck.

Brighida and I climbed into the back of the cart. Mister Angwin helped Claris in a few minutes later, while Mother got up on the driver's seat with Mister Tucker.

"Yes, mistress," Mister Tucker said over and over all the way back to the cottage, flicking the whip with increasingly loud snaps over the rump of his mare.

We arrived at our cottage just after dark—hungry, tired, and blood-smeared.

"Every day, Gus," Mother called to Mister Tucker as he checked his wheels before setting out for home. "She must take those bandages off and air those wounds."

"Yes, mistress." He waved his hand over the back of his head and climbed up onto his high seat.

"Dora's a dead woman," Mother muttered, shaking her head as she walked out to the well. She filled a bucket and lugged it into the cookroom.

Claris ladled some of the water into the kettle of pottage hanging over the smoldering turf.

"Thank goodness for Morwen and Aleydis," she said. "This smells delicious." She reached up, snapped off some herbs from the drying rack, and crumbled them into the kettle.

Mother carried the bucket into the workroom, Brighida and I following close behind her. As soon as Mother had returned to the cookroom, Brighida dipped her hands into the water. Splashing it on her face, she whispered to me, "I watched you today. You're meant to be a healer."

I sat down beside her. Pretending I hadn't heard, I splashed water onto my own face and began to scrub off the blood.

"Just open your mother's book," Brighida whispered.

Pink water dripped from my hands and face into the bucket.

"You nearly did it once," Brighida said. "Just open it."

Opening that book would finally make me one of the family. And it was the only thing that would. Perhaps it was time—

Murderer, came the hoarse whisper.

My heart hurled itself against my breastbone. Had Brighida heard that? I searched her face, but her expression showed no sign she had—none of the fright that had set my heart pounding.

My fingertips began to sting just as they had the first time I'd heard that whisper. My thumbs started moving frantically over my fingertips as if rubbing a slip of fabric between them. The room felt suddenly hot. I could hardly breathe, and I could not speak.

I dried my face with the hem of my dress and went back to the cookroom, trying to still my fluttering fingers before Mother saw them.

Mother, Claris, and Brighida ate a hurried supper, none of them noticing that I did not touch mine. Mother and Claris gathered their capes, and Brighida took down her hooded cloak from its peg. Mother reached for my cloak, but then her hand stalled. Lips pursed, she paused for a long moment.

I held my breath. *Please don't make me go.*

Finally, Mother shook her head and dropped her hand.

"Morwen will be along for you shortly, Margaret. She'll take you down to the lodge."

I watched through the window as they crossed the pasture. The slope was already dotted with the torches of women gathering for cures. Mother would not be back until long after I had fallen asleep.

I was safe.

CHAPTER 5

"Aren't you feeling well, Megge?"

Morwen came into the cookroom just as Mother, Claris, and Brighida disappeared into Bury Down. I shook my head, unable to tell even her about the whisper. About that word. *Murderer.*

Was I a murderer? Would I one day become one?

She took my face in her hands, turned it toward her, and looked into my eyes as I calmed myself.

"There. That's better," she said. "The color's come back into your cheeks. Will you tell me what's frightened you?"

I shook my head.

"Well, then, come with me. I've something for you."

She put her arm around me and walked me out to the sleeping lodge. I lay down on my pallet and pulled up the blankets and hides.

"Here, Megge. Hold out your hand."

I did as she asked, and she placed something cold and hard in it. I sat up and ran my other hand over it, held it up to inspect it. The candlelight reflected off metal.

"Careful," she said.

There were two pointed blades joined in a sort of loop at one end. Sheep shears!

"A May Day gift." Morwen took them from me and squeezed them together. They rasped. "They're dull," she said. She let them spring apart. "These were made for my hands." She opened my hand and laid them back atop my palm.

"They're just right for me," I said.

"Yes. And on the morrow, I shall teach you to shear. Together, we'll fill a woolsack with your very own fleece to sell at market."

I pulled up my blankets, but when I closed my eyes, I saw Mother reach for my cloak and then shake her head. I heard her words. *Can this truly be my daughter?*

But I fell asleep to the sound of Morwen's lilting promise. *And on the morrow I shall teach you to shear.*

"Megge." Morwen shook my shoulder and whispered, "Wake up, child. Work to do."

I pushed my hair out of my face. It was morning. We were going to shear! I threw back my covers.

"Quiet now," Morwen whispered.

I slipped out of bed and carried my boots outside. The breeze was gentle, the air fragrant with honeysuckle, the birds already making a racket.

"Hold out your hand." Morwen gave me a piece of cheese, and we started up the hill toward the pen. I shoved the cheese into my mouth but stopped chewing when I heard the noise. Squeals and grunts.

"Hold still, ye—"

"Mister Gynneys is already at work," Morwen said. I ran to the open side of the barn.

A young ram was scrambling, fighting Mister Gynneys, the shearer. Mister Gynneys caught the ram from behind, steadied his head, backed him up, and wedged him between his legs. The ram relaxed, and Mister Gynneys picked up his shears.

Morwen laughed and applauded. "See how it's done, Megge?"

"Morwen." The man smiled and held out his shears. "Care to have at this youngster?"

Morwen scratched her own blades together.

"In a moment." She dug into a pocket in her skirt and pulled out a flat, grey stone that perfectly fit in the palm of her hand. "Whetstone." She handed it to me. "It's for you. Keep it always near you when you shear."

I ran a finger over it. "Rough."

"Let me show you how to use it."

I handed it back to her, and she scraped one of her shears' blades over the flat side of the stone, stroking it away from her, flipping it over, then stroking it back. She did this until the blades made a swishing sound when she opened and closed them.

"That's what sharp shears sound like."

"This the lass?" Mister Gynneys, his hands steadying the ram, lifted his chin toward me.

"Aye, this is Megge, George." She looked down at me. "Megge, surely you know Mister Gynneys."

Suddenly shy, I looked down. I knew who Mister Gynneys was, although he had never paid me any mind. A herder, he did the shearing every spring and summer. He and his wife had lived in the village, but they moved up to Bronn Wennilli, the Hill of Swallows, when their boy was born—around the same time I was. A monster, it was said by the few who had ever seen him. They said his face was frightful, his mouth somehow broken.

Mistress Gynneys had died of childbed fever soon after the boy was born, and for a long time, Mister Gynneys only came down to do the shearing and go to market. He rarely spoke to anyone but Morwen; he just stayed in the barn until his work was done and then took his pay and went back up the hill.

But that was long ago; now they lived much closer, and although Mister Gynneys had never spoken to me, he had become a good friend to Mother and Claris, always seeming to know when they needed him and always coming down to help with the flock. He seemed especially fond of Morwen, smiling at her today and then smiling down at me.

"Morwen tells me you're to be a shearer. Let me see your hands." His voice, low and calm, put me at ease, so I looked up at him and held out both hands. He took them in his and frowned. "Let's see if they'll do."

Morwen knelt beside him and ran her hand over the ram's belly.

"Here's where we start, Megge. You hold the shears like so." She gripped the blades in her right hand, palm down, but tilted up toward her. I tilted my hand to mirror hers.

"You see how soft this skin is?" She touched the ram's belly. "Here. Touch it, so you'll know. You don't want to cut it. You tighten it, like so, before the first blow." She glanced up at me. "That's what we call each cut. A *blow*." She pulled the skin taut with her left hand. "Cut the fleece short, but leave him some for himself, since the nights are still so cool."

In three deft blows, the ram's belly was clean. Appearing to have fallen into a trance, it lay back against Mister Gynneys, head lolling to one side.

"Now the inside of the back leg, and then we'll do the back of the leg and, finally, the tail." Morwen's tiny hands, so clever, brought me under her spell just like the ram.

"Use care here," she said as she started on the neck.

The ram showed the whites of his eyes and drew back. Morwen kept talking—nonsense words, crooning in Welsh; and as she clipped the thick fleece from the ram's neck and moved to the back of his head, around the ear, and then down the shoulder, he appeared to fall asleep.

"Let me lay him down," Mister Gynneys said, "and let's see if your Megge here can clip the back."

Already? But before I could speak, Morwen had pried the shears from my hand. She sharpened them while Mister Gynneys settled the ram on its belly.

"Nothing to it." Morwen opened my hand and placed the shears in it. "Like so."

She closed my fingers, and when she took her hand away the shears snapped opened.

"Now you try it." Morwen tugged a loose string from her tunic and held it out for me to cut. I snipped it.

"Atropos!" Mister Gynneys said.

Morwen laughed, "Oh, go on with you! What would you know about the Fates, George?" She sat on the ground beside the ram and pulled me down beside her.

"Everyone knows about the Fates. And the Morrigan. And the giant King Bendigeidfran. Isn't that right, Megge?"

I nodded. "'His face to this day stares at faraway France,'" I said, quoting Morwen and shivering as I recalled her tales of the frightening Morrigan—"three goddesses in one"—and the Moirai: "Clotho, Lachesis, and Atropos: three sisters who spin, measure, and cut their lengths of silvered string."

"Aye, they tell those stories around the nights' fires on the hill as well." Mister Gynneys waved a hand in dismissal when Morwen's look, much like the one Mother often gave me, seemed meant to silence him. "But of all those gods and goddesses and faeries and pixies, it's only Atropos I fear, as it is she who clips the string of life." He laughed. "But you'll not be doing any of that today, will you?"

"Just the fleece, George," Morwen said. "She'll just be clipping fleece today."

Guiding my hand, she slid the points into the fleece.

"Careful now, child, stay away from the skin"—and tilted my hand up a little—"That's it"—and with a snap and a little tug, she closed the shears.

"Aghhh!" Mister Gynneys fell back as if dead.

"Never mind him, Megge. You shear like one born to it." She lowered her voice. "And I've always thought you more like Aerten—one of our own Fates, the goddess who chooses the victor in battle—than the Greek sister with her scissors and thread." Winking at me, she smiled. "Now, shall we try it again?"

"It's a skilled shearer she will be," Morwen said as we sat down to supper one evening after I had been shearing with her and Mister Gynneys every day for just over a week. Starving from our day of work, I picked up my bowl of pottage and lifted it to my mouth.

"Manners, Megge," Claris and Brighida said in unison. Mother handed me a narrow plank of hard bread, and I scooped another mouthful with it.

"The sheep follow her about like puppies, and she shears them like a man." Morwen rubbed the top of my head.

Reaching down, I touched the small sack of fleece Morwen had allowed me to bring back to the cottage.

"Just this once," she'd said. I glanced toward Brighida to see if she had noticed. *Pride, Megge.* I could almost hear Aunt Claris's frequent warning.

Mother pulled the corners of her mouth in. "And just who made her your apprentice, Morwen? Megge has other work to do. Already Brighida can name the constellations. She knows the healing to be done beneath each planet. She can read the runes. Why, she's nearly mastered Murga's symbols. Claris has fulfilled her duty, but I might never fulfill mine."

Her lips moved now over clenched teeth, and her breath came quickly through her nose. She slapped her hands on the table and forced a look onto Morwen.

"One charge my sister and I were given in this life. One task. One vital duty, with everything to lose." She looked as if she were about to weep. "I have vowed to face flames rather than fail.

"And I am failing. Megge will not even look at our book. Anyone can shear a sheep." She pointed at my sack. "Stop touching that dirty thing. You're in the house now, and we're eating. We all see your wool."

Face flames? Mother had vowed to face flames? What did that mean? And where had I heard those words before?

This had something to do with that book. And with me. Everything that was wrong in our lives, even that expression on Mother's face—worn, fearful, discouraged—was all that book's fault.

I sat up straight and wiped my hands on my apron. My eyes cut to the shelf above the sideboard where Mother kept the book. I sneered and stuck my tongue out at it.

"Never mind that," Mother said without looking up from her bowl.

Morwen looked up from hers, though, and shook her head gently. *Never mind, child*, her expression said.

That night, as Brighida and I snuggled down under the hides, I pulled my woolsack into bed with me.

"Morwen," I said in a hushed voice, "someone must protect Mother from the flames."

"Don't worry," she said. "Someone will." Then, as she folded our dresses and piled them neatly at the foot of our pallet, she told us the tale of a young shepherd who had faced a giant and vanquished him with naught but a stone.

"No one else in the kingdom, not even the biggest, strongest warrior, could bring him down," she said. "It took a shepherd."

I pulled the warm hides up to my chin and curled around my full woolsack, thinking *I could do that.*

whisper woke me as I was about to hurl a rock at a black-garbed, violet-eyed giant.

"Come, Megge, it's almost daylight. Quiet, now. Don't wake Morwen." Mother pulled back the corner of my blanket as the giant's violet eyes faded away. "And bring that sack. We're going to market."

Brighida, already up and dressed, sprinkled a few drops of her mother's floral-scented water onto her hair, wound her braids around her head, and covered them with her pristine white cap. I pulled my shift over my head, grabbed my dirty, fleece-covered cap, and started out the door behind her. As I closed the door, I noticed that Aleydis's bow and quiver were gone. I squinted back into the lodge at Morwen and Aleydis's pallet. Only Morwen lay upon it. Aleydis had gone hunting. We would have meat tonight!

I slung my woolsack over my chest and ran to catch up with the others. Brighida was out at the roost gathering eggs for market.

"Brighida, that's my job."

I reached for the basket, but she held on tight.

"Your mother told *me* to collect the eggs."

"Girls," Aunt Claris called, "come now and eat."

We broke our fast with the previous night's cold pottage and bread. When we had finished, I rushed to the door. I had wool to trade! Aunt Claris took down bunches of herbs from the drying racks and divided them between two baskets.

We set out for the village, Mother and Claris carrying bags of wool and baskets of eggs and herbs. I walked alongside them, and every few minutes dipped my hand into the woolsack slung across my chest, my satisfaction palpable if unexpressed.

Mother caught me at it and smiled at my cousin.

"Brighida, I need a big girl to help me." She held out the basket in which I had always carried the eggs and herbs to market to trade for fresh fish. "Can you carry this basket without breaking any of the eggs?"

Brighida drew in a breath and reached for it.

"Yes, Aunt."

I chewed on the inside of my lip as Mother settled my basket over my cousin's arm and walked alongside her.

"There's a good girl."

There's a good girl. Lovely. Such a lovely girl.

I hung behind them fingering my fleece and staring at my love-ly-good cousin until my eyeballs went dry. I blinked. I was glad not to be weighed down by that basket. I was happy to be away from Mother's book and out from under her eye, walking out of doors in air that smelled of gorse instead of musty pages or my cousin's perfumed hair.

Claris bent down and picked shoots, putting them in her apron pocket. Butterflies rode the warm breeze, Dropping my sack, I ran after them, my arms stretched out like wings, following their looping routes until they landed on white flowers or dipped into purple bells.

"Yarrow clusters. Foxglove." Brighida pointed them out to me as she named them.

Tiny, cupped petals cascaded from the cherry trees, and I had to stop. I must have sneezed a dozen times before I was through.

When I pressed a finger to each nostril and blew, no one hollered, "Margaret!" Mother, Brighida, and Claris had gone on ahead of me.

I picked up my sack and crossed the field at a trot, unlatched the churchyard gate, and hurried past the grey stone church, recalling Morwen's admonition.

"We live amongst them, Megge. We must not be strangers. What people don't know, they fear. And what they fear, they hurt."

The church windows leaked the smell of burning tallow. A single low voice inside intoned a ghostly call, to which the parishioners replied as one, their response a dirge. My mind's eye called up the tonsured monk I had seen every time Morwen had made me attend Mass. He had stood at the stone altar beneath the vaulted ceiling, his back to me, murmuring words I did not understand.

My woolsack had grown heavy, so I set it down. Bees hovered over a hedge of honeysuckle, moving in and out of the buttery yellow blooms as though at work. Were they working? What was their work? They made honey, somehow, and Morwen made mead from it. But how did they do it?

Did *The Book of Seasons* mention bees? I could ask Mother to teach me about bees. Perhaps that would satisfy her. I could ask her to open the book and show me if there was a notation, and then I could stand far away from her when she opened it. If I stood far enough away, it wouldn't burn me again. I could do that.

I shall do it, I promised myself.

Satisfied, and eager now to be with my mother and show her what a good pupil I could be, I slung my sack over my other shoulder and bent so no one would see me through the church window. I shuddered as I walked past the patch of weeds where Dora Tucker had lain.

When I reached the wide stone steps at the front of the church, I glanced at the top step—no one was standing upon it—and then down the rutted road toward the marketplace at the other end of town. There—Claris's hair. And beside Claris were Mother and

Brighida, in front of the church. I would ask Mother about bees right now, and I would ask her to show me a drawing of a hive in her book when we got home.

I jumped and waved to catch Mother's eye, but she and Claris and Brighida had crossed to the other side of the road, probably believing I was still with them. I called out and waved again, but they kept walking.

I ran to catch up with them, but just then the church service ended, and churchgoers carrying baskets streamed out into the road, jostling me and blocking my view. They greeted one another but did not tarry, nearly all of them moving toward the market.

Only three women held back—those three jowly old women, large-bosomed and thick-middled, clad in black from hat to hem, who always seemed to stand on that top step passing judgment. The Whispering Women.

The tallest of the three, whose lips I could see below the shadow of her hat—a crimson sneer—lifted her hand, and the other two quieted. She pointed to the far side of the road and drew her companions close, each lifting a hand to hide her mouth, like three vultures whispering behind their wings. After a moment, the hat brims began to turn, tracking something that moved from the edge of the road to the weaver's cottage. The hats halted when Mother and Claris stopped at the Tuckers' door.

Mother rapped, but no one answered. She rapped again. When there was still no answer, she picked up her basket to leave. The hat brims began to turn again. They followed Mother and Claris down the road to the candlemaker's shop.

I wondered if those old women somehow knew us, or if they were just admiring my aunt, for the hat brims were trained mostly on her. Claris was certainly lovely in her soft, flowing dress, her loose hair lifting in the breeze. She strode to the next shop, shoulders straight, eyes soft, a dancer wading through deep water. Was it any wonder people gawked?

Mother took clipped steps after Claris, her torso pitched forward and her face tight as a fist. Brighida followed just behind Mother, still gripping that basket of eggs and herbs.

I dawdled outside the church, plucking at the wool in my sack and scuffing my boots in the dirt while I tried to hear what those women on the step were saying. As an excuse for moving closer, I pretended to notice something on the ground near the lowest step, and I knelt as though to pick up a trinket or a shilling dropped in haste by one of the churchgoers.

Children shrieked and the ever-present street hawkers called out their wares; but one coarse voice stood out from the others, gritty, as if something loose rattled in the speaker's throat. I cocked my head to listen and looked up at the women to see who was speaking. The grinding words fit the movement of those crimson lips.

As the leader of the women spoke, she began to tuck stray hairs up under her hat. When she lifted the hat for a moment, I saw her face.

I knew her. She was the old woman who had pinched Vivienne's arm and told her not to dance with Brighida and me. She looked out toward the street, and the sun hit eyes so pale blue they appeared silver. Eyes, I realized, that were not admiring Claris. They were stalking her.

I sat down on the lowermost step and ran my fingers back and forth over it, brushing away dirt as I listened.

"Even as a young thing . . ." she rasped, ". . . a seductress."

"All that land . . ." said one of the others.

"A boon, they say . . ."

"Cursed," came the rasping voice.

Cursed? My heart slammed against my breastbone.

Just then, the church door opened and a slender woman emerged, a veil covering her hair and face.

"Jenifer," said the rattling voice.

The young woman whirled around and flung back her veil. It was Mistress Penneck, Vivienne's mother.

"Mother. What are you doing back here?" Without looking away from her mother, Mistress Penneck reached back and held the door open. "Come, Vivienne," she said over her shoulder.

The old woman sneered. "I came to see for myself if what your brother said was true. I went to the fair, and I've seen. It's true."

Vivienne came out of the church holding hands with a boy. When she caught sight of the old woman, she held up her hand, still clasping the boy's, and called out in a high, sweet singsong, "Good morning, Grandmother."

"Vivienne." The old woman coughed out a derisive laugh. "Already taking after your mother, I see."

Vivienne's mother yanked Vivienne's hand out of the boy's grip.

"Stay away from her," she ordered him. Then she turned to Vivienne. "Where is Gwyneth?"

"She's with Father," Vivienne said.

The church door opened, and the man who emerged was square-hewn as a slab of granite. A warrior's shoulders strained his fine tunic. He held the hand of a dark-haired girl who went suddenly quiet when an old monk approached. The little girl remained silent, her brown eyes staring at the wooden cross resting upon his teardrop paunch.

The brother put out his hand. "It's good to see you, Mister Penneck."

"A fine idea, Brother, to hold church services on market day. When we have guilds in this village, no doubt there will be vespers every night." His voice dropped. "My son Harold has left our tithe at the priory."

The monk opened his mouth to speak; but the old woman on the far side of the step coughed, and both men turned. Mister Penneck's face, already ruddy, went deep red about the cheeks. He pulled a grey wool cap out of his pocket and tugged it low over a gathering brow. Releasing the monk's grip, he picked up his daughter.

"Pardon me, Brother."

He stalked over to his wife, his heavy boots shedding clumps of dried mud with each step. He took her arm, but she seemed caught in her mother's malevolent glare and did not budge. He tugged.

"Come, Jenifer."

Mistress Penneck looked first at her husband and then at the old woman with the pale eyes.

"Stay away from me, Mother. Go back to Tintagel."

"Jenifer, Vivienne. Come." Mister Penneck took them both by the arm and led them down the steps. "Harold is here with the cart."

A slat-sided cart had drawn up before the church, wobbling and creaking, and stopped right in front of me. The bullock shifted its weight under the loose rein of a lanky boy with a shadow over his upper lip and lifted its tail. Steaming clods thudded onto the dirt and flattened like rotten apples. The unflinching Mister Penneck released his wife and daughter and walked right up behind the beast. He jiggled the front cartwheel.

"Harold," he called. "The hammer."

Harold reached beneath the driver's plank, pulled out a hammer, and tossed it to his father, who sat down in the road right beside the steaming heap of dung. He wiggled the pin that held the wheel to the axle and then tapped it into place.

I looked from the man in the dirt to the boy atop the cart. This was the father-and-son team who hauled vegetables to market. I could hardly recognize in the well-dressed Mister Penneck the dirty and unshaven carter who normally wore a homespun tunic and leather jerkin with those workman's boots as he made his rounds in his cart.

This fancy Mister Penneck helped his family into the back of the cart, caught the front rail, slung himself up onto the driver's seat with surprising grace, and clucked to the bullock. I sat, entranced by the jingle, creak, and clop of the cart making its way to the market stalls.

⁓

"What are you doing here, Megge?" Aunt Claris had come up behind me and now leaned over my shoulder, her fragrant hair brushing my face. "We've searched everywhere for you. Come, we must get to the market if we are to make it home before dusk."

At the top of the church steps, the hat brims were now touching. Those silvery eyes glared at my aunt.

"Scorned, reviled," the old woman whispered, now turning those eyes on me. "They'll die by flame!"

"Come, Megge." Claris grabbed my hand and pulled me to my feet.

"Aunt Claris?" I stumbled as she pulled me from the step. "Who is going to die by flame?" I tried to look back over my shoulder, but Claris was pulling me down the road. "Me? Am I going to die by flame? Are you?" Then I remembered Mother's outburst. "Is it Mother? Is Mother going to die by flame?"

When Claris did not reply, I pulled on her hand.

"Aunt Claris, I saw that lady at the fair. She pinched Vivienne. Who is she?"

"Hush, Megge. She's no one. She has no power over us."

"Did she just curse us? Is she a sorceress?"

"No one is cursed, child. And she is no sorceress."

"Aunt Claris, what's a boom?"

"A boom?" Claris stopped for a moment, frowned, and then started walking again. "Boon, Megge. A boon is a gift."

"Who gave us a boon?"

"No one. There was never any boon. Hurry now."

I tightened my arms around my woolsack and ran to keep up.

"Aunt Claris, who is going to die by flame?"

She led me past the shops of the weaver, the chandler, the blacksmith, two cobblers, the potter, and the carpenter. We reached Mother and Brighida just outside the stonemason's hut, next to the market. Claris took Mother aside and whispered to her, frowning and pointing toward me with a tilt of her head.

"No, no, no." Mother made brisk, up-and-down, turnip-chopping motions with every word. "It's too soon."

Without another word, Claris turned from Mother, took Brighida's arm, and led her into the market. Mother pulled me into the stonemason's shop. The big man, covered in fine white dust, looked up from the name he was chiseling into a headstone shaped like a cross.

"I'd like to thank you, Robert," she began.

Mister Angwin waved her off. "Just a mite of a thing, our Dora. Y'hardly needed me." He looked down at me. "You and your mother are taking good care of her."

Not I, I thought, not daring to look at Mother. *I've been shearing sheep while Mother's been seeing to Dora.*

Mother spoke as if she hadn't heard. "You've plenty of work to do. We'll leave you to it."

"Nine headstones commissioned, Mistress," the mason pointed with his chisel at great blocks of rough stone. "And my apprentice not yet schooled to the task."

A young man as broad in the shoulders as his master and, like him, covered in fine white dust, tapped hammer against chisel, fashioning a tablet with a rounded top from a rough slab of granite.

"Your son?"

"Yes, Mistress."

"How fine that your child honors your profession." She turned her back to me and ran her hand over one of the smooth granite tablets.

Was I not at her side in the healer's hut as she applied plasters and set bones? Had I not proved myself worthy with Dora Tucker?

The mason's son needed no book—the very dust that covered him confirmed his apprenticeship. And the nonsense words Brighida muttered confirmed hers. But not even blood confirmed mine.

Chapter 7

Taking my sleeve, Mother bade the mason good day and led me through the crowd to the market.

"Let's see if we can find some linen. And then we'll see to Dora."

A breeze carrying the reek of the fishmonger's stall drew my eye to Brighida. *She's probably naming the fish in Latin*, I thought. She handed her basket over to the merchant, and he took out the eggs and set them aside. Then he slapped a dozen or so salted fish into the basket and handed it back to her. She covered the fish with a cloth and followed her mother to Mister Tucker's crowded market stall.

Mother stopped for a moment to talk to Mistress Trelawney in her husband's pottery stall. They spoke quietly for a few minutes, and then the young woman whispered a question.

"Come to us at the half-moon," Mother said.

Mistress Trelawney blinked fast, but could not stop a tear from rolling down her cheek. She took a clay vase from the shelf and put it in Mother's hand.

Mother shook her head. "No, thank you, my dear." Then she took my arm and led me away. "If I had an apprentice," she muttered, "she could come to the grove and learn how we cure a barren woman."

Claris and Brighida had already selected and paid for a piece of muslin and were running their fingertips over flax, boiled wool, and even some lace when Mother and I joined them.

"Feel this, Megge." Brighida held out a supple linen.

"Soft," I said.

Mother ran a hand over it. "But who could make anything so fine on our old loom?" She doubled it over her arm. Taking my elbow, she guided me to the scales.

"Come, Brighida." Aunt Claris took her daughter's hand, and they walked around the baskets of clean fleece that divided the weaver's stall from the chandler's. A moment later, they were bargaining with the candle-maker. Then Claris counted out four coins, and he handed Brighida six tall tapers and two squat, honey-colored candles for the lantern.

"Mother," I said as we waited our turn in line, "there was a lady at the fair, and I saw her on the church steps. She was watching Aunt Claris, and she said—"

Too late. Mister Tucker was reaching for my wool.

"Give Mister Tucker the woolsack, Margaret."

Margaret. I would get no reply here.

I handed over my wool and looked with some regret into the empty bag Mister Tucker returned to me. But then he weighed the wool and slid a silver coin across his table. My first penny. I slipped the woolsack over my shoulder and put the penny in my pocket.

Mother paid for her linen. "Now, Gus, where's Dora? I knocked on your door, but there was no answer. Put her to work already, have you?"

I crooked my finger to Claris.

"Yes, Megge?"

She bent down, and I whispered in her ear, "Mother won't take me to the butcher shops, so will you please buy me some bacon? It's for Morwen."

Mother always said that a butcher shop was no place for a child, even though she took me to births, and I could not see how a butcher's shop could be any more gruesome than a birthing chamber.

"Consider it done, Megge." Claris took the coin and put it in her purse. "How delighted our Morwen will be."

Just then, a high, sweet voice called out from the other side of the weaver's stall, "Mistress! Come, look."

Dora Tucker stepped out on her right leg and swung the left around to meet it.

"It's ever so much better."

"That's fine, Dora," Mother said. "Though you've no business being up and about. Let's go and see to that leg."

"Must we? I'm sure it's fine. No need to worry yourself."

Mother squinted at her. "Dora. You remember your last child . . ."

"Now, Mistress, I didn't know—"

"The fever, going on four days, and you shut up in that hut, alone."

"It was the festival. How could Gus—"

"You lost the child. Will you lose the leg, now, on top of it all?" Mother called over her shoulder, "Megge. We're leaving." As we passed, Mother pressed her new linen into Claris's hands. "Will you mind this for me?"

I followed Mother and Mistress Tucker out of the market and down the road.

"We knocked at the door on our way to the market, believing you would be at home resting that leg," Mother said. "I hope you're not out every day, walking about from dawn to dusk. But, knowing Gus, I imagine that is exactly what —"

"It's not his fault," Mistress Tucker interrupted, stopping and turning to speak to me rather than to Mother. "The warm days—already we have such a surplus—we had to set to work at dawn to get it all to the stall in time for the market."

Mistress Tucker's rolling gait was not all that was amiss, I saw. Her face was nearly as white as our fleece.

"Aren't you going to ask me how well I feel or tell me how good I look?" Mistress Tucker asked Mother.

"I would ask if you drank the yellow dock tea I left last time I came, but your pale lips show me that you did not."

"But I did, Mistress. Four cups of it." She lowered her voice. "Then I got the flux."

"You drank too much. Three cups in a day—no more—to feed the blood. The fourth cleanses the bowel."

When we arrived at her cottage, Mistress Tucker was still describing the flux she had suffered.

"Like thin gruel it was. And oh, the smell! Why, I should think the place reeks of it still."

Close and dank, the black-walled dwelling smelled of old smoke and something rotten. Not the flux. Rotten meat? Spoiled fish?

There was no window in the main room of her cottage, which also served as Mister Tucker's shop, so Mistress Tucker lit a candle. She fixed it in a holder and handed it to me as Mother took out her shears.

"Over here, Dora." Mother clipped the knot on the soiled cloth that covered the wound. "Megge, take off that woolsack and bring me the candle."

I dropped the sack onto a pile of pallets lying by the door and took the candle to Mother just as she was removing the dressing. The soaked, yellowed plaster fell to the floor, and the smell of rotten flesh hit me. I drew back, gagging.

Never wince, Margaret, I could almost hear her scold.

"The light, Megge. Bring back the light." Mother wiped away foul-smelling pus, and I brought the candle closer so she could examine the tight, angry flesh surrounding the jagged wound. I could not help but wince. I thought I would vomit.

"It's been three days since I changed this bandage," Mother

said. "Have you not cleansed the wound, Dora?"

"How can I? I can't see it." She tried to look at the back of her thigh by bending her leg behind her, but her large buttock blocked her view.

"And Gus would not bring you to me."

"How could he, then? You've seen for yourself how busy he is with folks selling their wool. And there is so much weaving and tucking to be done—"

"You still have the healing potion Claris made for you?"

"It's over there." Dora motioned with her head toward a pitcher in the corner of the room.

"It's doing you no good over there, Dora." Mother fetched the pitcher then unrolled her pouch and removed three squares of white cloth. "Megge. A bowl."

"Over there, dear." Mistress Tucker nodded toward the open fire. When I had left them, I heard her ask Mother in a childlike voice, "Is it so bad, Mistress?"

I found a shallow wooden bowl on her table and gave it to Mother. She filled it from the pitcher and dropped the cloths in.

"Shall I lie down?" Dora began to lower herself to the floor.

Mother took her elbow.

"No. It's better if you stand. The dirty water can run away from the wound." Without looking away from Dora's leg, Mother said, "Megge. Fresh rushes."

"You will find them in the kitchen, too, dear."

I brought back an armload of fragrant husks and piled them near Mistress Tucker's feet.

"Stand on these," Mother told her.

Mistress Tucker stepped onto the husks, and Mother poured the liquid into her gaping wound. Mistress Tucker panted like a dog, but she did not cry out.

Keep them talking, Megge, Mother often whispered to me as she worked, *and they will feel less pain.*

"Do you remember being gored, Mistress Tucker?" I asked. It was the wrong question. I knew it the moment the words left my lips.

"Margaret . . ." Mother shook her head.

"Oh, yes," Dora said, eager to talk about it. "It's all come back to me. A dreadful, filthy thing that boar was, rooting around under the oak. I was taking fresh altar cloths to the sanctuary, and before I could get the church door open, it charged me." She groaned when Mother touched a wet cloth to the wound and wiped away the thick pus. "Well, I dropped my linens and ran," she said through gritted teeth, "but that hog was already upon me, pushing me from behind, ramming that filthy horn into the meat of my leg. I thought he would tear it off. I screamed, and the boar pulled back, perhaps to charge me again, but I had swooned dead away. Something else must have caught its attention, for it did not finish me off."

"Megge, come here and hold this open."

I knelt beside Mother. When I beheld that gaping, ragged hole, I started to retch.

"Don't you dare, Margaret," Mother said through gritted teeth.

I looked away and breathed through my mouth.

"The boar gored Dora behind the knee. See? Look here." Mother pointed to the deep puncture. "And tore the flesh all the way up to the middle of her thigh."

I nodded, my lips tightly closed.

"The tusk is as sharp as a knife, Megge," Mother continued, now master to pupil. "A mighty butcher's knife. And what it doesn't tear to pieces it rots with its filth."

She placed one of my palms on each side of the deep trench. When she moved them apart, I could see inside. The clean wound looked like raw meat with a fine, whitish web covering the deepest portion. The corners had already begun to knit.

"You see, if the wound is kept clean, it will draw together on its own. In a few months, there will be only a scar to remind her."

"How fortunate I was," Mistress Tucker said, her breath coming easier now we were nearly through, "that you happened to find me, for surely I would have bled to death had you not stopped."

"You were so brave." I picked up the sodden rushes and wrapped the stinking cloths in them.

"Nonsense, child," Dora said. "It's your mother who was brave. And you, little Megge. Why, that beast could have come back and—"

"Where should I put the husks?" I had never thought of the boar coming back. If it could do such harm to a woman the size of Dora Tucker, it might have tossed me into the sky, impaled me on its tusk, and carried me back to its lair, flailing about, fresh raw meat to serve to its young.

"Oh," she said, "just throw them out the door, with all the rest."

I opened the door in the rear of the cottage and tossed the wet rushes out onto the piles of rotted food, char, and human and animal waste, understanding now why the cottage had no window. I returned to the blackened shop grateful to live in a clean house with a window and a chimney.

Mother gathered her shears and forceps, cleaned them in the scented water, and dried them. She handed each one to me, and I slid it into its pocket in her pouch.

"That wound must be cleaned, Dora. I will do it if you can't." She lifted her apron, tied the pouch around her waist, and dropped the apron back over it.

Mistress Tucker smoothed her dress over her leg. "Gus will bring me to see you when he can."

"Three days, Dora, no more," Mother called over her shoulder. "That will be Sunday, a day of rest even for a merchant. Tell your husband that if he brings you, Claris will pour him a refreshing ale for his trouble. If he makes you wait another week, our Megge here will go out to the woods and fetch you a sturdy tree limb to walk upon, for you will surely lose that leg."

Dora and I both sucked in our breath. Nothing worse could befall one. It was even worse than losing an eye.

Dora swept her hand over her backside again. "Yes, Mistress."

"Sunday, then." Mother looked out the door and took my hand. "Claris and Brighida are waiting outside. Come, Megge."

"Goodbye, Megge." Mistress Tucker rested a soft palm on my cheek. "You're a fine apprentice."

My woolsack was still lying on the floor by the door, where I had left it. When I picked it up and slipped it over my shoulder, Mother dropped my hand and went out the door.

Chapter 8

s we walked home, Brighida pulled the muslin out of her basket. I reached over and rubbed it between my fingers. It was rough, but with washing would soften. I brought it to my nose and sniffed. It smelled of smoke from the weaver's shop.

I took care not to fall victim to pride but could not help feeling something akin to it as we neared our tidy cottage. The aroma of a meat stew rising from the chimney made my mouth water. Taking the parcel of bacon out of my sack, I ran toward the scent. Aleydis's bow and quiver leaned on the wall of the cottage, and a small hide, mitten-sized, was tacked down on a plank to dry. I flung open the door and ran inside.

"This is for you." I thrust the parcel at Morwen.

She set down the turnip she was chopping and lifted her gift out of my hands. Just as I had done, she brought it to her nose.

"Is there any better smell in all the world?" She kissed my cheek.

"It's from the fleece," I said.

"From the fleece, you say?" She unwrapped it. "Then perhaps we should have some this very night. Think how good it will taste in the stew."

Mother picked up the bacon, sniffed it, and, for the first time that day, smiled at me.

"Good girl," she said and got to work chopping the turnips Morwen had left on the sideboard.

Brighida put on her apron and began pulling the papery skins off the onions. Claris plucked dried parsley leaves and handed them to me. I crumbled them into the pot. Aleydis, busy grinding bones for meal and thinking her own thoughts, as she always did after a day of hunting, paid us no mind.

"What took you so long returning from the village today?" Morwen asked as she chopped the bacon into small squares. "A trip to the market takes but a morning. Was there a dancing bear in the green? A piper playing tunes? Did you dance the day away?" She smiled at me as she dropped the chunks of bacon into the pot then pulled out a chair and settled into it.

"No, Morwen," I said. "We cleaned Mistress Tucker's leg."

"And how is the poor dear?"

"Walking like a sailor on a rolling sea." Mother brought Morwen a cup of ale.

Morwen took a long drink, and her voice took on the bard's lilt.

"Well, if she's up and about, we have cause to celebrate. And with that bacon we shall have ourselves a feast. And a tale."

"Tell about Natalje and Gytha," I prompted. "What happened after Natalje took up Gytha's book?" I hoped Morwen's story about my grandmother, who died so young, would shed some light on what could happen to a girl who accepted her mother's book.

Morwen spread her hands, closed her eyes, and began . . .

"It is said," Gytha told Natalje on her ninth natal day, "that *The Book of Time* holds wisdom gleaned since the dawn of creation. That it has passed through the hands of the greatest of seers. Your finger is tracing a symbol etched a thousand years ago by a valiant young woman named Anwen, who defended Murga's pupil, Bryluen. Together, they wrote down the symbols Murga had taught her pupil and preserved the teachings of the first Seer of Bury Down.

"Had it not been for Anwen, the archer Murga summoned to defend Bryluen—whom we call the Guardian—we would long ago have lost the power she protects to this day, the power we call on to summon the Mentors."

"The Guardian?" Natalje asked. "How does she guard the power if she lived so long ago?"

"By returning to the living world and choosing the heirs to this and another great book, and by crafting destiny so that each heir is born precisely when and where she—or he—is needed. Even now, the Guardian is crafting the destiny of a very special child."

A cloud moved across Natalje's face, and she whispered, "Are you the Guardian, Mother?"

"No, child. I am but a seer."

"Who, then, is the Guardian?"

"I cannot say who she is in this life," Gytha told her, "only that she returns to the living world from time to time, no one knowing when or as whom. Maybe a king, a countess, a mason, a priest, a scullery maid, or even the one-legged man begging alms in the road. We never know when we are in the company of the Guardian, daughter."

As Gytha taught Natalje to read the runes, the stars, and the symbols and incantations of the heirs, the Welsh serving girl—a young woman now, silent and small—gleaned the teachings along with Natalje, and she, too, grew in wisdom and understanding.

Finally, the day arrived when twelve-year-old Natalje had mastered the teachings that would unlock the unknowable. And on that day, the Lady Gytha closed her book.

"You have listened with your ears and seen with your eyes," she said to Natalje, "and now you must learn to perceive with your mind the thoughts, the secret dreams, the conflicting desires that guide men, for they alone will reveal what lies within the heart." She spoke to Natalje, then, silently, using the language of the great book, — *For that is the seat of their discontent.*

Now Gytha taught entirely in silence, and the minds of her pupils opened. Vivid images assailed them—visions—which they grew to trust. The girls learned to tell visions from dreams; what was real from what was hoped—or feared. They heard their master's unspoken thoughts, even as Gytha heard theirs and knew she had taught both daughter and servant. And Gytha came to understand that the young poet, the lost daughter of the wandering bard, would one day see her child home.

Later that night, as Morwen tucked me in and blew out the candle, I wondered what would have happened if, like Natalje, *I* had inherited *The Book of Time.* I fell asleep wondering what it would feel like to be a true woman of Bury Down, the beloved of the family rather than the outcast; and I awoke the next morning with the touch of Gytha's rich linens soft against my cheek.

In my dreams, *I* had been the child seated alongside Gytha, learning in the glow of tapers and torches, a child apprenticed to a seer. I had taken up my book and learned to perceive and to speak without words. And my yellow-haired sea-captain father had tossed me, his beloved girl, into the air and promised me the world. *I shall show you the world! The world, Megge!*

Then Mother snorted in her sleep. Brighida rolled over and exhaled, her breath smelling of onion, and I remembered—I was no one's darling. I lived on a sheep farm outside a tiny riverside village in the Cornish hills, and I slept alongside my cousin, deep in the side of a hill.

That thought made me sit straight up in my bed.

Why *did* we sleep in a cave? Did everyone? No. Dora Tucker's family didn't. Their pallets were right there in their cottage.

I walked up to the cottage as if in a dream, scattering grain to the chickens, retrieving eggs from the roost, and then breaking my fast in silence, still wondering why we slept hidden beneath the ground. As I ate, I recalled the words of the old woman on the church steps: *They'll die by flame.*

That growling threat joined with Mother's words: *I have vowed to face flames rather than fail.* Together, the horrific refrains echoed inside my head until I could think of nothing else. Finally, I went back out to the roost to try to sort out what those words could mean to me and my family.

The chickens had eaten much of the grain, so I reached into the barrel to scoop out another handful for them. My breath came short, and time seemed to stop.

Closing my eyes, I dug deeper, the grain sliding through my fingers. That feeling—my hand in that barrel, the scratch of grain against my skin—seemed to mean something. The grain itself suddenly seemed very important. But why? It was only grain.

Casting a handful to the chickens, I felt a stab of remorse. *You're wasting food.* Then I felt a wave of giddy relief. *But there is plenty.* Then a surge of guilt. *Why have we such bounty when others have none?*

What was wrong with me? Why were these thoughts assailing me, and why did I suddenly feel as if I were about to faint? A high-pitched sound began to ring in my ears, and I felt myself floating high above my own head, everything appearing small and far away.

Brighida came out to the well with the dishes and watched me for a moment, an odd expression on her face.

"Megge? What's the matter?"

I shook my head. I didn't know what was wrong.

I watched Morwen and Aleydis, talking quietly, walk past me on their way to the lodge. As they passed, a deep sense of comfort enveloped me. Little by little, I began to come back to myself.

When my heart once more was at ease, and I felt I could breathe again, I squeezed Brighida's hand, and she nodded gravely.

"I know what this is," she said. "A moment in spirit. You've just lived in memory for a moment, Megge. A memory, perhaps, of another time."

"What other time, Brighida? All I did was reach for some grain, and all at once everything seemed to be moving away. Or I was moving away. Far away. And thoughts—awful thoughts, Brighida, and awful feelings—swept through me."

She nodded as I spoke.

"I thought I was dying," I said.

She whispered, "I know, Megge. I feel the same way every time a woman comes to us in the grove to tell us her child has died. I feel as if it were *my* child that died, and I have to look away from the grieving woman until the spell passes. Mother says I've chosen to forget a former life that wants to be recalled." Brighida put her head close to mine. "But it frightens me, and—please don't tell my mother—I try very hard not to remember."

A former life? What was Aunt Claris teaching Brighida?

Brighida said no more, so I helped her wash the bowls at the well and then returned with her to the cottage. Mother and Claris were at the sideboard talking quietly as they peeled and chopped vegetables for the day's pottage. In front of Mother was a growing pile of papery white husks and curling purple skins. On the cutting board in front of Claris were a bowl of garlic cloves and a pyramid of turnips. *This is how it should be*, I thought. *Everyone working. No one studying those awful books.*

I picked up the broom, happiness overtaking me, and began to sweep with zeal; but I soon stirred up so much dust Mother called over her shoulder, "Enough, Megge. Brighida's already done that."

I put the broom back in its corner, happy to have been scolded, for it proved that nothing in my world had changed.

I went back outside and was on my way to the roost when a bullock cart rumbled up to the door, raising dust and scattering the chickens. Cries rose from the back of the cart. Mister Penneck, the carter I had seen at the church on market day, jumped down from the driver's seat and lifted his keening son from the back.

"Be still, Harold," the carter growled.

"But Grandmother says they're—"

"I said be quiet, boy." The carter hoisted his son into his arms. "You want to lose that leg?"

Harold fell silent for a moment, his head dropping back on his father's shoulder, and it was only then that I saw the arrow. The barbed tip of the blood-smeared shaft showed on one side of the boy's thin calf, the feathers on the other. Blood streamed down his leg and dripped off the heel of his boot.

"... cursed," he whimpered.

Chapter 9

"Mother! Aunt Claris!" I ran into the house shouting, but they had already tucked their knives into their apron pockets. Mother rushed past me and out the door, the smell of garlic trailing her.

"Lay the boy there, Francis."

I backed away and held the door open as the carter carried his son into the cookroom and laid him on the table beneath the window. Mother watched him carefully.

"How did this happen, Francis?"

"An accident, Mistress. His brother didn't see him."

"His brother?" Mother's eyes narrowed. "Tinker? He's come back from Tintagel?"

"Aye, Mistress."

As Mother moved the leg into the shaft of sunlight, Aunt Claris turned away. Keeping her back to the carter, she reached up to the shelf above the sideboard and took down three small leather pouches. She handed them to Brighida, who opened the drawstrings and sniffed. Claris crossed to the hearth, took up the bellows, and blew air into the embers until they glowed again. She touched the water in the kettle.

"Still hot. Hand me those, Brighida."

"Yarrow, thyme, and lavender," Brighida recited the names as her mother reached into each pouch, took out pinches of dried flakes, and sprinkled them into the water.

Claris swung the pot back over the heat. "That's right. Let's go prepare an image while these steep."

I held my breath, wishing Claris would hurry and be gone before Mother could ask for her book. But she was too slow.

"My book, Claris."

Mother blocked Mister Penneck's view as Claris reached behind the curtain and took down *The Book of Seasons*. Hiding it beneath her apron, she spirited it into the workroom. Mother laid it on her work table and mumbled, bloody hands clasped behind her back. Then she closed her eyes, nodding as if someone were speaking to her. She wiped her hands on her apron, caught my hand, and led me to her loom, where she reached into the basket of scraps, pawed through the fabric, and selected a crooked piece of soft broadcloth.

"Tear this into strips."

I pulled at the edge but could not tear it, so I tried biting it. Mother took it from me, slit the edge in three places with her knife, and handed it back to me.

"Tear."

She unrolled her pouch, took out a wooden stick with a slim metal rod protruding from one end, and set the handle on a hearth-stone so the tip jutted out over the embers.

"Watch this," she said. "But don't touch it. It'll be hot. Tell me if it falls in."

Squatting next to the hearth, I watched it, but I also watched the boy. His white face had gone blotchy from crying, and his tears were carving rivers into the dirt on his face and carrying it straight back into his ears.

Unmoved by his fear, perhaps because she had not looked at his face, Mother took a pair of curved shears out of her pouch and laid it next to the squirming, keening Harold. As the rod heated, she tried to inspect his twitching leg.

"Francis," Mother said.

The carter bent down and hissed something to Harold, and the boy went rigid.

Sunlight glinted off the head of the arrow. It had passed straight through the right calf and was scratching the inside of his left leg. Imagining how it must have felt to be struck by such a thing, I covered my face to hide my grimace.

"Look here, Megge." Mother tied a piece of thick cloth over the arrowhead and closed her hand over it. Opened it, closed it. Showed me her hand. "Unharmed. Now we can remove it." She pointed at the wound with her chin. "See this?"

Blood pulsed out around the arrow in small bright bursts that clung to the shaft and trickled down into the feathers.

"It doesn't appear to be bleeding much, but . . ." She glanced up. "Leave that, Megge. Come here and look."

I got up and reluctantly went to the boy's side.

"It's pumping," Mother said, pointing to the blood coursing around the arrow's shaft. "It'll bleed when the shaft is removed unless I seal it. That's why we leave it in place until we're ready. It stops the bleeding." She spread the boy's legs. "Claris!"

Claris, her apron doubled over a bunch of tiny yellow flowers she had picked for the infusion, dropped the flowers on the sideboard and hurried over. Mother twitched her head toward the hearth.

"Get the rod and bring it over here."

"What are you going to do there?" The carter slapped the table top, but Mother did not flinch.

"I'm going to stop the bleeding, Francis." Mother turned her head very deliberately and gave him her *look*. "Or would you have him bleed to death here on my table?"

Francis Penneck's chin jutted.

"The surgeon sewed him last time. A long cut on the hip it was. Needle and thread, like a tailor." He mimed the sewing.

"And where would you have me put the stitch? This is no cut. The thing went through and through. Can you see where the blood's coming from? No. The wound is somewhere deep inside, and you can't reach in there with a needle and thread. It must be done with a thin, heated rod. Hot and quick. Then a good long lean on it. That will seal it and stop the blood. Now, can I get back to my work, or have you more to teach me?"

Claris picked up the stick with the glowing rod and positioned herself between Mother and me.

"Get ready," Mother told her. Without looking at me, she said, "Claris will put the handle in my hand quickly when I tell her. Watch now." She laid a hand on the leg, steadying it. "Turn his head, Francis."

Mister Penneck turned the boy's head to the side and held it with both hands.

"Quiet now, Harold," he said. "Lie still."

Mother picked up the shears, and Harold sent up a whine. Mister Penneck drew back, grimacing, but before he could say, "What are you doing there?" Mother said, "Now!"

She snipped off the feathered end of the shaft close to the skin, dropped her shears, and took the rod from Claris. Pulling the arrow out by the tip with her left hand, she slid the rod in behind it with her right. She withdrew the rod so fast, the boy screamed only once. Mister Penneck and I screamed, too.

"Remember this, Megge." Mother pressed a thick wad of cloth to the wound and leaned hard on it. After a long time, she lifted the cloth and peeked under. Slowly, she took it off. The bleeding had stopped.

Claris brought over a pot of the herbal infusion, set it on the table, handed Mother two cups, and patted the boy's arm.

"This will ease the pain."

Mother filled one of the cups then poured the liquid back and forth between the two cups to cool it. She dribbled the remedy over the wound, swaddled it, and gave it a pat.

"There. Keep it clean, Francis. Use this to wash it." She handed Mister Penneck the jug. "And keep him away from Tinker," she said as the carter carried his son out the door. "For that was no accident."

As Mister Penneck helped Harold out to the cart, Morwen and Aleydis arrived, each carrying a basket filled with dried fish and balls of cheese they had brought up from the spring house.

Morwen whispered to Mother, "What happened to the boy?"

"His brother," Mother said, one eyebrow raised, "shot an arrow through his leg."

Tinker? Morwen mouthed.

Mother nodded.

"We danced with Harold's sister, Vivienne, at the fair," I said. "Have you ever noticed that Vivienne Penneck looks just like Brighida?"

Claris coughed, spilling some of the water she had been swishing in the pot. She took the pot outside and poured the water on the ground.

"Brighida," she called from the doorway, "tell me again. What did we use in the infusion?"

As Brighida obediently recited the names of the herbs, Morwen and Aleydis exchanged a long look then took out their knives and got busy chopping the garlic and turnips Mother and Claris had peeled.

I went back out to the roost, daring myself to put my hand back into that grain barrel, and had just lowered my fingertips into it when Mother came out of the cottage with her book under her arm.

"Megge," she said in the same tone Claris used when speaking to Brighida, the master coaxing the apprentice, "why do so many come to us for a cure for lameness?"

I absently felt around in the grain barrel as I recalled mothers unwrapping their babies. *It's twisted, Mistress. Can you help?*

I saw Mother unwrapping Dora Tucker's dressing. *Do you want to lose that leg, Dora?*

Blood dripping off a boy's boot. *Do you want to lose that leg, boy?*

I saw the cripples in Morwen's stories of miracles, their litters abandoned in the street, their crutches hanging from the walls of churches or left lying at the sacred stone circles. The lame getting to their feet and proclaiming, "I can walk!"

I saw myself climbing hills and chasing lambs. George Gynneys holding a sheep against his legs as he sheared it. Men tilling fields, hauling rock from rivers and quarries. Village women carrying goods to market. How could anyone do their work on just one leg?

"Because we can't do our work on just one leg?" I asked.

"Because we can't do our work on just one leg." Satisfied, Mother headed toward the grove.

Suddenly realizing that nothing had happened to me—that I hadn't had *a moment in spirit*—when I touched the grain, I was about to take my hand out of the barrel and scatter some for the chickens when the cock stepped slowly through the grass, parting it with his feet. Chortling, he tipped forward, picked up a grub, and dropped it on the ground. Then he picked it up again, swallowed it, and stepped forward once more, parting the grass with his stick-like legs. *Even the cock needs his legs if he's to find something to eat*, I thought.

In my mind's eye, an arrowhead flashed through the calf of another sticklike leg.

"Mother," I called, "will Harold lose his leg?"

She kept walking. "Not if his mother keeps it clean."

I recalled Mistress Penneck's soft brown eyes.

"I'm sure she will."

Then I saw Mistress Penneck's eyes meet her mother's glare on the church steps, and I remembered what the old black-hatted woman had said about us.

"Mother," I called to her back, "why does Mistress Penneck's mother say we're cursed?"

Mother stopped, her book tight to her chest.

"Mother?"

She bent and picked a delicate yellow flower. She brought it to her nose and inhaled. When I caught up to her, she held it out to me.

"Coltsfoot. Smell it, Megge."

I stuck out my nose and sniffed.

"Sweet. But, Mother, why does Harold's grandmother say—"

She ignored me. Bending down again, she picked more of the yellow blossoms and dropped them crosswise into a pocket that spanned the front of her apron and could hold a dozen plants as long as my arm.

"What are they for?" I asked, for I knew I would learn nothing more about Jenifer Penneck, her awful mother, or the curse that now seemed to hang over us.

Mother took my hand and led me up the hill to her healer's hut, a long, low thatch-and-shingle woodshed just outside Bury Down circle, on the back side of the summit of the herder's slope.

"Let's go check the book."

Chapter 10

I was trapped.

Mother closed the door of the hut and took off her pouch. She set it and the flowers on the table along the front wall and propped open the shutters covering the small window. With great care, she set her book down beside her pouch. She opened the heavy wooden cover, and a musty smell rose from the pages. It tickled my nose and made me want to sneeze.

"Look away if you must do that," she said.

I looked away. Between sneezes, I could hear her finger brush over one of the pages. I thought, *This is my chance to please her.*

Mother was studying the very top page in the book. I squinted at it.

"This is the newest page. Parchment," she said. "Made from sheepskin. My father—Arjen was his name—wrote this notation."

She slipped her hand under the pages and opened the book to the middle. Brown and dry, the pages crackled like old husks.

"This is vellum," she said, turning the pages with care. "Very old." She pointed. "Look here, Megge."

I knew she wanted me to ask her a question, so I crossed to the other side of the hut to keep her from catching my hand and making me touch the page.

"What does it say?"

Mother closed her eyes and mumbled for a moment, then began to speak.

"Grown in the damp, in the full of the sun, coltsfoot will take root wherever the seed heads blow. Pluck them in the early hours." She opened her eyes. "When we call on *The Book of Seasons*, we are calling on the spirits of the Mentors. The Mentor who wrote this summoning incantation . . ." She stroked the page. ". . . tells us how things grow, Megge, and where to find them. To one who would ask, the Mentors will impart their knowledge of all things that grow in or walk upon the earth."

I desperately wanted to speak the words that had come to me in the churchyard: *Mother, would you please tell me about bees? Mother, would you please show me a page in the book that has a picture of a bee?* But the longer the book lay open, the more I just wanted to get out of that hut.

Mother, who had not looked up, who had not seen on my face the signs of my struggle, simply went on.

"*The Book of Time* speaks of this flower as it is used in healing, in spells. Coltsfoot, Claris will tell you, brings love and serenity. It also brings great wealth, but only to one who plants it as the Mentors in *The Book of Seasons* prescribe, picks it on the day *The Book of Time* orders, and prepares it just so, under the proper constellation of stars and the precise phase of the moon."

She stopped, waiting for me to ask a question.

"Could you do that?"

"Only if I knew the meaning of this symbol." She ran her finger over a notation on the page, stopping at the final symbol. "But the meaning of these and many other symbols, the most powerful ones, are found only in *The Book of Time*."

Finally, I thought, *a way to get us out of this hut.*

"But you can look in it, Mother. Brighida is steeped in it even now." I opened the door and stepped out. "Let's go back to the cottage."

She shook her head. "Only the one destined to unite the books may look upon them both, Megge. I may not, nor may Claris. We must never even open them in the same room at the same time.

"Claris has learned the seer's uses for this flower, and I the healer's. The rest . . . well, the rest is for the Guardian—and the Guardian's chosen one—to know." She closed *The Book of Seasons* and passed through the curtain that divided the hut into a healer's room in front and a wood-drying room in the rear. She returned with three small logs, some tinder, and a handful of straw. She laid them on the ground within a ring of stones just outside the hut. Then she reached into her pocket and took out her fire kit. She struck the flint and when the char cloth caught touched it to the hay, blew on the sparks, and fanned the flame with a stiff piece of tanned hide until it caught.

She came back in and reached beneath her table for a palm-sized crock covered with a stone lid.

"Are you going to boil the flowers, Mother?"

"The coltsfoot is for Claris. I have been making something for you." She hung the crock from a small tripod over the fire. A moment later, she came back in and opened the book all the way to the back. "These are the earliest notations," she said. "The symbols Anwen inscribed at Bryluen's instruction. The incantations of Murga herself."

Would Murga speak to Mother? Worse, would she call my name? I looked away and hummed a tune.

She pointed to the pages as if I were looking at them with her.

"Tin, for courage," she read. "For bringing about dreams. Zinc, for spiritual revelation. Bismuth, to ease the transition from the physical to the spiritual world."

Courage? Revelation?

"How do you know the meaning of these symbols, Mother, if you cannot look in *The Book of Time*?"

"Morwen taught me . . ." Mother started, but went suddenly silent. She closed *The Book of Seasons* and went back outside. Kneeling beside the ring of stones, she picked up the lid with her tongs. The stuff inside was grainy. Was it grey, silver, white? It was hard to tell.

"Melted," she said, "it will resemble silver." She set the lid back down on the crock. "When it cools and hardens, it will be ready."

"What are we making?"

She sat back on her heels. "I am making a stone. For you. To bring you courage."

Did I need courage?

. . . they'll die by flame.

But Grandmother says they're . . . cursed.

Mother set the lid down and pointed to a hawthorn stem on the table.

"Bring me that stem."

I took it to her, and she drew out her knife and cut off the end so it came to a point. When the molten metal had cooled into a soft lump at the bottom of the crock, she took it out and rolled it between her palms, making it into a small ball. She pushed the pointed green hawthorn stem through the middle of it and set it on the table.

"We will study while your stone sets."

I spent the rest of that long afternoon listening to her read incantations from *The Book of Seasons* and watching metal cool. Finally, she said, "It is time."

She picked up the silver lump and tried to sink her teeth into it.

"Rock hard." She studied it closely, turning it around and running her fingers over it. Satisfied, she slipped a slim leather thong through the hole the hawthorn twig had made.

"Come here, Megge." Standing behind me, she put the necklace on me and tied the thong in the back. "Wear this stone always, Daughter. For—"

"For courage," I said, rolling it between my fingers and wondering why no one else in the family had to wear a silver lump around their neck.

That evening, with Mother's stone to bring me courage, I sat down to a supper of pottage, thick bread, honey, and cheese. At the end of the meal, Morwen poured each of us a cup of her mead.

"Made by queen bees from the priory's honeysuckle hedge. Do you remember all those bees, Megge?"

I nodded, too sleepy to answer. My eyes were heavy. I could not think about the bees.

Aleydis tipped her head toward the door and gave Morwen a nod.

"The others will be leaving for the grove soon," Morwen said. "I'm tired, too. Let's go on to bed." She led the way with her lantern even though the full moon, nearly as bright as my new stone, would have shown us the way.

I lifted my stone so I could see it.

"Morwen, why do I need courage?"

"We all need courage, Megge," Morwen said. "But even when we're filled with courage, it's good to remember there's always some-one who will protect us." She laid her hand on the door to the lodge.

"Wait." I stopped her. "Why do we sleep under the ground?"

Morwen thought for a moment then patted the heavy door.

"Because long ago—you were no more than a babe at the time— someone burned down the house of the Bodmin midwife, a pious Christian woman called Clarissa. Clarissa Gloyn. No one ever learned who it was nailed her door shut and set the torch. Some said the hand of God had struck her down for cursing her neighbor's lit-ter of pigs, but none of us believe that."

"Mother and Aunt Claris talk about her sometimes."

"A frightful thing it was, Megge. And here we were—four women, two of them healers, one with child and the other with a newborn babe—living out on this farm in a house of wood and peat and thatch. No men around, of course, for your fathers—master craftsmen to the earl—lived at the castle."

"Did they give you a stone to make you brave?"

"No, child. I didn't need a stone, for I already had this." She held up her right hand. On her longest finger was a ring made up of what looked like intertwining silver strings.

"And your father and Brighida's father gave us something much more helpful than a ring or even a stone—a lovely home that would keep us safe. They dredged the Fowey for river rock and dug slate from the land. They spent that whole summer piling stone upon stone. A wall. A hearth. A roof of slate. Then, after they had covered the walls with shingles and the roof with thatch, so it would look as humble as any farmhouse in the Cornish hills, Brighida's father hung the lovely shutters into which he had carved those beautiful vines and nesting sparrows.

"No one ever would have guessed that we lived in a fortress to rival Restormel Castle itself. But even that wouldn't do. When they were done, they dug the sleeping lodge deep into the side of this hill." She patted the door. "Then, Brighida's father put in this strong oak door he had built and stained with woad. Hidden here among the grasses, you can only find it if you know where to look.

"'They'll never find you as you slumber here, little ones,' your father said. And six days after your father and uncle set this door on its hinges, the flux swept through Restormel and took both of them from us. Good men they were, and they took good care of us. Always remember that."

"But who takes care of us now? Is that why Mother gave me this stone?" I held it up for her to see. "Because there is no one to protect us?"

"Oh, Megge. Child, this is what you must understand—Fate brings people to love and protect us without our ever knowing. Why, just think about your grandmother Natalje. Did she know the girl she saw only as her mother's servant had been sent to protect her? Did she ever dream that a man would come from afar to marry her? Surely not. But life conspired to bring to her everyone she would ever need. And it all began with a nobleman's wish."

Lighting the way with her lantern, Morwen led me inside the lodge and held back the covers on my pallet. As I settled beneath them, she sat on the edge of my pallet, closed her eyes, and called forth one of her hypnotic sunrises.

✍

Watch closely, Megge, as the red, red sun rises from the sea. Keep watching. Can you see it climb into the clear morning sky? Higher, higher, and . . . there. Two masts. The Navigator's masts have pierced the eastern horizon beyond the rocky cliffs of Cornwall and bloomed into canvas sails tinted pink with the rising sun.

Down came the gangplank! And out stepped the great sea captain. Alongside him was a giant—a veritable Bendigeidfran—whose yellow hair and gold-flecked eyes Natalje had seen in her visions.

It seems the Earl of Cornwall desired a final resting place. And not just any old box to bury his bones in, mind you, but a proper place where an English earl might sleep the eternal night away alongside those he loved. So, he sent Adaem to find the greatest builders and craftsmen within the reach of his ship. And that meant, of course, any land at all.

Well, Adaem sailed back to his homeland, the seaside village of Aldestowe, far to the west, that looked over the Celtic Sea and into the setting sun. And he returned to Lostwithiel with masons and surveyors and carvers such as the earl had never known. And to lead them all: Arjen Magor.

Arjen Magor. A man possessed of uncanny, unsurpassed knowledge of the ground beneath his feet. A mason, a stone carver. An artist.

Shoulder to shoulder, Arjen and Adaem strode across the earl's land, Arjen bending down here and there and scooping a handful of dirt, which he tasted with the tip of his tongue.

"Copper," he would say. Or "Arsenic."

And Arjen's Uncle Egbert, a very short, very round man Arjen called "Rudh" for the color of his fiery hair, would write *Copper* or *Arsenic* in his tidy ledger book.

Finally, Arjen made up his mind.

"Tin and copper and slate abound around here. But slate for a mausoleum? Slate for a rich man's church? Take me to the moors, Adaem. There we will find granite for your nobleman's grave."

Well, twelve-year-old Natalje, slender as a blade, watched in awe as Arjen hefted his tools and an armload of rocks, and set off at a jog up the hill to the moors.

Summers came and summers went, and still they dug and still they built. By day, Arjen and his men hewed granite and drew plans for the church. For by now, Megge, that is what it had become. And by night, Arjen regaled those around the fires with tales of his home.

"A harbor cursed by a lovesick mermaid who to this day strands unwary ships upon the treacherous sandbar they call Doom."

And when Arjen finished his story, his bald-headed surveyor, the shy, silent, slumping Odo Fregys, Arjen's greatest friend, would dig a pair of dried white bones from the pocket of his vest. Holding the bones twixt the fingers of one hand, he would straighten his spine and send every girl a smile to melt her heart, and then he'd come to life. He would set those bones to clattering against his thigh while the Lostwithiel girls danced all around him. And I must tell you, little one, by the first Michaelmas, he could have had his pick of us.

Such a festive time it was. So many weddings. Why, even Odo and Egbert found wives in Lostwithiel. And when the building was done, they returned to the west, where their families abide to this day.

So, as Arjen told his tales and Odo played the bones, the Lady Gytha watched Natalje fall in love with the stonemason from Aldestowe. And when the last stone had been laid, and the earl had given his heartiest thanks for the living, breathing chapel, the exquisite place of worship Arjen had built instead of a chamber for the dead, Gytha led Natalje and Arjen to her grove. And there, in a rocky, mossy clearing, under a canopy of oak and rowan, she blessed their union.

Chapter 11

I dreamed that night of a wedding in the grove, and I awoke with a hundred questions about Natalje and Arjen. Surely, Natalje would return with Arjen to his ancestral home. How, then, would she become a seer like Gytha? It would be as if I were to leave my teachers, Morwen and Mister Gynneys, and set out for a distant land. How would I ever become a shearer like them?

Morwen and I set out for the pen under a stingy dawn; and as we walked, I asked, "Morwen, did Natalje go back with Arjen to his family's home?"

"Aye, very soon after they were wed."

"How, then, could Natalje ever hope to become a great seer like her mother?"

"Clever girl." Morwen smiled and nodded. "Natalje asked her mother the very same question. And Gytha replied, 'My path is not yours, Daughter.'"

I stopped and stood very still.

"What did she mean? What did Gytha mean?"

"You must understand, Megge, that we all have our own work to do. Even Natalje had her own work to do, work that would be nothing like Gytha's. But the lessons she had learned from *The Book of Time* had prepared her to do her work well."

"What did she learn, Morwen?"

"She learned a secret that gave her the courage to face whatever would come—that she was never alone."

But I was not concerned about courage that day. I wanted to learn how to stay away from Mother's path, because the only way down it was through that book. I pressed on.

"Morwen, did Gytha really say, 'My path is not yours, Daughter'?"

"Aye, child, she said those very words," Morwen said as we neared the sheep pen.

"Well, if it isn't Atropos herself," Mister Gynneys called from inside the fence.

"Not Atropos," I whispered to Morwen. "Aerten!"

Already he had sheared three ewes and had full bags of fleece leaning against the wall to show for his labor. He brushed off his tunic.

"Are you ready to get to work? Today you'll learn to do bellies."

As we sheared, Mister Gynneys and Morwen turning my hand this way or that and whispering instructions as I worked, I wondered if Mother knew that Gytha had not ordered Natalje to follow in her footsteps. I tried to imagine Mother saying, "My path is not yours, Daughter," as Gytha had said to Natalje.

I moved my lips over the words. *My path is not yours, Daughter.*

That afternoon, when Morwen and I reached the cottage door after a long morning of shearing, I listened for talk or for the clatter of dishes, but the cottage was quiet. Opening the door just a crack, I saw Brighida hunched over the deepest pages of her book.

I whispered, "Where is Mother?"

Brighida did not even look up, so I went inside, ladled cold pottage into three bowls, and set them on the table. I pushed one over to her, but my cousin was so lost in her book she did not notice. Nor did she pull her book away or try to hide it from me, as she usually did. Her eyes were fixed on the page with an intensity I had never before seen.

"What is it, Brighida?"

Still deep in the world of the book, she whispered as though exhausted, "I've gone dry."

My breath caught. My ears began to ring. Everything around me went small and bright and very far away. A feeling of dread overtook me, and I could not speak. An image seemed to be coming to me as if in a dream, a vision of a young woman, haggard and near to death, a blue-hued babe in her arms. I tried to see more clearly, but the image was hidden in shadow.

Morwen coughed, and then doubled over in a fit of coughing, and the spell was broken.

"Brighida," she said between gasps. "Brighida, fetch me something to drink."

Brighida got up slowly from the table, shaking her head just as I was doing, as if to dispel a nightmare. Like one awakened from deep slumber, she slowly dipped a cup into the bucket of ale and handed it to Morwen.

As Morwen sipped, she finally stopped coughing.

My ears had stopped ringing, but all I could do was stare at Brighida.

"Here, Megge," Morwen finally said, giving me a sip of her ale. "Eat something. You are so pale." She placed one of the bowls in front of me and watched me carefully while I ate. It felt as though my arm and hand were moving on their own. My mouth opened and closed, and I chewed and swallowed, but I tasted nothing.

I've gone dry . . .

I left my food and went into the workroom, thinking about something Brighida had said that day at the grain bin: *My mother says I've chosen to forget a former life that wants to be recalled.* I sat down on the stool beside the loom, and as I thought about those words, I picked up a handful of wool from the basket beside it. Rough and oily, it had burrs and twigs embedded amidst the tangles.

I've gone dry. I shivered as the words echoed in my ears, for I suspected they had something to do with a life *I* had chosen to forget.

I put the fleece back in the basket. I would card it that evening while Brighida and Claris spun, Morwen and Aleydis played their music, and Mother wove and cursed. But for now, I had to get as far away from the cottage—and from Brighida—as I could.

Mother would be back soon. Seeing Brighida studying, she would place her book before me and tell me to open it.

Then I remembered Gytha's saying, *My path is not yours, Daughter*; and I decided to think about those words rather than Brighida's, for they gave me hope.

I needn't follow in Mother's footsteps.

But if I was not meant to follow Mother's path, then whose was I meant to follow?

The story Morwen had told was about Natalje, who would follow Arjen to his homeland far to the west. But it was also about Arjen, a stonemason just as my own father had been. Was I to follow *their* path? Had I somehow missed that part of the story?

Aleydis can tell me about Arjen, I thought. He had been her brother, after all.

"Brighida," I called into the cookroom, "where is Aunt Aleydis?"

"I'm out here," Aleydis called from the garden just outside the window. "Let's go let the sheep out, Megge."

I ran outside, grabbed her hand, and pulled her across the chicken yard. Wanting to hear about Arjen as quickly as possible, I ran ahead of her to the pen, slipped the leather thong off the post, and flung open the gate. Mister Gynneys had finished his work, so Aleydis and I guided the sheep out onto the lawn, where they would graze for the rest of the day. Then we climbed to the top of the hill to sit on our boulders and watch them.

When I was very young, Aunt Aleydis always held me in her lap and taught me about the sheep.

"Why, your own dress is made of their beautiful wool. So are your warm leggings and the soft blankets that cover you at night as you dream." She also taught me to protect them. "You must watch the fields and the hills for animals that might hurt your flock—predators, such as wolves, that come out to hunt at dusk." She even fashioned the stick I would carry as I guarded them. "You can use this to frighten them off," she said raising it above her head and shaking it.

But I wasn't interested in wolves that day. I wanted to know how Natalje could have found her path if she strayed from her mother's side.

"Aleydis, would you tell me about my grandfather? About Arjen?"

She smiled. She had lovely pink lips and nearly all her teeth.

"Arjen." She pronounced it *Ar-chen*. "Arjen was my older brother," she began slowly, "and he was magical. Oh, not in the way you might think, not like your mother and aunt. Arjen's magic had come to him from Father, an artist.

"Father sculpted unearthly images from stone, and those who envied him said he was in league with the devil himself. But that was not true. He simply had an eye that saw within the earth, and he brought out his visions in rock.

"He came from a village called Bude, to the north, and he found himself in Aldestowe when his boat ran aground on Doom Bar. He loved the seaside village at first sight, and so he stayed and made Aldestowe his home. And when he first glimpsed the woman who would be my mother, the copper-haired Beatrix Couper, he fell in love with her, too, at first sight. They married and soon had a son, whom they called Arjen. And three years later, I came along.

"Would it surprise you, Megge, to learn that my father carried with him a great book? He guarded it with his life, though he claimed it held no more than a stonemason's knowledge of the earth.

It had come to him from his mother and was intended for his heir. He took great care to safeguard it from all other eyes."

Just like Mother and Claris, I thought. "Aunt Aleydis, what was the book called?"

She gave me a wry smile. "It was called *The Book of Seasons*."

"That's Mother's book!"

"Yes, Megge. It is the very same book."

"And it was your father's? Doesn't the book pass from mother to daughter?"

She shook her head. "Only *The Book of Time* is kept amongst the women. *The Book of Seasons* passes to boys or girls, for both men and women work the earth, serve as healers, and learn the ways of the physical world.

"My grandmother, his mother, an artist whose mosaics graced the walls of churches all along the coast, passed the book down to him." She waited a moment for me to consider this. "*My* mother," she went on, "was a sorceress—well, perhaps only a conjurer of sorts— as was her younger brother, Egbert, who studied alchemy.

"Like many who lived in the villages to the west, my mother and uncle envied the descendants of Anwen the Huntress, as she was known. Since they were children, my mother and uncle had heard the tales of Anwen and Murga and *The Book of Seasons*, and they believed that if they could but glimpse its pages, they would be able to harness its power.

"And so, when she had come into womanhood, and the very man who held the book came to our village, Mother set out to win his heart. A beautiful girl with hair like fire and skin like cream, she did just that.

"One day, not long after she had made me her apprentice, Mother found Father's book and took me aside. 'It is time for your first lesson in power,' she said. Her green eyes glinted, Megge, and though I was very young and knew nothing of that book, I knew that what we were doing was wrong.

"Well, Mother opened it. This was no stonemason's manual. It was written in symbols she had never before seen. Symbols I somehow seemed to know." Aleydis nodded, appearing satisfied, then looked at me and smiled. "But they did not give up their secrets."

She paused for a moment to think, her fingertips stroking her jawline and then pulling on a tiny chin hair.

"Mother begged Father to make me his heir, but Father paid her no mind. Arjen was already his apprentice and was learning all Father could teach him—of stoneworking, of building, and of their book—and when Father died, the book passed to Arjen.

"We were grown by then, of course. But ever since seeing those symbols, I knew who I was and where my path lay." The corners of her mouth turned down, and she nodded to herself in an expression of certainty and pride.

"Days after Father died," she said, "*The Navigator* sailed into port, and Arjen left for Lostwithiel with Adaem, his book hidden amongst his belongings. Mother never again saw its pages." Her expression went somber. "When Arjen himself was dying—so young—he asked your grandmother Natalje to swear she would pass his book to their child." Aleydis's gaze drifted into the distance. "I was with them, Megge, tending his ravaged skin as he died. 'Swear it, Natalje,' he said. And though she trembled, Natalje took her oath. 'I swear it, Arjen.'" Aleydis's gaze settled on me. "And that vow opened the door to Natalje's destiny. And to yours."

Afraid she was going to tell me about a frightening destiny that would require the courage Mother had said I would one day need, I ran down the hill to the sheep. Aunt Claris found me out on the lawn, down on my hands and knees with two of the lambs.

"Your mother is asking for you." Claris held out her hand to me. "Let's go see what she has for you, Megge."

It was going to be that book.

Claris walked ahead of me while I dawdled, picking up twigs, kicking stones, and swinging around the smooth trunks of saplings. When we reached the cottage, Mother came outside, took my hand from Claris's, and led me around to the side of the house.

"There is something I want to show you, Daughter," she said. She spoke fast, and although she did not quite smile—Mother never smiled if she could help it—her eyes were bright. "Now, we must be very quiet."

She pointed toward the hawthorn that stood against the cottage, just beneath the window, and put her finger to her lips. We tiptoed toward it. The bush was very dense, and beneath its branches grew sprays of high grass. Mother parted one with the tip of her stick and pointed to its depths.

"Look, Megge."

Tufts of soft, light-grey fur, with twigs and leaves on top.

"What is it?"

"Look closely. Can you see it move? It's a nest. Baby rabbits are hidden beneath the fur."

Only their burrowing, huddling movements were visible, but I could now see the outline of their tiny bodies. I touched the pile of fluff, so soft I could barely feel it, and they squeaked.

Mother pulled my hand away, and I squatted and watched them until my legs began to shake. She reached down and pulled me to my feet.

"The mother built her nest where her babies would be safe, instead of in a hedge where a predator might find them. Here, she will raise them and teach them how rabbits live. She will protect them, Megge—with her life if she must." She caught my eye and held it. "Protecting life is a sacred trust, Daughter."

I looked from the rabbits' nest to the pasture, where the ewes grazed alongside their young, and I wondered if Mother would protect *me* if she was ever forced to choose between me and that book.

Chapter 12

"No need to worry about me," Dora Tucker said at the market the following week. "I've hardly a limp." She handed Mother our empty woolsacks and a fistful of coins, and we purchased our candles, fish, and cloth and then started for home. When we had passed the church, Claris pointed to a path that led to a wooded ravine.

"Let's leave a tithe at the abbey."

"The Blackfriar abbey?" Mother stopped at the edge of the ravine, her face hard. "We'll not give those murderers a thing,"

"A couple of fish, Sister. A salted cod or two. The friars have so little, and they ask for nothing. They demand no tithe."

"After what they did to Clarissa Gloyn?" Mother demanded. "It was their whispers that got her killed."

"Whispers do not kill." Claris lowered her voice. "The Blackfriars rave, but no one listens anymore. In fact, when was the last time we saw them or heard a word from the abbey? The friars have kept very quiet, very much to themselves. And some are so old. They can't take care of themselves. Look around. It is May, Sister, the dying month. You know they have nothing to nourish them but their zeal."

"They have their orchard."

"This?" Claris waved her hand over a dozen withered apple trees veiled in cobwebs.

"One fish, then," Mother countered.

"Two."

Claris bargained with Mother as we descended the steep path, careful not to slip on the mossy stones.

The abbey sat in the hollows behind ancient oaks and moss-covered gates, the flagstones leading to the door canted and cracked, tall grasses growing up between them.

"Mother," Brighida said looking about the place, "who will eat the fish? No one lives here."

Claris closed her eyes for a moment. "There is hunger here."

A chill shot through me.

I shivered, and Brighida squeezed my arm and whispered, "Someone's just walked over your grave."

Claris wrapped three salted fish and two candles in muslin. She pushed open the gate, stepped carefully on the uneven flags, and pulled on the door's heavy iron ring. The door did not open, so she laid the parcel at the threshold.

Mother pulled a mossy rope and rang the bell.

"Let us be away from here."

Claris looked up at the dark windows of the abbey with pity.

"There is suffering here," she said.

I shivered again. I wanted only to be away from that desolate place.

"Come, Megge." Mother led me back through the gates. As I passed through them, I looked back at the abbey just as the door opened and a bony hand reached out and drew our meager offering inside.

I hurried to catch up with Mother, staying close to her as we climbed the steep path that led up the other side of the ravine. With each step, my unease grew.

I kept hearing Claris's words—*There is hunger here*—as, again and again, I saw that hand, all knuckles and sinew, reach out for the food we had left.

A cold wind came through that evening, so after we finished our supper, Mother closed the tin door over the cookroom hearth and opened the much larger one that covered the high, wide hearth in the workroom. Heat rushed into the room, and by the time we were ready for the evening's work, each with a cup of warm mead, the workroom was so cozy I wanted only to sleep.

But there was no moon that night, so no one would be visiting the grove. We would all be together. I would stay awake with the others no matter how sleepy I felt.

Mother sat down at her loom and Claris at her spinning wheel. Brighida and I sat on low stools by the hearth, picked up our baskets of wool, and began carding. Morwen and Aunt Aleydis pulled their chairs close to the fire and took down their musical instruments from the mantel. Morwen blew fine, high notes on her flute while Aleydis accompanied her on the gemshorn.

They repeated a little tune—three notes rising and one note falling. The notes merged with the words Claris had spoken—*There is hunger*—and brought forth once more the image of that gnarled hand.

Morwen stopped playing and slowly lowered her flute, something clearly upsetting her. She turned her chair to face me.

"What is that you're singing, Megge?"

"Singing?" Had I been singing?

I tried to pull my mind's eye back from the abbey and from the image of that hand reaching for food, and realized I must have turned Claris's words into song.

"There is hunger," I sang in a tentative voice to the tune Morwen and Aleydis had been playing. Speaking those words aloud conjured an even clearer image of that grasping hand and filled me with unutterable sadness.

Aunt Aleydis, a look of concern on her face, put down her gemshorn and moved her chair close to mine.

Why had my singing so upset my aunts?

"Morwen," Mother said sweetly, although her teeth were clenched and she was looking with vexation into Aunt Claris's eyes, "haven't you a story for the girls?"

Morwen turned her chair around to face the room.

"Well, let me see," she said, looking to the ceiling. "Oh, yes. When we left them, Arjen and Natalje had just become husband and wife." She took a sip of mead and looked at Brighida and me. "Well, girls, when the nuptial feasts were through, Arjen and Natalje set sail aboard *The Navigator* for Arjen's home on the cliffs to the west. When Adaem and the crew and the other servants returned to Cornwall, Natalje's serving girl stayed with her but kept her gaze low, a dull-eyed scullery maid beneath the notice of the family.

"Before a year had passed, Natalje was with child and young Arjen was very ill. As his great strength waned, he begged Natalje to pass *The Book of Seasons* to their child. 'Swear it, Natalje.'

"'I swear it, Arjen,' Natalje vowed. But though she said nothing, she was troubled. She was meant to pass her own book to her child. How, she wondered, would one child ever be able to master both *The Book of Time* and *The Book of Seasons*?

"Well, the answer came very soon. For, that night, the moon drew about herself a misty shroud and rose to her zenith, taking Arjen with her into the next world. And before the dawn could shine upon his still countenance, before his body could grow cold, before his bride could even wipe away her first tear, the time came for their child to be born. And, oh, what a birth it was. For a day and a night and a morning, young Natalje strained to deliver her firstborn."

Mother and Claris, who seemed to be squabbling, got up and stalked into the cookroom, hissing at each other, their backs very erect and their heels striking the floor like hammers. I rarely saw them face each other in anger, but now they stood by the hearth, red-faced, arguing in hushed voices. I stiffened in fear and moved closer to Brighida. Was this fight about the same thing that had upset Morwen and Aleydis? Was it my fault?

Claris gestured toward Brighida and me.

"She needs to hear it—"

Mother began chopping at the air, just as she had that day at the market when Claris spoke to her about those horrid old women on the church steps. *No. No. No.*

But Claris would not be deterred.

"Better she hear this story than—"

"Than what?" Mother barked. "Than 'There is hunger'?"

Claris looked away, shamed. My throat tightened for her, and I began to cry. Brighida, her face in her hands, was already sobbing.

"Isn't she frightened enough already?" Mother went on, heedless of Claris's humiliation and our tears. "Do you want her to flee?"

Flee? They couldn't be talking about me. Never had I fled.

I looked at the sobbing Brighida, whose wide, frightened eyes went from her mother to me. Would Brighida flee? Surely not, I thought, no matter how frightened she became.

Aunt Aleydis got to her feet, put herself squarely between my mother and aunt, and leveled a look at each of them, silencing them. She went to the basket beside Mother's loom, pulled out a small square of cloth, and handed it to me, smiling and miming blowing her nose. Then she squatted down beside Brighida. Handing her a square of cloth, she spoke to her, one hand on my cousin's shoulder, until she, too, stopped crying.

When Mother and Aunt Claris returned to their chairs, Morwen went on with her story as if nothing had happened.

"Well, girls, that very night, Arjen's mother—who was called Beatrix—and his sister, your very own great-aunt Aleydis, helped Natalje bear not one but *two* baby daughters, each child born with the caul.

"And Natalje declared, right then and there, that *The Book of Time*, which had come to her from her mother, would pass to her firstborn, whom she named Claris, and that *The Book of Seasons*, which had belonged to Arjen, would pass to her second-born, the babe still without a name."

Morwen lowered her voice. "But Beatrix practiced the dark arts and wanted nothing more than to possess *The Book of Seasons*." Her voice was now a whisper. "For its symbols were said to hold the secret of life itself."

Brighida and I held our breath. Although I had winced at the mention of *The Book of Seasons*, and although I wanted to get up and leave the room, I sat very still and said nothing. That book was part of this story, I now understood, and Claris had just told Mother that one of us—either Brighida or I—needed to hear it. I willed myself to listen.

"And so," Morwen whispered, "Beatrix bent to the fire, jabbing it with her poker until the sparks leapt and the flames danced. And then she spoke these words: 'The books, when joined by blood or name—'"

"Morwen!" Mother shouted.

Morwen's hand flew to her chest. Brighida jumped. My breath caught, and my heart pounded.

"That will do." Mother was now on her feet and moving toward Morwen.

Now that I was finally ready to hear about that book, Mother would put a halt to the story? Why?

I stood up. "Why mustn't Morwen finish, Mother?"

Mother did not reply. Instead, she put out a hand and helped Morwen to her feet.

"Enough for tonight."

Morwen shrugged and reached for her lantern. She lit the candle from the hearth fire and shepherded us before her.

"Come, girls. It's late." As we passed Mother, Morwen whispered to her, "She *needs* to know about the curse, dear."

✍

Feeling certain the words Morwen had been about to reveal—*the curse*—had something to do with *The Book of Seasons* burning me, I pestered Morwen all the way back to the lodge.

"*Who* needs to know about the curse, Morwen? Do I? And who is going to flee? Is it me? What did Mother mean—"

"Hush for a moment, Megge," Morwen said, her mouth as tight and hard as Mother's. "Let me think."

I quietly got into my pallet. Never before had I seen Morwen so upset. As I covered myself in blankets and hides, I asked a different kind of question.

"What does 'joined by blood or name' mean, Morwen?"

Morwen's face finally relaxed, and she sat down on my side of the pallet.

"It simply means that something is held by two people who are from the same family, or who have the same surname."

The books, when joined by blood or name . . .

"The books are held by Mother and Aunt Claris," I whispered.

"Aye, Megge." Morwen got up from my pallet. "Your mother and aunt hold the books. For now. Time to go to sleep now."

Your mother. Claris always called my mother *Sister*, and Brighida called her *Aunt*. Even her friends just called her *Mistress*. I reached out and tugged on the back of Morwen's cloak to stop her.

"Morwen, what's Mother's name?"

Morwen's breath caught. "Your mother . . ." She sat back down. "Your mother has no given name, child." She took my hand. "Your grandmother Natalje reasoned that if her second-born daughter had no name, then Beatrix's words could never harm them." She tucked my covers under my chin. "Now, go to sleep."

The words Mother had once said to Morwen came back to me. *I have vowed to face flames rather than fail . . .*

Brighida already had fallen into a restless slumber, but how could I sleep with a curse and that awful vow ringing in my ears?

I sat up on my pallet, my voice urgent now.

"But the books are still joined by blood, Morwen. By sisters," I whispered. "Will something happen to Mother and Aunt Claris because they are sisters who hold the books?" I held my breath while I waited for her to answer.

"Not if they pass them to the one the Guardian has appointed."

Something in the air changed, and I felt dizzy. I had to lie back. As I fell asleep, I felt I was on the verge of knowing something.

CHAPTER 13

I awoke gasping from a dream of the hatted women knowing the words spoken by my great-grandmother Beatrix, "The books when joined by blood or name . . ." ended with the ones spoken by the black-hatted, silver-eyed old woman on the church steps: "Scorned, reviled, they'll die by flame."

I knew now that it was Mother and Aunt Claris who were cursed. *I have vowed to face flames . . .*

Terrified, I decided not to go back to sleep. I would stay awake, and in the morning, I would face Mother. I want to know about the curse, I would say.

For I was certain it was Beatrix's curse I had felt writhing within the book, and that the fire that had burned me had come from the conjuror's flames.

The conjuror. My own great-grandmother.

But the night was long, and I drifted back to sleep despite myself, although the words I had rehearsed filled my dreams: *Tell me— now—tell me about the curse.*

The curse.

Finally, when it seemed morning must be near, I slipped out of bed and dressed.

Mother must have risen much earlier, for she was already in the cookroom when I opened the door. Still in her cloak, she was facing the hearth and working the bellows, bursts of air making the embers blossom. I stamped the water off my boots, but the sound did not startle her. It seemed she was expecting me.

Without saying a word, she put down the bellows and went to her shelf. She thrust back the curtain and took down her book. I steeled myself.

"There is no curse *within* our book, Daughter," she said, her voice and shoulders weary as she carried it to the table. She pulled up two chairs and sat, motioning for me to do the same.

I stayed on my feet, standing far behind her and trying not to look at that wooden cover or the symbols etched on it. I looked away when she opened it.

Her spine stiffened, and her voice went hard.

"You will look at it, Margaret. Look at this book."

Although I continued to look away, I could see her movements out of the corner of my eye.

"This . . ." Mother opened the book, her finger floating above the bottom of the page. ". . . is the summoning notation your grandfather Arjen wrote the day he died." She looked up to see if I was watching. "And this . . ." She pointed to the symbols just above it. ". . . is his father's. These symbols will bring forth all their knowledge, all their artistry. Speaking these incantations will bring forth their very spirits. Don't you understand, Megge? This book holds the spirits of all the Mentors. Of every heir to the books. One day, it will hold mine and Claris's. And Brighida's. Just look."

The Mentors' spirits are inside the book? Was it the Mentors who burned me?

I looked instead at the drying herbs.

"Stones, rocks, crystals, the soil—the earth itself. This was the stuff Arjen and his father knew. This is what they swore to teach the one who would come to the book and ask. They knew these things just as I know the limbs, the skin, the birth passage. As Claris and Brighida know the stars and planets, the celestial images—as they know what has passed and what is to come."

She hesitated for a moment before looking over her shoulder at me. "I wish I could tell you more, but I cannot. It is not for me . . ." She ran her hand through her hair, scrubbing at her scalp as if to tear the hair out at the roots.

"When you come to the book of your own accord, the Mentors will reveal themselves to you." Shaking her head, she pushed back her chair. "Our time here is so brief, Daughter. Soon, dark days will be upon us."

Frustrated, she got up and began to look around for something. I followed her outside to the roost. The sun was coming up, and the chickens were pecking in the dirt.

"This cock . . ." She pointed to the strutting bird, who lifted his head, threw out his throat, and crowed. "He knows he is neither hawk nor lark. He knows what to eat, where to sleep, when to crow, how to mate." She looked at me hard. "He knows what he is."

She took my hand and drew me back inside to the table. To the book.

"You are my daughter. The next heir to *The Book of Seasons*." She stopped. "Yet, you close your ears to me, claiming to be a herder. You close your eyes to the book. But can you not see what you are beneath the herder's cloak?" She pushed me away, held me at arm's length.

Finally, she let go. "Come." She motioned for me to sit beside her.

I remained on my feet.

"All this long night, Daughter, you spoke aloud of curses. You cried out. You kicked in your sleep. What is it you fear?"

I looked her in the eye. "I fear whatever lives inside that book, whatever called my name and then burned me. If it was not the curse, then what was it? Was it the Mentors?" My fingertips were fluttering wildly. "And I fear what I will become if I open that book. What path will it take me down?"

Mother sat back for a moment, her pursed lips moving from side to side until, finally, she leaned forward.

"You did feel something the first time you touched the book, Margaret." She got up and looked out the door, and then out the window. Finally, she sat back down and looked into my eyes. "What you felt was power. Life-sustaining power entrusted to us. That is why we live as we do, protecting the books and adding our knowledge and wisdom to them. We have been given a sacred trust.

"What you felt was not a curse, nor was it the spirits of the Mentors. It was power, Megge. And what you heard at your ceremony was your destiny beckoning you."

Murderer.

Was I destined to do murder?

"What *is* my destiny, Mother?" I wrapped my arms around my chest and rocked. "The book said 'Murderer.' If I open that book, is that what I will become?"

"Stop that nonsense, Margaret. How can a book make you something you are not? And you are not a murderer. Now, sit up straight. Look me in the eye. Put your hands in your lap. You are grown. Stop sniveling." She slid her book before me, opened it to the middle, and pointed. "Look upon it, Daughter."

Mother slipped her hand beneath the bulk of the pages and lifted them with great care, opening the book to the earliest notation. She pointed to it and spoke the words.

"*Scientia nupta sapientia potestas est.* Knowledge wedded to wisdom is power. But knowledge wedded to wisdom also brings courage." Her voice dropped, and she spoke quietly, rapidly, without taking a breath. "If you would but open that book—oh, Megge, I would tell you what's to be if I could—but if you would only open it, you would know everything. Most of all, you would come to know who you truly are."

She glanced furtively toward the door. Then she grabbed my hand and pulled it to the book, her voice hushed but her expression urgent.

"Just touch it, Mur—"

"Megge." The door swung open, hitting the wall and giving off a thunderclap that silenced Mother. And Morwen, tiny Morwen, stood in the doorway. Her eyes held Mother's, although she spoke to me. "There's a lambing. Aleydis needs you."

CHAPTER 14

"An easy birth," I said, watching the ewe lick her lamb clean. "Now that it is done," Aleydis said, "we can say with a light heart how easy it was."

She pulled the wet straw out of the barn while I brought in dry bedding. As she spread the sweet-smelling straw around with her rake, she said, "It's always easiest when they have lambed before. They know just what to do. And they are so calm."

I thought of Mother's saying "Knowledge and wisdom also bring courage" as I watched the ewe finish off the afterbirth. No one had taught her to do that. Did knowledge and wisdom come naturally to animals? If so, then perhaps I, too, already possessed them. Perhaps I could find them within myself without ever opening that book.

"Aunt Aleydis, do you think this ewe had knowledge of birthing?"

She leaned on her rake. "Well, for her, I would say knowledge of birth comes as . . . as nature's wisdom. But her calm comes from having lambed before." She paused. "Is that knowledge? Perhaps it is."

I went out for a bucket of fresh water. So, ewes had knowledge—nature's wisdom—and courage. I had seen women deliver their second and third babies, each one with greater calm.

"What about women, Aunt? Do knowledge and wisdom give a woman courage?"

"Well, let's see. Every woman learns with her first child that birth is very painful and that she could die. That the child could die." She raked slowly, going over and over the same patch. "And many babies do die, so every mother wants many children. Nature gives her this wisdom." She had stopped raking and was nodding to herself now. "So, yes, Megge, I believe that by knowing what is to come and by possessing the wisdom to have many children, a woman is able to face the pain with courage."

As I leaned over to dump the fresh water into the trough, my necklace fell off. I picked it out of the water and fingered the stone. It reminded me of the story Morwen had told the night Mother gave it to me. The shepherd in that tale had known his enemy. And he knew his own skill with a stone, so he had the courage to face the giant so feared by the warriors.

But I did not know my enemy, the thing that had come to life and burned me when I touched *The Book of Seasons*. I did know, though, what I might become if I ever opened it.

"What if we don't know, Aunt? Can we still have courage if we don't know for certain what it is we fear?"

"Well, we can't always know what is to be, can we, Megge?" She spoke to me over her shoulder as she put the young ram to the ewe's teat. "We must simply face what comes in life." The ram began to suckle, and Aleydis sat down and leaned against a hay bale.

"That day Dora Tucker was gored," she said. "You stayed with her, and then you went for help even though the boar could have come back."

"But I didn't know if it would—"

"No, you didn't. But, tell me, Megge. Did you even stop to ask yourself whether the animal that had hurt Dora might also harm you?" She did not give me time to answer. "And all the nights we spend out on the slope guarding the sheep. Have we ever asked ourselves if there was something out there, something out in the woods, in the hills? A wolf, a bear—a man—that could harm us?"

I shook my head.

"And when you take my place out on the rock one day, when you alone guard your flock, will you fear?"

"Not for myself."

She leaned on the rake and got to her feet.

"Now, let me ask you one more thing. What do you think makes us do these things with no thought for ourselves?"

In my mind's eye, I saw Natalje vow to protect *The Book of Seasons* so it could be passed from her husband to his heir. I saw Mother and Claris and the Bodmin midwife, healers all, protecting the lives of the women and babies of the village. I saw the cock—neither hawk nor lark—protecting his flock. And I saw myself protecting mine.

What was it Mother had just said? Protecting life is . . .

"A sacred trust," I replied, wondering how Mother—my protector—could ever ask me to open that book knowing the curse that would fall upon me and Brighida, and the path the book might lead me down.

But then another thought occurred to me. Perhaps *The Book of Seasons* offered two paths: the one Mother wanted me to take—that of protector—and one she knew nothing about, the one the book seemed to be luring me toward. *Murderer*. And perhaps it was I who would choose.

Aleydis cocked her head. "Let's go back, Megge," she said, putting up her rake. "Morwen is calling for you."

Chapter 15

November 16, 1282 C.E.

Thirteen years old today," Morwen said, and the cough that had plagued her since summer made her stop talking until she could catch her breath. "Practically a woman," she said, her voice rough, when she had recovered from that fit.

She closed her fingers over mine. "Three full years a bard's apprentice, and you've learned all my stories. Why, it's a bard you could call yourself now."

She laughed to herself, and then coughed until Aleydis brought her a cup of ale.

Morwen's cough sent her to her bed that night and deepened with the winter's rains. As the days grew shorter, the cough worsened until she was no longer able to recite a long tale. Soon it became a struggle for her to speak.

"You must remember the stories," she insisted. "You must remember everything. Everything, Megge."

By mid-December, only one remedy calmed Morwen's cough.

"My mead, Megge. Just a sip."

"She can't sleep here," Mother said, looking around the lodge. "It's too cold and damp. Let us move the pallets to the workroom, where we can keep her warm."

Clouds moved in as Brighida and I carried the last pallet into the cottage. By the time we had arranged them around the hearth, a drizzle was coming down.

"Thank you, girls." Morwen's teeth were clenched, her face flushed.

A storm raged outside that afternoon as Mother and I coaxed Morwen to eat. Claris gave her an infusion, and she dozed on her pallet before the hearth. Before long, though, the fever claimed her once more and shook her till her teeth chattered despite the blankets and hides we heaped upon her.

"We've not much peat left," Mother called from the cookroom. "Fetch some wood, Megge. The oldest and the driest you can find. And bring my fire kit and some tinder."

The best firewood was stored in the back of Mother's hut. I chose six seasoned limbs. Although thin, they were too long to carry easily, so I took down the axe from the beam she always hung it on to keep the head from rusting. I chopped the long pieces in half and ran back to the cottage with them.

I arranged the firewood in a loose square over the peat, looking up when someone knocked at the door. I glanced into the workroom, but Morwen had not awakened, though she tossed and winced, restless despite Claris's potion.

"I brought this for the wee wisewoman." Mister Gynneys came inside and handed me a small parcel wrapped in linen and tied with gut.

"I'll give it to her." I held out my hand. "She's sleeping, and she is too ill—"

He unwrapped the cloth. "Let me show you." Inside was a trinket made up of four silver rings. "'The guardian's knot,' Morwen calls it, probably because my boy, Alfred, was meant to guard sheep. A herder he is." He traced each of the four rings. 'It will bring him courage.' That's what Morwen said when she gave this to Alf when he was but a boy. The only kindness he's ever known. He's asked me to give it back to her now. 'To ease her way at her passing,' he said."

Who was this boy? I wiped my tears on my sleeves and folded the cloth over the rings. I thanked Mister Gynneys and took the parcel to Morwen when she awoke. When I put it in her hand, she closed her eyes and smiled. Then she spoke for the first time that day. Her eyes were clear and her voice tender.

"My ring. The circles of life. Of death. Of transition. Of rebirth. The boy is every bit the one I knew him to be. I'm satisfied with him." She opened my hand and slipped the ring onto the long finger of my right hand. "And I'm satisfied with you, my Megge."

A burst of coughing overcame her. When it had subsided, she smiled.

"Do you remember the day your mother gave you this stone?" She touched my necklace. "You asked if I had a stone, and I showed you this ring, the very ring I gave Alfred soon after that day, at a time when he needed comfort and courage to get through the whispers and meanness he found aplenty.

"I told you that night there were many who would protect you, and I began to tell you Natalje's story." She took a sip from the cup by her side. "By now, you've heard me tell the story of the birth of your mother and aunt many times. That's because you needed to know about the curse. And of all the stories you've learned by heart—all the tales I've told you a hundred times and that you could now tell better than I—Natalje's is the one you must never forget.

"Tonight, though, I shall reveal much that I've never told you and all you will ever need to know when hard days are upon you. My breath's nearly gone from me now, so you must listen closely. So you'll remember. Fetch Brighida, will you?"

Brighida brought Morwen another cup of mead, and the three of us—Brighida, Aunt Aleydis, and I—sat beside Morwen's pallet as she raised herself onto one elbow and took a sip. Looking at each of us, she set the cup down and began.

∽

For a day and a night and a morning, young Natalje strained to deliver her firstborn . . .

My eyes closed, and I saw, as if in a dream, a young woman gripping the seat of a birthing chair, grunting and straining, her hair stuck to her face and hanging in tangles across her shoulders and down her back. Her lips were cracked. Her thin shift clung to her. She slumped forward, and I could feel her fatigue. I breathed the sticky, fetid air she breathed in the dim birth chamber.

"She can't go on. Help her up." The copper-haired midwife—Beatrix Couper—and her apprentice, a young Aleydis, took Natalje's arms, helped her to her feet, and guided her to a pallet beneath a closed window. Natalje fell back onto it, sending flakes and dust and bits of straw swirling in the heavy air.

"Help me, Beatrix," she moaned, her eyes rolling, bleary.

"You are so large. It may be the child can't come." Beatrix's green eyes glittered.

Heaving herself up into a squat, Natalje curled around her great belly and filled her lungs. She bore down hard, and the baby's head slid from her.

The child's face, covered by a glistening membrane, was as serene and contemplative as the Virgin Mary's. Beatrix reached behind her for her knife. The child opened its eyes and stared as Beatrix cut the membrane away and held it out.

"Take this, Aleydis."

Natalje pushed again and delivered the baby. Still panting, her fingers grasping and releasing the sides of the pallet, she lifted her head and saw Beatrix tie and cut the cord.

Another spasm.

"The afterbirth." Beatrix said.

She laid the baby in Aleydis's arms and moved into place to receive the placenta. Natalje's fists pulled back at her sides as if rowing a boat against a swift current. She bore down . . . and another head crowned, also covered by a membrane.

"Natalje, push," Beatrix ordered.

"I see only eyebrows," Aleydis said.

The eyebrows were followed by swollen eyelids, tightly shut. Tiny purple spots began to appear on the baby's brow.

"Push harder," Beatrix ordered. "The baby's dying."

Natalje bore down, and the head came out fully out, the face still and blue beneath the yellow-stained membrane; but when she paused to take a breath, the head withdrew into the birth canal, like a turtle's head into its shell.

Beatrix pushed Natalje's legs back.

"Hold these, Aleydis. Now, *push*, Natalje."

The head delivered once more, and then neck came into view, wrapped in a tight blue collar.

"The cord. It won't let the baby come." Beatrix ripped off her own stiff collar and flung it aside. She slipped a finger under one of the tight blue coils. "Aleydis," she called out. "The string."

Aleydis, shaking, fumbled with the string. She cut off a length and handed it to her mother. Beatrix passed it beneath the cord, tied it, and held out her hand for a second piece.

"Now, Aleydis!" She took it, passed it under the cord in one deft movement, cinched it down, and slit the cord with her knife. She unwound the cord—once, twice, thrice—and slim shoulders slid out in a gush of yellow water. Natalje fell back on the straw.

The baby's chest was still. Beatrix rubbed it hard. She breathed into the slack, open mouth, blew into the bruised, flattened nose. Yellow liquid bubbled up from the child's mouth.

Silence forced Natalje's eyes open. "What's wrong?"

When no one answered, Natalje held her breath and closed her eyes. She concentrated, mustering all her power and urging her daughter to live. Moments passed.

"Mother," Natalje wept, "help this child."

Aleydis slapped the sole of the baby's foot—hard—then the other, but the legs hung limp.

Then the baby's eyes slammed open. She gasped, then held the great gulp of air. Held it . . . held it . . .

Beatrix mumbled over her. Aleydis stepped back to make room for the child's spirit to come. And still the mottled baby held her breath, legs slack, skin blue.

Natalje breathed deeply enough for both of them, her eyes closed, willing her daughter to cry. *Mother, she won't cry. Let her cry. Please, make her cry.*

A long moment passed, the room silent, the women holding their breath. Then the child arched her back, threw out her arms, and screamed, her tongue a rigid pink petal quivering with rage.

A small young woman with light-brown hair and warm brown eyes pulled the curtain aside and looked into the room. She nodded and slipped back into the cookroom. The curtain fell back over the doorway.

Beatrix held the raging child close and covered her with a soft cloth. She wiped her own face with the corner of it as she murmured to the baby.

"There, there. You cry, child, that's right." She held the furious baby close while her own breathing slowed.

Natalje fell back, but a moment later another spasm racked her.

"No, not another one." She took in a deep breath and pushed, and the afterbirth slipped out in a gush of blood. Aleydis picked up the bloody maroon disc.

"Lay it on a cloth on the floor," Beatrix said, placing the spotted baby in the cradle alongside her twin, who lay awake but quiet, her unfocused blue eyes blinking.

The second child railed, kicking off the blanket the moment Beatrix turned her back. Aleydis swaddled her while Beatrix knelt and picked up the afterbirth. She felt between the umbilical cords that arose side by side.

"Nothing between them. One afterbirth and one sac," she said to Aleydis. "They will be as one."

She picked up the piece of drying membrane that had covered the firstborn's face and carried it to the table, folded it, and set it aside. Then she bent over the second child and whispered into her frowning, sucking, blue face, "No one will ever know you had one."

Even before she had wiped the sweat from her own face, Natalje knew which of her daughters would inherit *The Book of Time*. It would be her firstborn, whom she already had named Claris for her clear blue eyes, for the clear membrane that had given her the second sight, and for the clarity of vision that would enable her to see people and know their hearts.

She feared for the second child, the babe with the angry, mottled face, who had been born strangling and without the veil that would have endowed her with the grace and intuition her sister, a caulbearer, would possess.

Then, remembering, she sat up, holding her blanket to her throat.

"Arjen's book," she whispered. "She's Arjen's heir." She lay back thinking, *But, who will teach this child?*

The clatter of dishes startled her from her reverie, and the aroma of rich chicken soup drew her eye to her serving girl.

"Morwen," Natalje said.

Morwen passed the bowl and a thick piece of bread to Natalje, unlatched the window above her head, and threw it open. A thrush chortled, and a gust of warm, fragrant air blew in. Natalje breathed deeply and then caught Morwen's eye and spoke to her with a thought.

—Arjen's book. How will I keep it from Beatrix?

—You made a vow, Natalje. Morwen nodded to her. *The Guardian will help you keep it.*

Beatrix came back into the room and poked the embers in the hearth with a long metal rod, awakening the fire. It crackled and spat.

Without turning from the fire, she tilted her head and spoke in a gentle voice.

"*The Book of Seasons* must pass to the next in my husband's line." Avarice leached through her healer's mask. "To *his* daughter. To Aleydis, a caulbearer."

"Mother," Aleydis called from across the room. "The second child's cord is too long. Can you bring me your knife? It's in the kitchen."

The curtain fluttered behind the old midwife like a magician's cape when she left the room, and Aleydis leaned close to Natalje.

"The babies both were born with the caul."

"I saw no caul on the second babe. Your mother said there was none."

"There was no time to save it, Natalje. The baby was dying. But I saw it, and so did Mother. She was born under the veil, like her sister. I was not. It is not for me to inherit my father's book. I heard my brother's dying wish. I was with you when you swore your oath. *The Book of Seasons* is meant for his child. Morwen and I will help you keep your vow."

Beatrix returned with a knife and bent over the naked, kicking child. Aleydis rested a hand on the baby's legs to still them. Morwen moved close to the crib, elbow-to-elbow with Beatrix. Beatrix brought up her arm to move Morwen away, but she did not budge.

Beatrix tied a short piece of string around the cord, closer to the baby's belly, cut off the free length of it, and returned to the fire. She spread her hands before her as if to hold back the flames, and then dropped the length of cord into them. She jabbed the fire, and it leapt as if she had stabbed it.

"Now," she said. "You must declare."

Morwen moved to the head of Claris's cradle. Aleydis held the unnamed baby close.

Natalje brushed her fingertips over the face of the sleeping Claris.

"To my firstborn, whose birth was foretold by Gytha, will pass *The Book of Time.*"

Beatrix narrowed her eyes and murmured into the fire.

"To the second child, my husband's heir, will pass *The Book of Seasons.*"

Seconds passed in silence, then a minute, then two. The breeze stilled, the thrush went silent. Beatrix bent low over the flames, murmuring, then her chant rose in timbre and volume until the words became clear.

"The books, when joined by blood or name, will bring the bearers naught but shame. Scorned, reviled, they'll die by flame!" She cast a handful of sulfur into the man-sized hearth, and great tongues of putrid flame crackled and sparked. The curtain fluttered behind her departing back.

"Morwen, Aleydis . . . What did she say? Die by flame?"

Mother, she cried out silently. *This witch has cursed my children.*

Natalje's eyes went black, and her breath came fast. Morwen whispered Gytha's words to her.

"You are not alone, dear one. Never alone."

In her cottage at the foot of Bury Down, in the Land of the Second Sight, Gytha awoke with the dream still alive within her. Her daughter's pleas had drawn her into the stifling room where Natalje lay racked in childbirth. She watched as Beatrix lifted the caul from her granddaughters' faces and then cursed them. The midwife's dark words scrolled before her eyes.

Adaem gathered the crew of *The Navigator*, and Gytha came before them on the quay, storm winds whipping her cape.

"My daughter is in danger." Her words cut through the thunder. "She and her infant daughters must be returned to me from Aldestowe."

A wall of clouds blackened the sea. Some of the warriors crossed themselves.

Doom Bar. The men fingered their scabbards and reached behind them to touch their shields. Gulls hung above the sea, screaming into a sky that smelled of lightning and carried the tang of shipwreck, as Adaem's men loaded barrels and crates, then pulled in the gangplanks and loosed *The Navigator* from her moorings.

Aleydis ran to the window when the rattle of a cart sounded outside. She watched as her mother climbed onto the cart and snapped a knotted whip over the backs of yoked bullocks. When the cart had trundled away from the house, she closed the window and pulled the curtain over the doorway.

"Mother has gone, but I've only a moment to speak. We must go, and take the babes. They are not safe."

Natalje's hand went to her belly. "There is nowhere for us to go. How can we leave?"

"Morwen is waiting. She will take you, and I will follow. But we must be quick." She pulled Natalje's dress off the peg on the wall and threw it to her. "Put this on."

Natalje struggled into the dress. "Where are we going?"

"There is a place near the river where you will be safe. You will wait there."

"Wait there?"

Aleydis disappeared from the room and returned with a longbow and a quiver of arrows.

"Come. We must go." On her way out of the room, she picked up the fragment of Claris's drying caul and slipped it in her pocket.

Natalje and Morwen carried the babies through the copse along the riverbank.

"This is it," Morwen said. They had arrived at a shack overrun by rushes on the bank of the River Camel. The silvered planks had forced out most of the nails, so it leaned toward the bank. Morwen pulled open the door and went in. She gathered hay, straw, grasses and river rushes, made a pile of them on the floor, and covered it with a blanket.

"Here, Natalje, lie down."

Bats fluttered and hornets whirred in the rafters as the women hunkered in that hut. With each dawn, Morwen went out amid the cattails and followed the river to the seaport to await the ship that would carry them home . . .

⁂

Morwen sat up suddenly and coughed, and the spell was broken. Aleydis dabbed camphor on her lip.

"Breathe deeply, Morwen," she said.

Morwen took a long, whistling breath and motioned for Aleydis to continue the story.

"The day we arrived at that blessed little hut," Aleydis said as she dabbed more camphor on Morwen's lip, "I walked the floors with the crying, raging, unnamed babe while Morwen cradled Claris in her arms, whispering to her."

Morwen sat up. Brighida and I leaned in close.

"We stayed in that mean little hut," Morwen rasped, "for seven long days . . . waiting for *The Navigator*."

Aleydis poured a cup of mead and held it to Morwen's cracked lips.

"I hunted and fished," she said as Morwen sipped. "And I cooked and kept watch for my mother."

"And then the ship arrived," Morwen said. "*The Navigator*." She coughed, then leaned forward and spat into a cloth. Aleydis took it from her.

"Blood!" I looked to Morwen. "Morwen, there's blood."

"*The Navigator*." Morwen repeated, frowning at Aleydis. "I saw my master's sails." Morwen paused. "And what do you think I did?"

"You ran!"

"That's right, Megge. I ran." Morwen lay back smiling, her gaze moving from me to Brighida. "All the way back to the hut, to my lady Natalje, Aleydis, and the babes."

She began to cough again and motioned for Aleydis to bring her the cloth.

I knew the story's ending by heart, so I finished it for her.

"And then you gathered at the water's edge, as the winds over the Celtic Sea buffeted the screaming gulls, whose bellies shone pink with the setting sun. And a hundred men welcomed you aboard and saw you safely home."

Smiling, Morwen finished her mead and fell asleep.

The others went to their pallets. Aleydis shared Morwen's, while Mother and Claris shared one on Morwen's other side, and Brighida lay beside me. They all fell quickly into slumber, but I lay awake thinking about the parts of the story Morwen had never told me. The parts about the terrible danger Natalje had faced, and of all the people who had come to her aid—Morwen, Aleydis, Gytha, Adaem, and the crew of *The Navigator*. Had they all somehow known they were meant to save Natalje's life and the lives of her daughters?

A tapping noise drew my eye to Morwen's pallet. Moonlight shone through the cracks in the shutters, but it was still the middle of the night and too dark to see, so I lit a candle and went to her. She lay rigid yet shaking, teeth clenched and eyes rolled back.

"Mother!"

Mother rolled over, put out her hand, and felt Morwen's face.

"She's on fire." Suddenly fully awake, she stripped off Morwen's blankets and clothing and examined her skin all over, then covered her again. "Not the pox, not the flux . . ." She seemed to be thinking aloud.

Claris took the candle from me and held it close to Morwen's face. The flame barely moved.

"She's not breathing. And she's bitten her tongue."

Aleydis sat down and cradled Morwen's head in her lap, stroking her hair and whispering in her ear. Morwen's lips pulled back, the slow grimace cracking the dried blood at the corners of her mouth.

Her hands fisted and drew up beneath her chin, knuckle to knuckle, one finger pointing straight up over her lips as if to still us, and she exhaled one last time.

I could not stop weeping as Mother prepared Morwen's poor body for burial. After she bathed her, Mother dumped the water out the window and handed me the bucket.

"Go heat some more water, Margaret."

I had just brought up the fire and was about to take the bucket outside to fill it when Aleydis came out to the cookroom and took it from me.

"I'll go," she said. Her voice sounded strange, as if she'd had too much mead.

"Aleydis?" I called as she started out the door.

She turned. Her face ashen, she leaned heavily against the jamb and dropped the empty bucket to the floor.

"Can't . . ." she said out of the right side of her mouth. The left side hung slack, and her left eye did not blink. She shook her left arm with her right hand.

I tried to help her into a chair, but she slumped against the wall and slid to the floor. Claris ran to her side and looked into her unseeing eyes.

"Grief," she said. "She's died of grief."

She took off her apron and covered Aleydis with it. Her tears, which had never completely stopped since Morwen's passing, began afresh as she bent and kissed Aunt Aleydis's cheek.

"We owe her everything, Megge. One day you'll come to know who your great-aunt truly was."

I had rarely seen Claris cry, but she wept now for Aunt Aleydis just as she had for Morwen. I put my arms around her and cried along with her. My dearest friends gone, I was now alone. Brighida had Claris, but I had no one.

∽

Mister Gynneys came to us later in the day and asked if he could see to the graves. Mother and Claris exchanged a long look and then nodded.

Claris, Brighida, and Mister Gynneys climbed the herder's hill ahead of me and disappeared into the grove. I hesitated outside the stone ring, for I had been forbidden to enter until I was truly one of the women of Bury Down.

But it was here, in the grove, where my family would be laid to rest, so I stepped over the stone ring and, for the second time in my life, into Bury Down.

The morning was cold, so as I crossed the windy summit I kept my head down and pulled up my hood. The whine of wind passing through branches startled me, and I looked up. Before me was the gnarled rowan that had so frightened me the first time I had entered the grove. Another noise caught my attention, this one coming not from the tree but from somewhere farther away. I lowered my hood and cocked my head. It sounded like someone was digging into rock or frozen earth.

Had Mister Gynneys started digging the graves so soon?

The clanging was soon drowned out by a wail. Women, keening.

I pulled my hood back up and ran, heart thudding and lungs burning, until I saw Claris and Brighida deep inside the grove. But they were not weeping. They and Mister Gynneys were standing together talking in low voices. All was quiet.

"They will rest here, George," Claris was saying to Mister Gynneys. She brushed her hand over a flat stone as wide as I was tall. "Next to this stone."

She hadn't heard that wailing. None of them had.

Mister Gynneys dug the toe of his boot through the deep layer of rain-soaked leaves and into the ground next to the stone. He bent and pressed his palm to the moist ground.

"'Tis soft. Indeed, 'tis warm."

"What is this, Aunt Claris?" I ran my hand over the stone.

"It's Gytha's gravestone. The one beside it is Adaem's." Then she stroked a smaller stone. "This one is my mother's. Natalje's."

"I never knew." I knelt and touched the stones. I had never realized that people were buried here. Why had no one ever told me?

"Our people are all laid to rest here, Megge," Claris said, "their graves marked only by these bare stones. Only Morwen, who was born a Christian, shall have a true headstone. She asked the mason, long ago, to carve it." She smiled to herself for a moment and then looked at Brighida and me. "We, too, shall rest here. Never forget that."

I thought of the wailing, and the clang of shovels.

Who else rested here?

Chapter 16

SPRING, 1283

Mother cursed and stopped to untangle another knot before it made its way into the weaving. She worked at it gently for a moment then began to pull so hard I was sure she would soon tear the cloth off the loom if no one stopped her.

"Perhaps an ale for your mother, Megge," Claris said without looking up from her spinning.

Putting down the wool I was carding, I went into the cookroom and poured her a cup of cool ale. She took it from me with a nod, then got up and stretched her back.

"Let me, Mother." I sat down at the loom. As I worked out the snarl, something occurred to me. "You know, if you taught me how to weave, you might never have to sit at this loom again."

"It's bad enough wrestling with this monster to get my own work done." She nudged me off her seat and sat back down, handing me her empty cup. "I don't need to give lessons as well."

Too tired to argue, I went back to the cookroom and poured two more cups. Handing Claris and Brighida each one, I went back to picking snarls and twigs out of handfuls of wool then scraping it over the teasel hand. Aunt Claris took a sip and went back to spinning, while Brighida wound the soft grey yarn onto spools. It was tiresome work, and we had been at it since dawn. My eyes burned. and my throat felt swollen from swallowing the tears that never seemed to stop.

Something rattled outside the cottage.

"Shhh!" Claris closed her eyes and listened. "What is that noise?"

A shadow crossed the window.

I jumped up from my stool, but Mother thrust out an arm, grabbed a handful of the back of my dress, and pulled me back down.

"Wait here and be quiet. It sounds like a cart." She went to the door and opened it.

No one had come for cures all winter long, so stormy had it been. Now, here was this unlikely pair—a boy with long blond hair and wisps on his chin standing alongside an old woman, bent over and coughing, her hooded cape casting her face into shadow. Just beyond them was a cart with one wheel askew.

"Please, Mistress," the boy said, "my mother is afflicted."

"This woman is ill!" Claris nudged Mother aside and threw open the door. "Come in."

The woman was dressed all in grey, her head bowed and her back bent. Although her hood shaded her face, I could make out downcast eyes crosshatched at the corners. She shuffled in and, just inside the door, leaned forward, braced her fists on her thighs, and coughed. A gob of phlegm flew out of her mouth and landed in the rushes at her feet.

Mother and Claris led her to a stool while Brighida and I picked up the soiled rushes and carried them out. We brought in fresh ones and scattered them on the floor.

"This is my mother, Lowenna Caerlin," said the boy. "I'm called Martyn." He pushed back his mother's hood, revealing a full head of dark-brown hair.

"I'm Claris," my aunt said. "This is my sister . . ."

Mother was circling the woman, frowning, stewing, studying her from every angle, sniffing first the air and then the woman herself.

The woman coughed again, and a burst of yellow flew past her son's ear.

Martyn winced. "Can you help her?"

"What is that noise? Who is hammering?" Mother turned from the woman and looked out the window. "It's coming from that cart."

"We have a bad wheel," Martyn began to explain.

But Mother pushed past him and outside to the far side of the cart, where she abruptly stopped.

"Who are *you*?"

The blows ceased, and a low voice said, "I'm Hugh Caerlin, Mistress."

Brighida and I ran to Mother's side and, as she must have done, stopped and stared.

Getting to his feet, hammer in hand, was a bearded man twice as wide at the shoulders and a full head taller than Mother. At first glance, I thought he was covered in fur from the crown of his head to his ankles. He had thick blond hair that curled to his shoulders, and he wore a sheepskin vest and a tunic made from what must have been a full sheep's-hide. His arms and legs were covered in thick blond hair, and his neck, cheeks, and jaw in a dark beard.

In his hand was a hammer made from a crooked bough as thick as my arm.

Brighida pointed at it and whispered in my ear, "That looks like the *Was* scepter."

"The what?" I whispered, pulling my eyes away with some difficulty.

"That hammer." Brighida pointed again. "It's shaped like the symbol for the *Was* scepter—the scepter the gods were said to carry as a symbol of their power."

If anyone could carry such a thing, this man surely could.

"Maybe it is," I said.

"Stay outside, please—er, Hugh—while we see to your mother," Mother said, stepping backwards away from him. Brighida and I followed her back into the house.

"I'm sure we can help her," Claris was saying to the boy, her voice gentle, her hand settling on his mother's arm. "Why, my sister—"

"We've work to do." Mother gave Martyn her *look*. "Please leave us for a moment."

Touching his mother's shoulder, Martyn walked toward the door, but before he left he looked back, his eyes darting back and forth between Mother and Aunt Claris. Then, he crossed himself.

"Go now. Stay away from the window." Mother lifted her chin toward the door. "Close it, please. And keep your brother away from the window, too."

"Brother?" Claris looked toward the door. "Is that who was hammering?"

Mother nodded as she closed and latched the shutters. She turned to the sick woman.

"Let's take a look at you now. Come on, off with those things."

As Claris helped Mistress Caerlin loosen her dress, she asked her, "Tell me, Lowenna, how is it that we have not met?"

"We arrived only last season, Mistress, from Lostwithiel. We live not far from here, just beyond your grazing lands. My husband and sons are herders. They're clearing brush for the earl and turning fields overrun with gorse and blackthorn into grazing pastures." She lowered her voice. "The women at Restormel still speak of your family. Of Gytha, and of the two of you. They say—"

"How fortunate we are to have you as our neighbors," Claris said, taking the woman's arm to lead her to a chair in the workroom.

Mistress Caerlin planted both hands on her thighs and coughed again, bringing up an even larger wad of phlegm.

"Never mind, never mind." Mother twitched her head toward the floor, and Brighida cleared away the slimy rushes while Claris helped the wheezing woman to a seat.

"Megge." Claris pulled a square of fabric from her pocket, held it up to her mouth, and mimed a cough, raising an eyebrow to ask if I understood what she wanted me to do. When I nodded, she handed it to me. I stood by Mistress Caerlin's side. Being careful not to wince, I held it in front of her mouth hoping nothing would come out that I would have to catch.

"Cough," Mother said, putting one ear to the woman's back.

Mistress Caerlin mustered a weak cough and then bent over again, hands on knees, and began to hack into my hand. Mother moved all around her back and chest, one ear pressed to the woman's bare skin.

"Sounds like cats fighting in there," She muttered. She stood up and helped the woman close her dress. "How long have you been coughing?"

"Not so long." Mistress Caerlin's voice rasped. She cleared her throat. "Just since my husband and the boys began clearing the land."

Claris and Mother helped her to her feet and guided her to a stool at the table.

"Megge." Mother looked over her shoulder at me. "Fetch some wood. Dry. You know."

"Brighida," Claris said, "an apronfull of coltsfoot."

Brighida and I scrambled to our feet and ran outside.

As I opened the door to the woodshed, I looked over at the grove where Aleydis and Morwen lay side-by-side, Aleydis beneath an unmarked stone, and Morwen beneath a lovely clover-shaped granite cross embellished with a circle at its center.

"Megge," Brighida called out, "the wood." She was already halfway up the hill, her apron pocket bulging with long-stemmed flowers.

I ran to Mother's hut and piled several pieces of seasoned firewood into my doubled-up apron. The rough edges dug into my middle as I ran back down the hill. Claris met me at the door and waved me over to Mother, who was squatting before the hearth. Brighida followed me in, holding up the corners of her apron, and placed the flowers on the table.

Without looking behind her, Mother reached out a hand. I handed her the firewood one stick at a time, and she arranged it in a square around the embers then blew gently with the bellows. As the fire grew, she placed two larger pieces on top and swung the pot of water over the heat. What little smoke the fire made went straight up the chimney.

Mother turned to Lowenna. "Did you ever have a cough before your family came here?"

"No, not often." Lowenna held out her hands to the fire.

"And you say your husband and sons are clearing brush?"

"Yes, ever since we came." She lowered her voice. "Gorse and blackthorn."

Claris leaned forward, her head tilted to one side. "Are you using the brush to make your fires?"

She nodded. "They bring it home."

"Does your fire smoke?" Mother narrowed her eyes.

Mistress Caerlin nodded.

"Does the smoke make you cough?"

Lowenna nodded. "I never coughed before we came here, but now I can't stop."

"And the men? The boys? Do they cough?"

"Well, now, they're always out of the house, aren't they, so I can't say. But . . ."

"Margaret!" Mother called to me over her shoulder, keeping her eyes on the woman's. "Bring Mistress Caerlin's sons in."

Martyn and Hugh were sitting on the ground talking, their backs to the cottage door.

"My mother is asking for you." I led them inside. Hugh had to stoop in order to fit through the doorway.

"Can you help her?" Martyn asked Claris.

Mother answered the question. "Yes, we can help her. But it is you two and your father who will decide whether or not she will be cured. That racking cough comes from burning brush." Mother held up one of the logs I'd brought in. "She must burn either seasoned wood—cured over three summers—or turf, and you must let the smoke out properly. Claris will give her an infusion to quiet the cough, but the air must be clean if your mother is to be cured."

Claris went to her cupboard and took down one of her pouches. She opened the drawstrings and extracted a large pinch of dried leaves between her thumb and her first two fingers.

"Dried coltsfoot. Observe how I prepare it." Claris crumbled the leaves, dropped them into a cup, and poured hot water over them. "Prepare one cup for her every morning and night until the cough is gone."

Martyn moved in closer and studied Claris's movements as she made the tea, and we all waited for it to steep.

"See this color?" She pointed to the golden brew. "It's ready." She poured it through a thin cloth into another cup.

"Here, drink." She held out the cup to Mistress Caerlin.

She drank it, wincing, and, with an "Aaach," handed the cup to Mother.

"Burning gorse has nearly killed her," Mother said to Hugh and Martyn. "But if you give her this remedy and keep the air clear, she might live." She handed Martyn the plants and raised an eyebrow at Hugh. "I would advise you to bundle the brush and take it to the castle if you want to stay on the good side of Earl Edmund. It's his land you're clearing, so it is his brush to burn if he wishes."

Martyn nodded. Turning to leave, he looked into the workroom, his eye traveling over the squares of misshapen cloth Mother had woven. I flushed when he looked closely at the loom, for the treadles were uneven and the heddle bar had fractured and was now braced.

"Please allow me to repair your loom," he said, "to repay your kindness."

"You are a loom maker?" Claris asked.

"A weaver. Mister Tucker's apprentice. But I'll soon be a member of the Guild."

"Mother," I whispered. "He's a weaver."

"I heard him, didn't I?"

I looked up only as far as Mother's chin and whispered, "He could teach me to weave." I risked a glance at her face. "If I do the weaving, you won't have to."

Mother nodded to Martyn. "Thank you, Martyn. That would be kind."

"You have alder growing right here on your land. May I use it for the repairs?"

"Of course," Claris said. "Whatever you need."

"I'll be back tomorrow." He began to close the door, but Hugh held it.

"I'm a herder, Mistress," Hugh said to Claris. "I'm at your service if ever you need me." He closed the door and was gone.

Mother bent to the hearth and jabbed at the logs. I knew it would please her if I asked a question about healing, so I said, "How did you know about the smoke, Mother?"

She sat back on her heels and nearly smiled.

"I smelled it on their clothes. Smoke from fresh gorse smells nothing like smoke from turf."

"Will she live?"

"Mistress Caerlin is not nearly as old as her illness makes her appear," Claris said. "She will recover. Give her a month or two, and she will be bustling about." She smiled at me and Brighida. "And our reward for healing her will be seeing her renewed spirit and her vigor."

"And a new loom," I added.

"Wicked girl," Mother said.

I'm satisfied with you, Morwen had said.

Chapter 17

I walked up to my rock every day that spring and settled in just as Martyn was getting to work striking down alder limbs from the copse alongside the house. All morning long the axe blows would ring, echoing off the hills on the far side of the meadow. For weeks, as I tried to reconcile myself to herding without Aleydis and to going to sleep without Morwen's songs and stories, Martyn measured and sawed ever larger limbs, sanding them until they were as smooth as stone. He whittled sticks into rods and carried them inside. One afternoon, I followed him into the workroom.

"When might I use it?" I asked stroking the broken-down loom.

Martyn just laughed. "Are you a member of the Weaver's Guild?"

"I'm thirteen-and-a-half years old. I know very well what's required to be a weaver and will join when the time comes to sell my textiles and I have proved myself worthy."

"Very well, Megge." He set down his hammer. "If you are to be a weaver, it's not too soon to learn the workings of your craft." The new pieces for the loom, each precisely cut, were laid out so he could simply reach for the one he needed. "Let's begin."

He pried off the fractured heddle bar and held up the new piece. "Hold that end."

I held it, and he took half a dozen nails out of a pouch much like the one Mother used and put all but one of them between his lips. Then he set that nail just so on the new heddle bar and with three sure taps settled it into place.

"Do you wish to make fine textiles?" He spoke around the nails bristling between his lips.

Our lumpy woolen tunics and rough shifts were all I'd ever worn.

"I'd like to make soft ones."

"I'll teach you if you'll promise to work hard at it. Will you strengthen your arms and legs and hands so you can work this large a loom?" He patted the heddle. "This monstrous machine is a man's loom, you know."

"I'm already strong." I bent my arm, knotting the muscle. "Feel."

He held up a hand. "It's a good enough start. The first part, though, takes no strength. You must learn how yarn becomes cloth. Show me your hand."

Although I already knew how a loom worked, I held out my left hand.

"Spread your fingers, like this." Martyn separated his fingers. "Let's say your fingers are the warp yarns, the ones we'll string taut on the frame. And my fingers are the weft yarns." He stuck out his little finger. "The weft yarns go between the warp yarns, like this." His little finger slipped between my little finger and my fourth finger, and I took a sharp breath. "The next one goes like so."

When all his fingers were intertwined with mine, and I couldn't take a deep breath for my racing heart, he flipped our joined hands palms up, revealing the tightly woven "cloth."

"You see?" he said. "Simple." He gave my hand a squeeze. It took a moment for him to release it and untangle our fingers.

Martyn repaired the loom in the cool of the evening through the days of high summer, teaching me at every step how each piece worked. One morning in late July, as Brighida and I were sitting down to porridge and I was thinking about the day's weaving lesson, Mother came in and dropped her pouch on the sideboard.

"She's had a boy."

"Who's had a boy, Mother?"

"Mistress Trelawney," Mother said. "The potter's wife."

The barren woman.

"You cured her."

"She is delivered and safe?" Claris had come in with fresh water and poured it into the soup pot.

Mother, bending over and pulling off her bloody boots, just grunted.

"Megge?" Brighida whispered. "Why weren't you there to help?"

"I didn't ask her to come," Mother said. "Megge has other work to do. She's a herder now."

Mother had dark lines beneath her eyes.

I had heard Claris awaken last night and whisper to her, "It's time." Mother had hesitated by my pallet but had not whispered my name. Instead, she went out without me. I knew she was going to deliver a child. I should have gone with her. *Selfish girl*, I chastised myself. *Willful.*

I will do better, I promised myself. *I will.*

And then I realized what Mother had just said. *Megge has other work to do. She's a herder.*

She had just released me, and the only words I had ever wanted to hear as a child—*My path is not yours, Daughter*—fell upon me like rocks.

"I passed the Caerlin's cottage on my way home and spoke to Lowenna," Mother was saying to Claris.

Claris fanned the flame under the pot and spoke without looking up.

"Is she better?"

"Well, she wasn't coughing up egg yolks, I'll say that much." Mother sat down with a grunt, and I brought her a bowl of porridge and a cup of ale.

"I should have been with you, Mother."

"You've made your choice. You're a herder. And now, a weaver, besides." She took a long swallow of ale. "Keep to your work and learn it well." She ate her porridge in silence.

Claris stirred the pot. Brighida touched my elbow as she passed me on her way to the well with her bowl.

I took up my stick and climbed the hill to my rock. I should have rejoiced, but I felt like one apart, truly alone now.

"I knew I'd find you here," Martyn called from the foot of the slope. He ran up the hill and sat down on the ground beside my rock. I slipped off it to sit beside him.

"Your mother called on us early this morning," he said.

"Mother tells me that your mother's . . ." I struggled not to retch as I recalled those gobs of phlegm, ". . . that your mother's cough is better."

"My mother is a new woman, Megge, thanks to your family. We are all in your debt."

"But why was your mother burning brush instead of turf?"

"Father said the turfcutters here charged too much. And that the brush was free." He put up a hand, not wanting to say more about that.

He stood and picked up his walking stick. "Today, I will complete the repairs on the loom. And tonight, you must sleep well, for on the morrow you shall begin your apprenticeship."

Chapter 18

"Three and one . . . and three and one . . . and three . . ." Martyn called out the beats of what he called "the weaver's rhythm."

For a year now, my feet had worked the treadles in time to his count. Now he stood at my back, his hands guiding mine as I wove my first good twill.

A knock at the door jolted me, and I jumped up from my stool and looked out the window. It was Gwyneth Penneck. I didn't realize who she was until I noticed her sister Vivienne beside her and nearly mistook her for Brighida.

Oh, but didn't Gwyneth look awful. Red spots and scabs covered her face; and her hair, lank and greasy, hung straight down, covering all but a slice of her forehead, nose, and mouth.

"The Penneck girls are here," I whispered to Claris and Brighida.

Brighida got up from her carding and followed me outside, where Mistress Penneck now stood alongside Gwyneth and Vivienne.

"Mother," I called.

Mother, out in the herb garden, straightened and squinted, shading her eyes to see. Brighida and I walked Gwyneth and Mistress Penneck out to the garden.

Vivienne, though, wandered back toward the cottage, glancing over her shoulder at us as she tapped on the door. I stopped to watch her.

"Come in," Claris called.

Vivienne went inside, and Claris gently closed the door.

I ran to catch up with Mistress Penneck and Gwyneth, who had just reached Mother. Without a word, Mistress Penneck lifted her daughter's chin, pulled back her hair, and aimed the girl's face at Mother.

"Look," she said. "Is it the pox?"

Wiping her hands on her apron, Mother brought Gwyneth into the waning light. She took the girl's chin between her thumb and forefinger and turned it from side to side as if she were considering purchasing the girl and was about to bid low. Then she peered down the neck of Gwyneth's dress and ran her hand over the girl's back while making tsk-tsk noises.

"Lift your arms," she said.

Gwyneth stretched her arms over her head.

"Now your skirt."

Gwyneth raised her skirts to the knee, and Mother circled her, inspecting every inch of her.

"Not the pox," Mother finally said. "She'll live, though she won't be a pretty sight if you allow her to go on hiding behind that dirty hair and digging at her face." She called over her shoulder, "Megge, fetch willow bark. Brighida, witch hazel switches."

Mother went down to the house, and I took out my knife and cut the willow bark while Brighida cut switches. We ran back to the house with our arms full, but Claris and Mother did not hear us come in, huddled as they were by the hearth, heads together, speaking in low voices about tisanes. And about something else. Something to do with Vivienne. Something that had made their mouths go stern. I caught only fragments.

"I gave her nothing to make her lose it, Sister."

"Nor will I," Mother said, reaching for the willow bark.

Lose what? I wondered as I handed it over, but I knew better than to ask.

Mother stripped the bark while Aunt Claris made an infusion of witch hazel.

"The willow bark tisane will bring down the redness," Aunt Claris told Brighida as she poured the infusion through a funnel into a clay bottle, then rolled a piece of cloth tightly and pushed it into the top. "The witch hazel plasters will dry the sores." She dripped candle wax on the stopper. "Gwyneth must not touch the sores. They'll spread, and Vivienne and the boys will get them, too." She blew on the wax and touched it gently. When it was dry, she handed the bottle to Mother.

Brighida looked out the door to where Gwyneth and Mistress Penneck stood waiting. Mistress Penneck was looking all around. Finally, she came to the door.

"It's getting dark. Have you seen Vivienne?"

"I think I know where she is," I said and rushed back to the workroom.

Martyn sat at the loom, his feet busy on the treadles. Vivienne was behind him, smiling, her hands on his shoulders as he threw the shuttle. They both startled when they noticed me. Martyn smiled, but Vivienne narrowed her eyes at me.

"Mistress Penneck," I called out, "I found her."

Mistress Penneck stormed into the workroom. A moment later, she came back out pushing Vivienne ahead of her, jabbing the girl between the shoulder blades.

"I've warned you . . ."

Ignoring their arguing, Mother held out Claris's bottle to the seething Mistress Penneck.

"Pour this infusion on clean cloths. She'll need plasters—warm—twice a day."

Mistress Penneck pocketed the bottle, and Mother opened a cloth pouch.

"This is willow bark. Let it dry." Mother reached in and took out a big pinch of the bark and held it up. "One pinch in a cup of hot water. Steep it till it's yellow." She dropped the bark back into the pouch and handed it to Mistress Penneck, then she bent down and squinted into Gwyneth's face. "Drink the tea your mother gives you. A cup—no more—every morning. Stop picking. Wash your hair. Stand up straight. Look me in the eye. There. Good. Now, go."

Claris touched Gwyneth's shoulder and smiled at the girl.

"The disease will pass," she said while gently brushing Gwyneth's hair out of her eyes. "But the habit of looking away will not. You must learn to allow people to see you, sores and all, so you can see them. What we do not see, we fear."

Mistress Penneck threw Claris a bitter look.

"Come, girls," she said. She took her daughters' arms and led them away.

Why would anyone give Aunt Claris such a look?

When they were gone, I turned to my aunt.

"Why did she scowl at you, Aunt Claris? Is she angry at you?"

"She is afraid, is all." Claris put her arm around me. I turned and watched, through the open door, Jenifer Penneck draw her daughters close to her.

Afraid? I thought. What could a woman with two sons and a burly husband have to fear?

CHAPTER 19

The Blackfriars, Dora mouthed over the clacking and pounding of her husband's tucking mill the next day. She had waved to us as we crossed the market road, but before we could properly greet her, she pulled us into her house and closed the door. Mother, Claris, Brighida, and I, each of us carrying a full bag of cloth Martyn and I had woven, handed them to her.

"They're in the village again," she said. She set the bags aside. "They say they're hunting heretics."

She opened the door a crack and looked out. Pulling her head back in quickly, she closed the door again, her words punctuated by heaving breaths.

"Those zealots. They finally have an abbot. He's just arrived. Already he's out looking for heretics, claiming he's carrying out the pope's call to root them out. I have seen him. He's huge. Like no man I've ever seen. His eyes, Claris! Why, they're violet—"

"What is he saying, Dora?" Claris leaned in close to the flushed and sweating woman.

"That only the clergy may heal. That all others who call themselves healers are heretics doing the work of the devil." She crossed herself. "Everyone is frightened. Who hasn't applied a poultice?" She dropped her hand to her leg and lowered her voice. "Do you remember what happened to the Bodmin midwife the last time those friars cried witch?" She crossed herself again. Opening the door a crack and peering out, she spoke quietly. "Give me those bags. Gus will finish the cloth for you this week and bring it to you. You're not safe here. Go. Stay away from the abbey."

❧

"You know why this—abbot—is here, Sister," I overheard Claris say after we had all gone to bed. "The books are not safe. It is time. She must know the truth."

"You know she's not ready," Mother spat. "*We* must protect them until she is."

Who was *she*? Were they talking about me?

The fear in Claris's voice was unmistakable. Mother sounded angry, but it was often hard to tell with Mother what her anger was masking.

Claris's voice softened. "You took that detestable vow, Sister, knowing what he has done in the past and what he will not hesitate to do now. If she knows, then all will be clear to her. She will do her duty, your life will be spared, and she can choose to protect what is hers."

Questions plagued me, and I tossed through the long night. What would the abbot not hesitate to do? *She will do her duty and your life will be spared.* Was I *she*? Was it my fault the abbot had come and that the books were not safe? Was it because I would not open Mother's book?

Mother woke me at first light and took me to the cottage before Claris and Brighida stirred.

"Sit."

She pulled out a chair for me, and I sat down at the table. She took down *The Book of Seasons* and set it before me.

"Dangerous times are upon us, Megge. You must take your place in the order of things." She sat beside me, laid her forearms on the table, and leaned forward. "This book is your birthright, Megge. For nearly a thousand years, the Mentors have risked their lives to safeguard it so I could pass it to you. No more delays, Margaret. No more cowardice."

"But who wants it, Mother? Who are you guarding it from? The abbot?"

Mother sighed, and her voice softened. "There was once a man who craved the power of the books. Like the Guardian, he lived long, long ago. And, also like the Guardian, he possessed the power to return to the living world. But unlike the Guardian, who can craft destiny, this man—this unstill spirit—can return to the living world only through a kindred, someone in the living world possessed of avarice to match his own.

"Once united with such a soul, he seeks out those who hold the books and tries—through friendship, through seduction, through murder or mayhem—to make the books his own so he can wield their power. He cares not that the power exists solely to sustain the Mentors. Never would it serve him. If he stole the books, the power would simply vanish, and the Mentors would perish.

"The books must pass to their rightful heirs. To you and Brighida. Do you understand?" I nodded, and she went on. "Swear to me that you will protect *The Book of Seasons* from him. That you will one day add your own notation to it and pass it on to your own child."

I stiffened and drew back. *And curse my own child as Mother would curse me?*

Brighida and Aunt Claris came into the cookroom before I could reply, and Brighida set the kettle of the previous night's soup on the fire to warm. We ate in silence. Mother put her book away, but my thoughts still dwelt on the child I was being asked to burden with that book.

A hard knock on the door startled all of us. The door flew open, and Mistress Caerlin burst in.

"Forgive me, but you are healers. You must be told what is afoot."

She had visited us many times since the day she first came for a cure. Now a dear friend, she went to Mother's side and knelt beside her. No longer a crone hidden beneath a grey hood, she was a young woman, not much older than Mother herself.

"It's happening," Lowenna said. "All over again. An abbot has arrived to lead the godless Blackfriars. He has stirred up the village against women healers. I was there when it happened before, you know. In Bodmin. I was there when they..." She saw me and stopped.

I finished her sentence. "When they burned Clarissa Gloyn."

"She knows, Lowenna," Mother said.

"But, surely this is different," Claris said. It seemed she was trying to reassure herself. "That was over a curse. And these are different times. Surely, the monks will stem this zealotry."

"Will they?" Mother asked. "How? Benedictine monks have no rule over Dominican friars, and the friars claim to take their mandates from their Holy Father himself."

Lowenna cast looks all about the cookroom. "This is how it began last time. With whispers that came from the Blackfriars' ravine and were silenced only when Clarissa Gloyn was dead."

Having had her say, she left us with the assurance that she and her boys would watch and listen, and would alert us should any new happenings come to pass. When she was gone, I turned the sheep out and went out to my rock to dispel the doom that cloaked our house.

The sun had crested and was just beginning its descent when the sheep lifted their heads and sniffed the air, suddenly restless. I scanned the lawn as I bent to pick up a stone. A vole skittered over the shorn grass at the edge of the meadow, but nothing moved the deeper grasses. Nothing disturbed the tall weeds at the farthest edge. The skies were clear of hawks and vultures. The world was still. Yet the agitation grew, as before a storm.

I walked the edge of the summit at a steady pace, one hand shading my eyes and the other gripping my stick. As I searched the hills, the thuds of my stick punctuated my demand to whoever—or whatever—was out there. *Show yourself. Show yourself. Show yourself.*

There. Something was moving on the hill farthest to the west, behind my flock. Dogs.

Or were they? I squinted. Yes. A pack of dogs was coming down the hill.

And then I heard the howl.

Never in the daylight, Aleydis had taught. *Watch for wolves at nightfall. Listen for the yips through the night.*

But this *was* daylight, and there was no question, as the pack drew near, that the midday sun was falling on ragged coats that did not belong to dogs. And the wolves were getting closer.

I shucked off my cloak, raised my stick over my head, and ran, bellowing, down the slope and across the lawn. My flock edged away from me, black fleece merging with white into a grey mosaic that spread across the grass like a ghostly shadow, a wave that surged toward the pen and away from the wolves.

Safe.

Four of the wolves broke into a trot. When they had neared the sheep, they ran full out, belly to the ground, and cut a lamb from the flock. The lamb bleated, and a ewe ran to it, catching the eye of the pack. The wolves turned toward her, and she darted the other way, drawing them away from the lamb.

All at once she slowed. The grey coats circled, eyeing her. One went for her throat. She coughed once and was down, mute, the wolves tearing at her.

I swung around, now a warrior from one of Morwen's tales—slate blue, fighting naked with javelin and shield. With a hellfire cry, I went for the pack.

They watched me, whining. As I drew near, they left the carcass and trotted back across the lawn, snarling and snapping at each other.

Their howls lifted into the sky and fell into the hedges that separated the grazing land from the fields beyond. I kept vigil until the yips and howls came from the hills to the west, far from my sheep.

I quieted the bleating lamb and reunited it with the flock. With a heavy heart, I went for my cloak, spread it on the ground, and rolled the ewe onto it. The light was fading, so I moved quickly, pulling that valiant mother into the far corner of the pen and wrapping her tightly. This ewe would not be taken to be butchered; I would bury her in the morning.

I went back up to my rock. Aleydis had been wrong. I would have to ask Hugh to tell me about wolves. Or . . .

Mother's book.

Mother always said, "To one who would ask, the Mentors will impart their knowledge of all things that grow in or walk upon the earth." She had also said that protecting life was a sacred trust.

My flock was in danger, and I was its protector. I began to wonder if any of the Mentors had been a herder, or if any of them had ever written about predators in *The Book of Seasons*.

I was nearly grown. I could no longer remain ignorant when the lives of my sheep—and now, the lives of my family—were in peril and knowledge was within my grasp. I slid off my rock and paced, watching my shadow lengthen until night finally settled over the flock. Over me. Over the hills to the west. Over what else? What else was out there? *Who* else was out there? What else remained obscured? For how much longer would I remain in the dark?

I walked the summit, keeping watch as the heavens turned above me and the moon rode the night on distant howls and yips and cries. When the horizon finally showed itself, I was resolved.

I would open *The Book of Seasons*.

I penned the sheep and walked back to the cottage, hesitating at the table as I looked up at that curtain. Behind it lay Mother's book.

Once I opened it, it would be mine.

The books when joined by blood or name . . .

I was Brighida's cousin. If I opened *The Book of Seasons*, if I claimed it as my inheritance, it would still be joined to *The Book of Time* by blood, if not by name. And then, Brighida and I . . .

. . . they'll die by flame.

I sat down at the table and fingered the silver stone at my throat. I could almost feel *The Book of Seasons* high above me, hidden behind that muslin curtain.

"It holds the knowledge of all things that grow in or walk upon the earth," Mother had said. All things. That meant predators as well as flowers and healing.

"I am going to open it," I said aloud. I stood up and reached for the curtain.

. . . Scorned, reviled, they'll die by flame.

My hand froze.

Worthless girl, I accused myself. *Coward! Open that book!* Mother had overcome her fears and sworn her oath to make me her heir. Natalje had overcome her fear and sworn *her* oath.

But, I argued with myself, would Gytha ever have passed that book to Natalje if she had known it was going to be cursed? That her own granddaughters would be cursed?

"*Would* she have?" I shouted into the dark.

A woman's voice, soft and warm, seemed to wash over me.

— *You are as I once was, Megge, a child destined for a daunting task. I was meant to bring forth the caulbearer whose own child would unite the books, but I bore two.*

Natalje?

— *Understand me, daughter of my daughter. It is not for you to see your fate. Your duty will reveal itself to you and fulfill itself through you. This is my gift to you, Megge—be comforted. You are not the first to fear.*

Those not dismayed by destiny are fools. But you are not alone on your path. Never alone. Just as I was never alone.

I opened my mouth to object, for I felt very alone, but Natalje's voice went on.

— *Megge, why do you suppose Morwen made you her own pupil and for three years made you commit her tales to memory?*

I shook my head. "I did not know until her final night among us, when she showed me the horrors you endured at the birth of my mother and aunt. She told me to remember your story, for it would teach me all I needed to know."

— *That's right, child. Now, let me ask you this,* Natalje's soft voice coaxed. *What filled your mind and kept you from sleep the night Morwen passed into eternity?*

I remembered very well what had kept me awake.

"I spent that night thinking about all the people who came to your side when you fell victim to your husband's mother. I thought about Aleydis, who, when Beatrix cursed your babes, found the courage to defy her mother and take you away. I thought about how Morwen and Aleydis then protected you and Mother and Claris until Adaem and the crew of *The Navigator* braved the storms to carry you home."

— *But why did they come to my side, Megge?*

I thought back to the vision Morwen had conjured.

Mother, please make her cry.

Mother, she's cursed my babies.

"Because you asked Gytha for help?"

— *Yes, Megge. Because I asked for help. Just as you may do.* A long pause. *You have long been troubled, child, afraid you will not find your path in this life, afraid the curse laid upon your mother will lead her to a hard death that will have been your fault.* Another long silence. *One day soon, Megge, you shall be asked to face a truth more terrible than death itself. If you face it with wisdom and courage, you will be asked to make your vow. As you take your first steps into your new life, remember this: you are not alone. Never alone, child. The path we take to fulfill our vow often leads us into darkness and peril; but when yours does, you may trust in the kinship of the Mentors.*

From outside the cottage came the knock of wood on stone, and my questions for Natalje died on my lips. *What could be more terrible than death? And, what do you mean, darkness and peril?*

Claris came into the cookroom, closed the door behind her, and set her bucket down beside the hearth. She looked up at the curtain and nodded at me knowingly. Without a word, she filled a cup with fresh water from her bucket and handed it to me, holding on to the cup for a moment longer than necessary.

Lightning shot through me. *She knows.*

Mother kicked the door open with the toe of her boot and entered carrying an armload of turf. Brighida followed her with a basket of eggs, something green lying atop them.

"What's that on top?" I asked, feigning interest though my heart pounded.

"This is tarragon," Brighida said, lowering her head to the basket and sniffing.

"For . . . ?" I hated to ask.

"For wind," Mother said. "And for toothache."

"For breakfast, Megge." Brighida smiled. "Tarragon tastes good in eggs."

Aunt Claris took the basket.

"You have eaten it before, though you may not have known it at the time, since you are so rarely in here with us as we cook. You're usually out with the sheep."

"And how is it that you are here, Megge?" Mother laid a square of turf next to the hearth. "Who is tending the sheep?"

Still dazed, I just stared at her back as she fanned the embers and dropped the new turf into the hearth. She looked over her shoulder at me.

"Megge. Who is with the sheep?"

I went out to the pen and released the flock. When I had settled on my rock, I tried to bring back Natalje's voice but heard nothing. So, I closed my eyes.

The darkness soon gave way to Morwen's voice and to a crisp spring breeze and a crimson sunrise over that ramshackle wharf in Aldestowe. *We all gathered at the edge of the cliffs as the winds over the Celtic Sea buffeted the screaming gulls. And a hundred men welcomed us aboard* The Navigator *and saw us safely home.*

Morwen's voice fell silent, the river winds abated, and the vision faded. I sat for a long moment, and as I relived memories of Morwen and Aleydis, their courage and that of my grandmother Natalje washed through me. Sitting out there on my rock, knowing I was not alone—Never alone, child—I asked the Mentors to deliver me at last from ignorance and from childhood.

"Megge, are you awake?" Aunt Claris touched my shoulder, and the sky filtered into view. My chest felt hollow.

My aunt's eyes met mine. "The sun has risen, and tonight it will set, though never again on the same Megge." She set a cup of ale beside me and handed me a plate of eggs, speckled with green. "Tarragon," she said.

She smiled and sat on the ground beside my rock as I tried to eat. My mouth was so dry, I could taste nothing. The eggs seemed flavorless.

"Aunt Claris, Natalje spoke to me . . ."

"Yes." She nodded. "Your life—and your mother's and mine and Brighida's—are all joined to the lives of those who went before and to the lives of those to come. It was Natalje you summoned, but we all are one. We have all been in the living world many times. Even you, Megge, though you do not remember. Yet our destinies, though linked, follow very different paths. You have seen this, too, though you do not yet understand it." She smoothed my hair. "Soon you will."

She took my plate. "For now, work your loom. Guard your flock. Allow your eye to roam over your meadow and your spirit to be at ease, for you are in your place."

"But not on my path," I said. "Not yet. Something terrible—"

Claris tilted my chin up with a fingertip. "Look at me, Megge. You have long been on your path. You've simply not been ready to see where it began. Soon, though, you must."

Chapter 20

"We will not allow that—abbot—to cow us," Mother called over her shoulder to Claris that evening. She tramped the treadles of her loom harder than necessary. "We have business in the village like anyone else. I will not fear these Blackfriars. We go our own way; we cause no trouble. We do what we can to ease suffering and bring new life. Though one who hides beneath a friar's hood would call us heretics, our work takes nothing away from the clergy."

Claris, winding soft yarn around Brighida's raised forearms, said nothing.

And so, we took our goods to town on the next market day.

When we entered the weaver's stall, Mister Tucker took my sack, and his eye caught mine.

"How goes your weaving, Megge?"

"Slowly, Mister Tucker."

"Still," he prodded, "you are apprenticed, are you not? I taught Martyn myself. But we've weavers enough for one village, wouldn't you say? I daresay we don't need another."

Claris laughed and handed him her bag.

"I'm afraid Megge is her mother's only hope for escaping the loom."

Dora squeezed past me, took up all the sacks, and emptied the wool onto the scales.

"What is this?" Brighida, on the other side of the stall, held up a supple fabric.

Mister Tucker smirked at me. "Master weaver that you are, Megge, you tell us."

I unfolded the cloth, a lovely tweed. Three colors woven in diagonals. White, light grey, and black. A tight weave. I closed my eyes and ran a finger over it. Smooth. I turned it over to examine the wale. Martyn had taught me how to vary the number of weft yarns to create a fabric that would hang with more grace than my simple plain weave while holding warmth and shedding water.

Mother took a whistling breath.

"I'm sure I do not know," I said, dulling my eyes as Morwen might have done while playing Natalje's servant in Aldestowe.

Mister Tucker sniffed and fished three shillings from his vest pocket. He handed them over to Mother and held out the empty sacks to me.

"Your wool is fine, Megge. Keep to your sheep. You're a fine herder."

Dora gave Mother a quick nod and tapped her breast pocket. Claris touched my elbow and guided me to the door. As it closed behind us, she whispered, "Good girl."

I tossed my hair, a new habit that pursed Mother's lips.

"That was a fine cloth, Megge." Brighida smoothed my hair. "I'm surprised you didn't know what it was."

I pulled away from her. "Of course it was a fine piece, Brighida. Didn't I take it off my own loom last week and hand it to Dora myself? But I'll give Tucker no reason to carry a dispute against me to the guild for selling it before I'm a proper member."

"Never mind," said Claris. "Let's take our tithe to the church and go home. We have the three shillings from the wool, and Dora will bring us three more from the twill once it's sold. We will profit from your fabrics in time. For now, though, Dora is a fine friend to take such a chance selling it for us."

"Nonsense," Mother said while counting the coins into her purse. "Without us, she'd be walking on a peg."

We waited at the edge of the road as a small cart rattled past us, drawn by a pair of mules and driven by a young woman. Her hair was tucked up under a man's hat, and she wore a man's tunic and leggings. As she passed, she stared at Claris for a long moment and then looked straight into my eyes and snapped a leather whip.

"That's Francis Penneck's son," Claris whispered before I could ask.

"Son? That can't be—"

"It's his eldest son, Tinker," Claris said. "He still has a face as pretty as a girl's. He caused trouble when Francis married his second wife, Jenifer, so they sent him to live with his grandmother. He's been away in Tintagel since he was a boy. I don't even know his real name; they've always just called him Tinker. It was he who shot Harold with his arrow that day, when he was back in the village for a short time. Seems he's returned again." She lowered her voice. "It's said he hurts animals for pleasure. Sets them alight, so they say, and throws them in the river."

"*What?*" Brighida and I both gaped at her.

"Don't let his pretty face fool you," Mother said. "Keep your eye on that one."

We crossed the road, and as we neared the church to leave a tithe, the doors opened. At least half a dozen of our tonsured Benedictine monks came outside and gathered on the topmost stair with four hooded men in dirty black robes belted with fraying rope over dirty white tunics. The monks were not murmuring as they usually did; their voices and those of the hooded men were tense. Were they arguing?

The doors closed behind them, and the tallest of the hooded men pointed toward the road. The other clerics shaded their eyes and looked toward us. The pointing man, his hood casting his eyes into shadow, bent toward the others, and then all their heads came together.

"The Blackfriars," Mother said. She lifted her head toward the big man. "That must be their new abbot. The one Dora spoke of. What does he here with the good monks?"

Claris looked away from the men and put an arm around Brighida. Drawing her close, she smoothed Brighida's hair, looking closely at it and pretending to untangle a snarl. Mother, though, looked into the tall man's hood. Like me, she appeared to be searching for his eyes.

His eyes, Claris, Dora Tucker had said. *Why, they're violet...*

Like the giant in my dreams, I thought, and my thumbs began to stroke the tips of my fingers.

The church doors opened again, and two girls in dusty brown dresses came out, heads covered, eyes downcast. As they passed through the circle of black robes, they looked up. I knew Gwyneth Penneck's spots and scabs at once. As usual, she looked away. But her sister's eyes bored through Mother and then through Claris.

Vivienne edged into the huddle of men and spoke to them in a low voice, her eyes straying toward us. Then she spread her hands as if opening a large book. She stepped away from them and descended the steps arm-in-arm with her spotted sister.

Watching the girls leave, the Benedictine monks crossed themselves and went back into their church, leaving the disheveled Blackfriars outside on the stair. The big man, the abbot, whose hooded face still looked in our direction, nodded toward Vivienne and Gwyneth; and his ragtag band of friars took the girls by the arms and led them down the path to the abbey.

None of us uttered a word all the way home, but the moment Mother closed the door and laid her empty sacks beside the spinning wheel, she called Claris into the workroom. Their words came out in hisses and gasps.

"Vivienne has accused us," Mother said.

Brighida put a finger to her lips. Taking my arm, she drew me into the cookroom. We sat down at the hearth, kept very still, and tried to hear what they were saying.

"And now . . . with no husband," Claris said.

"Like mother, like daughter," Mother muttered.

"Stop saying that, Sister. Vivienne . . ." Claris looked into the cookroom through the hearth. She noticed me and went silent.

Vivienne? No husband? Did Vivienne need a husband? Why would a girl my age need a husband?

Then I remembered seeing her draped over Martyn's shoulder as he worked on the loom. Martyn would make a good husband. But did he want to marry? He had never said so, and he spent so much of his time here, it had never occurred to me he might want to start his own family. He felt so much a part of ours.

But what was it Mother had said? That Vivienne had accused them? Of what?

"What could she have accused you of?" I called through the hearth.

"Who knows what children brew up in their heads?" Mother said. "And who knows what the priests plant there?"

Claris hung a kettle of stew to warm. "This is just what happened to Clarissa Gloyn, though she was a pious Christian." Fretting now, she sat near the hearth to calm herself with her sewing, but her nimble fingers moved ever faster as she spoke. "First came the whispers—*a heretic among us*. Next, the accusations—*Clarissa Gloyn has cursed my pigs, drying up the sow's milk*. Soon, the neighbor children were telling the entire village they had seen Clarissa fly over the pastures by moonlight. Why, it's said the girls sought out the Blackfriars to accuse her. And the friars listened to them. They gave the children's words great weight. They said that children were not capable of lying."

"But girls lie." Brighida was near tears. "They deceive every day. Could the friars not see it?"

Claris kept on sewing. "It would not have mattered, for that very night, they—"

Mother interrupted. "Not 'they,' Sister. Someone. Someone boarded up Clarissa's door and burned her alive in her own home."

"Who was this someone, Mother?" I asked. "If it wasn't it one of the friars, was it a monk?"

Claris gave Mother a warning look and spoke to me.

"No, not one of our monks. But no one knows, Megge. It could have been the friars."

"I never believed that," Mother muttered.

But this time it *was* the friars. And this time it was Mother and Claris who stood accused.

I glanced up at the shelf, my fingers on my silver stone. Why could Mother and Claris not simply have been weavers or farmers? Why could we not be like all the other families? Why had they not found husbands after theirs died so young? How could we be without protection and at the mercy of a loathsome girl and a band of gullible friars?

Movement outside the window caught my eye. Martyn. He came in and pulled the shutters closed.

"I've just come from the village."

Claris put down her sewing. Mother came into the cookroom from the workroom. I did not move; my eyes stayed tight on Martyn.

"Tell us," Mother said.

"The Blackfriars have heard Gwyneth and Vivienne's accusations. For hours they questioned the girls."

"How does it stand?" Claris asked. "Do the friars believe them? Do the monks?"

"It doesn't matter if the monks do, for the Blackfriar abbot claims authority over matters of heresy and says he acts in the name of the pope." Martyn moved to the window. He opened the shutters and looked out. "Rain," he said, latching them again and disappearing into the workroom. "Storm's coming."

Mother and Claris sat down at the table, but a moment later Claris got up and poured a cup of ale. She handed the cup to Mother then went back to the hearth and began to season and stir the stew. Mother held the cup in her hands and stared at it, looking up only when a cart rumbled up to the cottage and Martyn's mother crossed the threshold, her step sure and brisk, her cloak swinging over the tops of heavy boots.

Lowenna pushed back her hood and raised her head, shaking out her hair. Defiant, I thought. Noticing me, she lowered her head and murmured to Mother.

"The child knows?"

"Martyn is here," Mother said, tilting her head toward the workroom where Martyn was busy at the loom. "He told us."

The thumping of the treadles slowed, and when the loom had stilled, Martyn came into the cookroom.

"More word?"

"Two more girls have brought accusations," Lowenna said. "Friends of the Penneck girls."

Claris, still stirring the stew, hung the long spoon on the hook above the pot so the rich broth dripped into it. Her gaze drifted to the drying racks. I thought she was going to reach up for an herb, but she just exhaled.

"More tales?"

"Outlandish ones. What they are saying . . ." She noticed me again. "Perhaps the girls . . ."

Mother reached behind her and opened the door a crack.

"Megge. The sheep."

"Hugh is with them," Martyn said.

"No, I'm not," came a voice at the door. Hugh stood in the doorway, the expression on his bearded face grim. "They're coming for you."

CHAPTER 21

H ugh rested one hand on the top of the doorjamb for a moment then bent his head and came in.

"I just saw the abbot's cart from the hill."

Brighida came to stand beside me. She took my hand and gripped it hard.

Mother opened the shutters and stared out for a moment. Then, in one fluid movement, she shut and latched them, reached up to her shelf, slid her hand behind the curtain, and pulled down the books. She handed them to Claris.

"Quickly, Claris."

Claris took the books and ran. Brighida let go of my hand and followed her. When they were out of sight, I looked back into the cookroom, and a terrible thought occurred to me.

Only the clergy may heal. The drying rack was full of medicinal herbs. The abbot could use the herbs against Mother.

"Mother, the herbs," I cried.

"For flavor, Daughter," Mother's voice went gentle. "They grow in our garden as they do in every garden. They are of no consequence. Every woman grows herbs." She shrugged. "We have nothing to fear. Let them see the plants."

Lowenna motioned for Mother to follow her into the workroom. She spoke so quietly, I could not hear a word she said.

"What do you mean, 'a bird'?" Mother shouted.

I looked through the hearth into the cookroom.

"They are saying that you change yourself into a bird." Lowenna said, flapping her arms as if they were wings. "A black bird. And that you fly into their houses at night while they sleep."

"Nonsense," said Mother. "What else did they say?"

Lowenna lowered her voice. "She said that you gave Gwyneth the spotted disease and took away Vivienne's womanhood."

Martyn frowned at Hugh. "What did she say?"

Mother spoke up. "That I took away Vivienne's womanhood. Her monthly bleeding."

Martyn shook his head and shrugged, so Mother was blunt.

"Vivienne is with child, and she has cast the blame upon me, saying that I flew into her house at night, as a bird, and cursed her. The girls are saying Claris consorts with evil and that it was a charm of hers that gave me wings."

Claris came through the door, and when she turned, a sudden shaft of sunlight glanced off the silver rose hanging at her throat. Mother absently touched her own necklace. Then she sucked in her breath. Catching Claris's eye, she gave an exaggerated tilt of her head, directing Claris's gaze to the rose necklace Brighida wore. Claris took a quick breath and nodded. Then she whispered in Brighida's ear. Brighida, touching the rose at her throat, nodded gravely.

"They're here." Hugh left the window and came to stand between Brighida and me.

A creak, then a rumble, and a bullock cart entered the yard, its slatted sides as tall as a man. The driver, a squat, burly fellow, hauled back on the reins.

When the squeaking and the rumbling stopped, the abbot stood. He smoothed his robe over his massive chest and drew his hood up so it hid his face, then climbed easily down from the cart and came right inside the cottage. A moment later, three dusty friars in torn robes, with hoods that obscured their faces, climbed out of the back of the cart and came to stand at his side.

The abbot drew a packet of papers from his sleeve. He was so close I could smell him; pungent, his scent made my nose burn. He looked with contempt at Mother and Aunt Claris, and the gloved hand gripping the papers clenched into a fist. The other pointed at them. His face remained in shadow.

He shook the papers open and held them out at arm's length, showing them all around the room for each of us to see. Claris pulled Brighida behind her as she stared into his hood, seeming to search, as Mother had, for his eyes.

Hugh stepped in front of Claris and crossed his arms over his chest. Martyn came and stood beside Mother and me. As Claris had done to Brighida, Martyn swept his arm in front of me and pulled me behind him. My cheek brushed his rough sleeve, and the smell of his sweat and the scent of sheep quieted me. None of us so much as breathed. The abbot, with his black hood, his enormous cross, and his display of parchment, had scared us silent.

The black hood aimed itself at Mother, and she notched up her chin.

"You, woman," the Blackfriar pronounced, "stand accused of woefully afflicting Vivienne Penneck and her sister, Gwyneth Penneck." Turning to Claris, he pointed. "*You* stand accused of heresy and of consorting with demons in the practice of necromancy. This warrant commands me to bring you bodily before the church to answer what has been presented against you." He stepped aside, and his men muscled in and searched the shelves and the sideboard, overturning the table in their zeal. They stormed past the hearth and into the workroom, where they dumped the baskets of fleece and shook out bolts of cloth.

"Where are they?" The abbot demanded of Mother, who stared into his hood, defiant. He turned to Claris, who looked away.

"Where are the demon's books?"

The friars tore the herbs off the drying racks. Brighida brushed twigs and leaves from her hair. I moved closer to Martyn and swallowed so many tears I thought I would choke. Would no one stop these men?

"Lowenna," Claris said, her voice urgent. "Take the girls outside. Please."

But it was too late. None of us could move as the shortest of the friars bound Claris's wrists. Another tied Mother's wrists and passed the length of rope around her waist, pulling her hands in close. Mother, breathing through pursed lips, stared at me. Then she closed her eyes for a moment, stilling herself. As her breathing slowed, mine quieted, too.

Hugh guided Brighida and me out the door, but I could not take my eyes off Mother, her eyes still closed, her lips moving.

The abbot and his men pushed her and Claris out to the cart. The driver came around to the back and dropped the hinged gate to the ground. Mother and Claris, heads bowed, climbed up the ramp and into the wooden cage. Rain began to fall, and unable to raise their hoods, they huddled together until the friars boarded the cage and pulled them apart.

One shoved Mother against the side and slipped a rope around her neck. She coughed and choked as he passed the ends between two slats and tied them on the outside of the cart. The other took Claris by the shoulders and tied a black cloth around her head to cover her eyes.

"Don't turn your evil eye on me, Witch." He struck her cheek with the back of his hand and bound her by the neck to the cage. I could not bear to look as the driver snapped his whip over the bullocks and the cart moved off.

Chapter 22

"Go after them, Hugh! You can stop them!" I ran to the door. "I'll go! Brighida, come with me!"

"No, Megge." Brighida grabbed my sleeve, pulled me back inside, and closed the door. How could she be so calm? I ran to the window. The cart was disappearing over the hill. What was she thinking? Why weren't we going after it?

"Are we going to do nothing?"

She was not listening to me; she was stroking her necklace as she spoke quietly to Hugh. He nodded then leaned toward his mother, but I heard only part of what he said.

"If we leave now, we will reach Restormel before dusk." He took Brighida's hand, and in an instant they were in his cart and away.

"Bless you, Hugh." Lowenna whispered, now weeping, her hands covering her face.

Restormel. They were going to see the earl. Why had I not thought of that? Earl Edmund! The rose on Brighida's necklace would give her safe passage.

My breath finally reached deep within me, and I thought of Brighida—for the first time ever, I believe—with admiration.

Martyn righted the table, and Lowenna dished each of us a bowl of soup.

"Enough weeping." She struck the table with the flat of her hand. "Sit. Eat. All will be well."

I took my bowl and a cup of ale out to my rock. Pulling the bowl against me, I scooped the salty soup into my mouth. I drank great gulps of ale and wiped my mouth with my sleeve. The back of my hand touched the silver stone at my neck, and the image of Mother and Claris bound to that cart came back to me. I dropped the cup. What was happening to them? And why was I out here on the hill when I should be helping them?

The wind picked up, blowing in low grey clouds to shroud the hills. I jumped off the rock and herded the sheep back to the pen where they could ride out the storm in safety. When they were in, I counted them as I closed the gate. I tried to slip the leather thong over the post, but it must have shrunk, for I had to use both hands. I wrestled with it, shouting at it, and when I finally got it over the post, I scraped my knuckles pulling my hand free.

I stalked toward the cottage, knuckles burning and bleeding and rage building with every step. Rage at the hooded giant standing on the church steps. Rage at the friars who had ransacked our house and tied my mother and aunt to the sides of that cart. Rage at the sneering Vivienne Penneck, at her sidelong glances at Mother and Claris as she whispered behind her hand to the priests. Rage at those books. This was their doing. Those damned, cursed books defended by sisters who would fight to the death to protect them.

. . . a hard death that will have been your fault.

I spun about and headed for the lodge instead. Where were they? Mother had beseeched me to keep them from the abbot. I would do that. Brighida was not the only obedient daughter. I, too, could be an obedient daughter. The abbot would never get his hands on the books because I would destroy them myself.

I threw open the door. They were here—I knew they were. I tore the covers off Mother's pallet and threw them aside. I pulled up the pallet, shook it.

Those damned books. They're here somewhere. Where are they?

My pallet.

I pulled back the hides. There. Something hard. I pulled on a corner but it was sewn shut with the books inside. I pulled at the knot and bit at the seam, but it held. Exhausted, I sat down beside the large, flat lumps.

Soon, my breathing quieted. My heart slowed, and its hammering ceased. I fingered my ring—the guardian's knot, my last gift from Morwen. Her gift to—and from—the boy with the broken lip. I had forgotten all about it, though I wore it always.

I'm satisfied with you, my Megge.

How could she have been?

I lay alongside the books, my arm draped over them. They calmed me, though I cannot say why. They were the cause of all our troubles. Yet, lying beside them, feeling them beneath my arm, I could not blame them. What were they, after all, but words—incomprehensible symbols—on a page?

I fell asleep . . .

and was in a dark stone chamber. A bar of silver-white moonlight fell from a high window and shone on Mother, who lay on the floor, her back to the wall, legs stretched out before her, arms hanging at her sides. Her dress was torn at the shoulders and pulled away from her throat, revealing three red marks that encircled her neck like a moist vermilion collar. Glistening red stripes crossed her palms.

I awoke, gasping.

"They've hurt Mother."

My elbow grazed one of the books when I rolled over, and I knew that had not been a dream.

Where was Brighida? I sat up. I needed light.

Something rustled. Someone was coming through the door.

"Who's there?"

Silence. But what was that scent? Loam. Musk. Sheep.

Martyn.

"Shhh, Megge." In the dark, he felt for my hands. When he touched them, my breath snagged.

"Calm yourself, Megge." He squeezed my hands. "You've had a nightmare."

"Yes," I said, though I knew it was not. "Is it morning?"

"You've only been asleep for a short time. It's still night."

Lowenna made her way to my bed and sat down.

"Hugh and Brighida will not be back tonight. And you can't leave your flock, so I will stay here with you. Martyn will sleep in the cottage and keep watch."

I walked outside with Martyn; and when he went up the path to the cottage, I breathed deeply, relishing the cool night air. The sky had cleared, and a gibbous moon shot hard white beams through the trees.

The same light that had shone on Mother.

As I paced, dew climbed my skirt and clung to my ankles. I went back to the lodge and leaned on the door, staring into the sky. A few of the stars outshone the moon. Claris could have told me the name of the brightest star, the constellation it belonged to, and the healing that could be accomplished beneath its glow. Brighida could do the same, and had often pointed to the night sky as we walked to the lodge.

"Ursa, the bear," she would say, tracing the stars with her finger. Or, "Aquila, the eagle's constellation."

Was she even now doing her mother's work?

Where *was* Brighida? Had the guards granted her entry to the castle? Or had they turned her away?

One of those bright stars flashed, and its sudden brilliance reminded me of the sun glinting off Claris's silver rose. How fortunate for all of us that Brighida was her mother's apprentice. That she went to the grove with her mother. That she huddled with her mother every day, learning from her. I knew little of my cousin's studies other than that they were constant. Numbers. Stars. Planets. Murga's symbols. And something else. Something that rose from *The Book of Time* itself.

Although it was hard for me to admit, even to myself, I envied Brighida. While Claris and Brighida had grown ever closer as mother and daughter, master and apprentice, Mother and I had grown ever more distant. Mother had wanted nothing more than to instruct an apprentice as dedicated as her sister's, but instead of teaching me how to read our book and heal sickness and deliver babies, she had been forced to watch Aleydis and Morwen teach me how to read the clouds and move the sheep when the weather was about to change; how to shear the sheep, feed them, heal their wounds, birth their lambs, and even cull the herd. And now she'd had to watch Martyn teach me to weave their wool into cloth.

Everyone, it seemed, even the sheep, had been my teacher. Everyone but Mother. Her book had lain too long untouched by the one person destiny had apprenticed to her. And now, when she needed me, my head held nothing that could help her.

A whisper, little more than a memory, sounded at my ear.

I asked for help. Just as you may do.

But I had not taken up my book. I had not taken my vow, so I had no right to ask the Mentors for help. I had no reason to expect them to hear me, no right to hope they would respond.

But recalling Natalje's promise—*never alone*—I murmured, "*Scientia nupta sapientia potestas est.*" And I begged, "Please, someone rescue my mother and aunt."

I slipped back into the lodge, careful not to awaken Lowenna, and got into my bed, lying with my back touching the books. Arranged lengthwise from head to foot, they felt like another body in the bed—they felt almost like Brighida—and I fell into a deep slumber, wondering if the four of us would ever share this lodge again.

Chapter 23

here did Martyn go?"

Lowenna had risen early and set out bread and cheese.

"A friend came for him at daybreak. 'A favor,' he said. Martyn's gone off to help him."

I cut a piece of cheese and ate it as I crossed the field to the pen. The sheep milled about, bumping my legs. They were ready to be led out to graze. But from the back of the barn came grunts. One of the ewes, lying in a nest she had dug in the straw, was straining to lamb. She lay on her side, flicking her tongue over her lips and nose as a hoof still covered in the glistening bag of waters slid out between her back legs.

I squatted beside her to see if the lamb would come. She struggled, her belly squeezing, but the leg unmoving. I moved around behind her, rubbed my hands over her back, and slipped a hand into the birth canal. One rear leg would come easily, it seemed, but the other was tucked up under the lamb.

I felt along the first leg for the hoof of the second. When I found it, I wrapped my hand around it and pulled the leg with one hand while rocking the lamb from side to side with the other, allowing it to find its way down the canal. There was a moment of resistance before the leg straightened and the hoof came out. Then, struggling to hold two hooves in one hand as the ewe's belly tightened, I pulled gently, and the tiny ram slipped out in a rush of slimy warm water.

The ewe gazed over her shoulder at the youngster lying in the bed of straw, soaked with blood and birthwater. As she licked the newborn's eyes and ears, he lifted his face to hers and blinked. A moment later, he gathered his back legs under him and lifted his haunches. His front legs were still folded, so he rested for a moment before lurching to his feet. After a couple of stumbling steps, he collapsed again and lay resting as the ewe licked the remnants of the birth sac off his haunches. A few moments later, he was suckling.

I sat back, recalling with satisfaction the many births I had attended. The first were babies Mother had delivered in dark, warm huts. Later, I had helped Aleydis with lambings in this very barn. With each birth, my teachers had instructed me in the care of the mother and newborn. Now, having done all the work on my own, I smiled.

Then I remembered. Mother and Claris were locked in cells beneath the abbey, suffering I knew not what. Seeing once again the rings around Mother's neck, I cried until I retched, until no fresh tears came. My breathing quieted, but somewhere deep within me, in some black, black place, hatred and anger began to seethe. To roil and bubble. It brought me to my feet, and I ran.

Down the hill I raced, and across the pasture. I stormed across the stream, the water splashing up over my knees. Coming out in the Penneck's hayfield, I caught sight of Vivienne coming out of her cottage lugging a bucket.

"Vermin!" I ran at her. "Vermin! Rat-faced, foul, stinking, lying wench!"

She dropped her bucket and turned to flee, but I hurled myself at her, landing on her back. We fell to the ground, and I forced her face into the mud. She reached back and took hold of my hair, but I grabbed the neck of her dress, hauled back her head, and mashed it into the slop she had spilled on the ground.

Heavy boots strode towards us, and frigid water splashed over my back. I gasped and looked up at the same time Vivienne lifted her face. It was covered with slop, and her lip was bleeding.

An empty bucket rattled over the dirt and stones, and a strong hand grabbed the neck of my dress and pulled me off. Vivienne's brother Harold, breathing hard, held me away from his sister while another man offered her a hand and helped her up out of the mud.

"Martyn?" The mud ran off my face as I gaped at him.

"Megge, what have you done?" Martyn shouted at me as he helped Vivienne to her feet. She stumbled around, wiping her bleeding knees and pulling down her dress to cover her legs. Jenifer Penneck came out of the cottage screaming at me and wiped the filth off her daughter's face with her apron.

"How can you ask me that, Martyn?" I pulled myself free of Harold's grip and picked up my stick. "She killed my mother. This horrible thing has killed my mother and aunt. I know they're dead. I saw my mother last night, beaten and bloody, chained in a tower."

"She's not dead, Megge," Martyn said. "Harold just came from the abbey."

"I'm sorry, Megge." Vivienne moved toward me, but I raised my stick.

"I lied," she said. "I'm sorry. I lied. We all . . . lied."

"The earl sent soldiers late last night, and they freed your mother and Claris," Martyn said. He shook my shoulders. "Your mother and Claris are still alive." He looked into my face. "Did you hear me? And Gwyneth confessed her lie. The abbot has Gwyneth, but your mother is alive."

I glanced from him to Vivienne. "She's alive?"

Vivienne nodded.

The earl had rescued them!

But that abbot. He would not give up so easily. All the girls would have to confess their lies if Mother and Claris were to be truly free.

I threw myself at Vivienne.

"Go. Now. Confess your lie." I looked all around. The cart was gone. "Where is your father's cart?"

No one moved.

"Martyn?"

"Megge. Don't you understand? Vivienne, her sister, and all the girls lied. They will face a harsh punishment. Mister Penneck is at the abbey right now trying to free Gwyneth."

Even if the earl had saved Mother and Claris, I knew the abbot would still demand a trial. He would come back for them if Vivienne did not tell the truth. If she confessed, this would end here and now. There would be no trial, and no more fear of this abbot. Why were we all just standing here?

"They could *die*, Megge," Martyn said.

"Who could die?"

"All the girls."

"Nonsense. Not even this abbot would kill girls."

"They accused falsely. That, too, is heresy." He let go of Vivienne's arm and came closer to me. "You saw the abbot. He's mad. Gwyneth slipped out of the cottage last night, somehow made her way to the abbey, and confessed her lie, and the abbot had his men lock her away." He paused and lowered his voice. "So, it will not end so simply, don't you see? He had to release your mother and aunt to the earl, but have no doubt—he will punish Vivienne and the other girls. We don't know what he's done to Gwyneth."

"But, surely, the earl will not allow him to hurt the girls—"

Hooves thudded in deep mud. An axle groaned. Cries. Shouts. The abbot.

The cart drew up the path to the Penneck's cottage, a string of keening villagers trailing it. Beside the driver sat the abbot.

Screaming, Vivienne and her mother ran inside and slammed the door while Harold Penneck blocked the narrow road, his hands raised in supplication. Martyn pulled me aside and took me behind the cottage.

Harold's voice was choked. "Your Honor, please—"

"I am not a judge." It was the abbot's rumbling voice. The cart creaked as someone heavy climbed down from it. The voice went deadly quiet. "I have been sent by the Holy Father, and I carry the authority of the Almighty." Silence. "Now. The girl."

A whine rose from the cage.

I looked out from the corner of the cottage. Three girls were in the back of the cart, tied to the sides of the cage by the throat. They gurgled and whinnied and mewed while their fathers and mothers fought the two friars guarding them. I gasped, and Martyn put his hand over my mouth and drew me back behind the house. He held me to his chest, one hand across my face and an arm tight around my waist. I clawed at the hand over my nose and mouth. Finally, I bit him.

He pulled his hand away, shaking it, and put his mouth to my ear.

"Be silent, Megge. Please, be silent. Please, Megge. Be silent. Be silent."

I could no longer see the cart, but I heard the gate hit the ground. Silence. And then the boards squeaked—the abbot walking Vivienne up the ramp, no doubt. She whimpered, and in my mind's eye, I could see those friars fit the rope to her neck, pass it out the slats, and tie the knot.

Pulling at the neck of my shift to keep from retching, I broke away from Martyn in time to see Vivienne's mother run out of the cottage screaming for her daughter and throw herself at the cart.

"This man is no abbot!" she shouted. "He is not even a friar. I know him. He is my—"

"Blasphemer!" The abbot ran toward Jenifer, stripping off his rope belt. He caught her, pried open her mouth, passed the rope between her lips as if it were a bit, and tied it behind her head. He handed her over to his men, and they strapped her to the cart alongside Vivienne.

The driver cracked his whip, and the cart rattled away with its whimpering cargo and its keening entourage.

He is her what? I wondered. *What is he to the Pennecks?*

Chapter 24

Lowenna pulled Martyn and me through the door the moment we arrived at the cottage.

"Come in, come in. Have you heard? Dora Tucker was just here. She said the earl sent his men to the abbey last night. They rescued your mother and Claris."

Martyn and I looked at each other but did not respond.

"What's wrong?" Lowenna asked, her smile gone. "Megge, why are you so filthy?" She pulled a twig out of my hair and wiped her fingers on her apron. "What's happened?"

"Did Dora tell you the girls lied?" Martyn asked.

"What?" Lowenna held me away from her and searched my face. "Well, of course they lied. We knew they were lying."

"Yes," Martyn said. "But Gwyneth went to the abbey last night to confess, and the abbot imprisoned her. That's why Harold came for me this morning. He thought the friars might come for Vivienne, and he wanted my help. His father is still at the abbey pleading for Gwyneth's life."

The door crashed open, and Hugh's bulk blocked out the light.

"Megge, Martyn, get in the cart."

"What do you mean?" Lowenna shouted. "What's wrong, Hugh?

Where's Brighida?"

"Father's coming for you," Hugh told her, ignoring her questions. "He's bringing Alf Gynneys here to tend the sheep. Go home with Father and stay there." He turned to us. "You two—go." He pointed outside. "Now. Get in the cart."

Martyn took me by the hand and pulled me out the door.

"In the cart," Hugh repeated. "Quickly."

I jumped into the back, and Hugh and Martyn swung up onto the driver's seat. Hugh cracked the whip, and the cart lurched out of the ruts. The horses broke into a trot, and then a gallop, their hooves throwing mud up into my face.

"Where are we going?" I shouted, holding onto the sides. "Where is Brighida?"

"Restormel." Hugh shouted. He snapped the whip again and sent the horses to the left, up the hill and away from smoke that was rising from the woods in a thick grey tower.

I moved as close to the front of the cart as I could and shouted, "Where is that smoke coming from?"

"The abbey," Hugh called over his shoulder. "They're burning Gwyneth Penneck. Vivienne and Jenifer and the other girls are next. And then the abbot's coming for you."

When we were well away, Hugh slowed the horses.

"Last night," he said, his voice calmer now, "I rode with two of the earl's men to the abbey." He handed the reins to Martyn and turned all the way around to face me. "We got there just as the abbot and his men were—" He stopped.

"Tell me, Hugh. I know they hurt Mother." I touched my throat as if it bore the same welts as Mother's had. "I want to know."

"The abbot had already prepared for the . . . execution. The stake, the wood, the gorse—it was all there. When we rode in, your mother and aunt were tied to the stake. One of the friars had a torch. When he saw us, he lit the gorse." Hugh paused and looked back at me. I nodded. "Your mother wasn't crying or screaming. She and Claris were whispering something. I could see their lips move."

I covered my eyes but could still see the scene. I smelled the smoke, felt the heat of the flames. I heard Mother and Claris whisper *Scientia nupta sapientia potestas est.*

"The earl's men ordered, 'Hand over the women!'" Hugh was shouting now, living it anew. "One of the soldiers handed the abbot the earl's writ. I got off my horse, but before I could even reach your mother and aunt, Alf Gynneys had sliced the ropes and freed them. The soldiers rode over, and one lifted your mother onto his horse and the other lifted Claris onto his.

"Brighida had asked to stay at the castle to await our return. She is there now, with your mother and Claris."

My hands still covering my face, I wept with relief. But then I remembered.

"What about Gwyneth?"

"Alf told me she was with the friars, inside the abbey," Hugh said. "She had run all the way there in the dead of night. When she arrived, she was crying, and she told everyone she had made up her story. But rather than free your mother and aunt, the abbot imprisoned Gwyneth and went on with the execution.

"Alf warned me the abbot was going to arrest Gwyneth's sister and the other girls, and he also said you and Brighida were in danger. When I told him I was going to take you back to Restormel, he offered to tend your flock until you return. I went for the cart and left Alf with my father. They'll come for my mother, and Alf will stay at your cottage."

I took a quick breath to speak, but Hugh held up a hand.

"Don't worry, Megge. Alf's as good a herder as his father. He will take care of your sheep."

I opened my mouth again. "What about—"

"And your chickens."

A castle guard granted Hugh leave to pass over the drawbridge and through the stone archway. My breath came quick and shallow as we drew up to the great hall of Restormel Castle. Surely, we would be safe here. A castle was full of knights, wasn't it?

Hugh led me inside.

"Wait here, Megge," he said and disappeared with Martyn down an echoing hallway.

As I waited for them to come back, shivering from the cold, I began to calm down. Coats of arms and brilliant tapestries covered the walls and stairways. *This is the earl's home*, I told myself. *I am safe here.*

"Megge." A young woman in a light-blue gown descended a narrow stone staircase like a wraith. "Welcome. Come with me." She held out a hand and led me to another staircase across the great hall. "I am Elizabeth," she said, "and I am a lady-in-waiting to the countess."

She doesn't know, I thought. *She doesn't know what's happening now, or why we've come.*

Elizabeth and I must have climbed twenty stairs before we reached the second floor and stepped into Lady Margaret's private chambers. Lady Margaret wore a silk gown the deep-green color of her eyes, with long, draping sleeves. Rising from a short couch crowded with colorful cushions, she extended a jeweled hand, and took mine.

"My dear, you're freezing." She touched my hair. "And muddy." She turned to Elizabeth. "Take Megge and get her out of these wet things. She'll soon be sick—"

"My mother, Lady Margaret. May I see my mother first?"

"Of course, dear. Elizabeth, a blanket for Megge."

The countess led me toward a small room just off her chambers, and Elizabeth followed a moment later with a soft blanket she draped over me.

"Megge!" Brighida jumped up and ran to me from across the room as we entered. She held me, her embrace tightening with each sob. Over her shoulder, I saw Mother and Claris sitting on a long couch. Mother wore a hooded gown that must have belonged to someone much shorter than she, for it did not cover her ankles, which were ringed with angry bruises edged with red cuts, still oozing. The gown's low neckline and short sleeves revealed similar bruises encircling her neck and wrists. What did her hood cover?

Aunt Claris's right cheek, the same color as Mother's neck, was so swollen it nearly closed her eye. Her neck, too, was bruised, and her eyes blackened.

I let go of Brighida and went to Mother. Afraid of hurting her, I knelt beside the couch. She bent forward and put her arms around me, holding me close, her head against mine. Brighida and Claris put their arms around both of us.

"Megge," Mother said, so tenderly I began to cry.

Finally, I managed to say, "Mother, they've taken the Pennecks."

She held me away from her so she could see my face.

"They have done *what*?"

"They've burned Gwyneth, and they're going to burn Vivienne and Mistress Penneck," I said, tears blinding me and my words coming out one at a time, punctuated by hiccups. "Hugh passed the abbey on his way home. He said the abbot was coming for us. That's why he brought me here." I tried to stop crying so they could understand me. "The abbot," I said, more clearly. "He was coming for Brighida and me."

"There must be some mistake, Megge," Lady Margaret said. "Whoever told you this was mistaken. No abbot would murder little children."

"I saw the smoke, Lady Margaret," I said. "It was coming from the abbey."

"Elizabeth," the countess said quietly, "take the girls to the kitchen and give them something to eat." Then she bent so her face was close to mine. "You are safe here, Megge. There is no danger. Nothing to trouble you. Surely, this is all a mistake."

Panic gripped me. "Are you going to send me home?"

"No, child. I am going to send you off with Elizabeth for a warm bath and a meal. Leave this to me, Megge. I shall speak to the earl, and he will take care of everything, you'll see."

Elizabeth gently pried me from my mother's arms and took my hand.

He will take care of everything . . .

For the first time in days, I felt safe. Someone knew. Someone who would take care of us.

"Where are Martyn and Hugh?" I asked Elizabeth.

"They are being made comfortable in chambers not far from your own."

"Our own?"

"Why, of course." Elizabeth laughed again. "You don't expect us to send you back to the hands of—well, back home—before the earl has seen to this."

Back home. Where a girl had accused my mother and aunt of heresy. Where Mother and Claris had been tortured and nearly killed. Where their accusers were likely dead now themselves. Burned.

I covered my face but could not stop seeing that column of smoke.

"Come, my dear." Elizabeth dropped to one knee and took me into her arms, mud and all. "You will bathe, and then you will eat." Even Brighida leaned on her for a moment. "And here is your chamber."

After leading us down a long, narrow corridor, Elizabeth opened a tall door that gave onto a room Morwen would have described as "the very blue of the Virgin Mary's veil." The color was one I had never before seen on a wall—soft blue, deep yet bright—the blue of a summer afternoon's sky. I touched it.

"Pretty, isn't it?" Elizabeth said. "The plaster itself was dyed.

Azure, it's called. The color has faded but is still pleasing, I think."

"Oh, yes." I touched it again. Dyed. How I would love to dye wool this color! *Azure*. I formed the word over and over in order to remember it, so I could repeat it to Martyn.

Hearing the sound of water splashing, I turned away from the lovely wall and followed the sound to a curtain on the other side of the room. A short, square old woman came out from behind it carrying two buckets. She lugged them out to the hall and dumped the water out a narrow window.

I ran out to the hall and looked out the window to the moat far below. When I returned to the room, Elizabeth introduced us to the woman, who now held in each hand a bucket of steaming water.

"This is Mistress Pounfrect, girls."

"It's Polly you'll call me. I'm not a countess, now, am I?"

"Polly has had a hand in raising most of the children in the castle." Elizabeth said. She hid her face behind her hand and offered me a grimace that made me snort. "Even me," she said in a normal voice. "Isn't that right, Polly?"

I realized Mistress Pounfrect appeared square only because her arms and shoulders were so muscular they strained the seams of her dress. I followed her behind the curtain and watched her dump the clean, hot water into a tub that looked just like a big barrel cut in half at its midsection. It sat before a wide hearth heaped with turf.

"Well, get in before it gets cold." Polly pointed to the tub with her chin.

"Off with those wet things now, Megge." Elizabeth pulled my dress and shift over my head. "Perhaps these can be washed outside," she suggested.

I remembered, then, how I had gotten so dirty—Could it have been just that morning?—and I thought about what had happened to Vivienne and the other girls.

They're burning at the stake.

Elizabeth nudged my elbow, and I stepped into water hot enough to make my head swim. Swaying, I put my hand to my forehead.

"That feeling will pass as the water cools," Brighida said. She went to the window and looked out over the bailey as she pulled a delicate comb through her hair.

Once I became used to the hot water, I cupped it in my hands and washed with it.

"Use this," Mistress Pounfrect ordered. She handed me a lump of white soap. "Lay your head back now," she said when I had finished washing.

I obeyed, and she poured water over my head. I blinked fast.

"Do I have to tell you to shut your eyes?" she asked.

I closed my eyes. As she poured, I ran my hands through my hair to loosen the clods.

"You're filthy, child. Look at this." She picked something out of my hair. "Straw and twigs. You have twigs in your hair. What were you doing? Wrestling in the mud?"

I pretended not to hear her as, once again, I saw the abbot drag Vivienne out of her cottage and load her into the cage. Would Brighida and I be next? Would we wail, as the other girls had done?

After Polly finished, I soaked a while longer. When the water began to chill, Elizabeth stretched out a hand.

"Let me help you up." Black water ran off me. "Polly, Megge must be rinsed again. Have you any more clean water?"

"Acchh," she said, "I've seen knights come in from the tiltyards cleaner than this one." She poured two more pitchers of hot water over me. "There. She's pink. I wouldn't have given you a farthing for her, but now she's . . . pink. Pink and, well, passable."

"'Passable' she says." Elizabeth winked as she wrapped me in a towel and helped me out of the barrel.

Polly got to work dunking her bucket into the barrel and handing the full buckets to two young serving girls, who together carried them one-by-one across the room. Instead of trying to pour them out the high window as Polly had done, they carried them to the other side of the room. When they reached the far corner, they opened a narrow door that gave onto a very small, dark chamber. I walked over with them and looked in.

Inside was a wooden plank with a hole cut in the middle. I could see light beneath it. I bent closer just as a stinking breeze rushed up from it. I turned away, grimacing.

Polly's laugh exploded. "What? You've never seen a garderobe?"

One of the girls opened the small door all the way, and together they lifted the bucket to pour the water down the hole.

Elizabeth laughed along with Polly.

"The waste slides right down the castle wall and into the moat. All this bathwater will give the wall a good cleaning." When we heard the water slosh out of the buckets, she sang out, "Over the wall it goes!"

She slipped a clean, soft shift over my head. I began to tug a comb through the snarls in my hair, but my arm went slack. Suddenly exhausted, I could not do it. Elizabeth took the comb from me, squeezed some of the water out of my hair, and laid a dry towel on one of the cushions on the bed.

"The room is warm, Megge, and you're safe here. Sleep now."

CHAPTER 25

By the time I had finally roused myself, the room was dark. Brighida, asleep beside me, woke with a start.

"Is it nighttime, Megge? Morning?" She got up and looked out the tall, narrow window close to her side of the bed. "The sun has almost set. It's still evening, but I feel as if I've slept all night." She lit the candle on the bedside table, and we noticed that someone had hung two lovely dresses on pegs beside the bed. Brighida chose the cream-colored one, the one with the bodice made for a woman.

"The pink one will look good on you," she said, handing me the shorter dress with the flat bodice. I wondered how cousins—daughters of twins—could look so different at the same age.

The silky fabric felt cool on my skin. I shook my hair and tried to smooth it over my shoulders.

"Oh, Megge. Your hair. Here, sit down." Brighida took up the comb and began to loosen the tangles. "It is like carding wool, Cousin. Nothing but snarls." Her touch was gentle. "Do you never brush your hair?"

Elizabeth knocked on the door, already ajar.

"May I come in?"

She handed each of us a pair of slippers, the corner of her mouth tilting up when she saw my hair.

"Perhaps we should have combed it before you slept." She held out her hands. "You've missed the evening meal, but you must be hungry. Come with me. Cook has prepared something special for you."

Brighida stopped fussing, and we both smoothed our dresses. Mine had a wide, loose hood, so I pulled it up over my hair as we followed Elizabeth downstairs to the kitchen. Even before we entered the generous room with its ovens and hearths, a sweet smell filled the air. Someone was baking with yeast, flour, honey, and something else. Something I had never smelled before.

"What is that smell?" I asked.

Elizabeth sniffed. "They're baking cakes. Perhaps you smell the cinnamon."

"Cinnamon. So, this is what cinnamon smells like." Brighida closed her eyes and inhaled, as she so often did standing alongside her mother preparing herbal potions. She would take a long, deep breath over some concoction and stand with her eyes closed, committing to memory the smell, the taste, the name, the uses, the dangers.

"Can *you* use this, Brighida?" I asked.

"Yes, for catarrh," she said. "And for other purposes."

I remembered Lowenna's cough.

"Instead of coltsfoot?"

"Well, yes," she said. "But not for us." She tilted her head toward mine and spoke low. "It is very dear."

"I never knew it could be used as a cure," Elizabeth said, "only that it tastes good in cake. You will try it."

We had a dinner of venison and boiled turnips before Elizabeth brought us each a small honeycake and a cup of mead. I ate until I could not take another bite.

Elizabeth guided us back up the narrow stairs and then down a dark passage. As she walked, she fished something out of a deep pocket hidden in the folds of her gown.

"A gift for you," she said. In her palm were two small leather pouches closed with delicate drawstrings. "Our baker liked you. She heard you ask about the spice and gave me this to give to you."

I put the pouch to my nose. Cinnamon. I dipped a finger inside and tasted it. Terrible. It made me cough.

"It needs cake."

Brighida held her packet to her nose.

"Cinnamon," she whispered. "May I give it to my mother? She can use it in her work."

"Of course, Brighida. And you, Megge, may sprinkle it on your gruel if you wish. It's yours."

I must have appeared a child—a greedy child—next to my cousin, who had thought to give hers to her mother. But compared to Brighida, what more was I, after all?

When we finally stopped walking, I saw we were back at Lady Margaret's rooms. Elizabeth held a hand out to stay us and entered alone. Brighida and I waited in silence until she opened the door again.

"Come in, girls," she said, extending an arm to guide us.

Mother and Aunt Claris sat in high-backed chairs beside the countess. Aunt Claris's lips trembled. Mother's face was so pale the bruises and cuts looked darker and even more sinister than they had when I first saw them in my vision. Even Lady Margaret, until now so composed, was close to tears.

"Come in, please. Sit." Lady Margaret waved her hand toward the long bench Mother had been sitting on the last time I saw her. Brighida and I sat down, put our hands in our laps, and waited. Brighida's fingers lay straight and still while mine clutched at each other, the dirty nails of one hand picking at the dirty nails of the other.

The countess crossed the room toward us, gown swooshing but slippers silent on the thick rugs. From across the room, her hair had appeared yellow, like Mother's, but as she came closer I saw that it had silver strands. She regarded Brighida and me from what seemed like a great height, her eyes swollen and rimmed with red. A countess, crying? Ladies of the court did not cry.

She knelt before us. "You slept well?"

"Yes, Lady Margaret, thank you. We slept very well." Brighida, so cool, nodded.

My fingers picked at each other while my feet swung beneath the bench. *Tell us what's happened*, I thought.

"The earl has returned from the abbey." The countess looked back at our mothers. "Shall I tell them, or would you prefer . . . ?"

"Please do, Lady Margaret," Claris said.

The countess placed a hand over my fingers to stop their picking.

"The Penneck sisters confessed to consorting with demons. Their mother confessed to blasphemy." She paused, and her voice dropped. "Your friend Hugh was right. They were put to the stake."

Brighida took a deep breath and closed her eyes.

So, it was true. But it was worse, somehow, to hear it from the countess's lips. Once again, my mind's eye saw the smoke.

I ran to Mother and put my arms around her. She, too, could have been burned alive. He would have done it.

"Earl Edmund could not stop him?" I asked.

At the same moment, Brighida said, "Hugh said the abbot was coming for us."

The countess went on. "It was all over by the time my husband arrived. And the abbot is gone. He and his men cannot be found. In fact, there was no one at the abbey but two old friars locked away in their cells. When the earl's men got them out, they said the other brothers—and there had only ever been a handful of them, half a dozen at most—have been gone for nearly a year, preaching in the hinterlands. The old men, who said they had depended for months on the charity of the villagers, did not know those four new men."

Claris looked at Mother and raised her eyebrow.

"The sheriff will find them," Lady Margaret continued. "And the earl has sent word to the bishop. Your friends Martyn and Hugh have returned to their home. While we await an answer, you will stay with us as our guests. You are safe here."

Mother brushed back my hood, her lips tight.

"We're safe," she said. Seeing my tangles, she pulled my hood back up and tucked in my hair.

"He killed Gwyneth, Vivienne, and their mother, and then he *fled*?" Brighida asked. "What will happen now?"

"This is not a simple matter," Lady Margaret said, "as it involves the Church. But the earl will not allow these men to go unpunished."

"How can we be certain the other friars will not act against us, or that the abbot won't find us himself and harm us?" I asked.

"They will not act against you, of this I assure you. Cornwall is a civilized place. Rest assured, Megge, the Church does not persecute healers. There is more to this than we know." The countess leaned a hand on the bench and rose, one of her ladies at each elbow. "Elizabeth, please take the girls back to their room."

Elizabeth led us back to our room and lit Brighida's bedside candle from hers.

"It's late," she said, her voice hushed but tinged with humor. "You've had a bit of slumber this afternoon, but after such a terrible day, you'll no doubt need more rest. I'll come for you in the morning. Sleep well."

"Goodnight, Elizabeth." I wanted to run to her and put my arms around her. Only Aunt Claris had ever been so tender.

"Goodnight, Elizabeth." Picking up her comb and brush and beginning the chore of untangling my rat's nests again, Brighida worried aloud.

"That man was no abbot. Something has begun."

I slept hard that night, not awakening until Brighida lifted a corner of the coverlet and got out of bed. She crossed to a bank of burgundy silk ceiling-to-floor curtains. She pulled one back and basked in the golden light of a beautiful summer day.

"Let me finish combing out your hair, Megge." She returned and sat behind me, and patiently untangled the last of the snarls. Then, she brushed it until the bristles floated smoothly from crown to waist. I picked up some of the brown strands that had fallen on the bed and held them up to the light. Gold glinted off them.

"They match your eyes." Brighida smiled. She put down her brush. "I see how he looks at you, Megge."

My breath caught. I went rigid.

"How who looks at me?"

She heaved a sigh.

"Why, Martyn, of course."

"Yes, I know," I said, my palms suddenly sweating. "I annoy him."

"Annoy him? How can you say that? He would marry you, Megge."

"*Marry* me?" My heart hammered my ribs. "He has no such thought, Brighida. And besides, it was Vivienne he looked at, not me."

The door opened, and Brighida took my face in her hands, eyes urgent, voice hoarse.

"You must never say that."

"What a pretty room." Running a finger over the lovely embroidered coverlet on the high bed, Claris admired the blue walls and the framed landscapes.

"Look at this, Aunt Claris." I jumped off the bed and ran to the small door in the back corner of the room, throwing it open just as a breeze swept up from the moat.

"Close it!" Mother, Claris, and Brighida shouted as one.

"Here we are, so graciously received, so safe. So fine," Claris said. She held out her wide skirt then ran a hand down the sleeve of Mother's dress. "Just a day ago, it was so very different."

"He hurt you," I said to Mother. I touched my neck. "The abbot."

"It's over," she said.

"Is it?" Brighida sat down on the bed.

Mother crossed the room and perched on a delicate chair with carved legs and an embroidered seat. I leaned on the garderobe door, lifting the latch and letting it drop.

"The earl has said ..." Claris paused and started over. "The earl's men searched the farms, hamlets, and villages for the abbot and his men ..."

Mother leaned forward. "What Claris cannot bring herself to say is that the earl's men found four friars yesterday afternoon, out on the moors between Camelford and Bodmin."

I jumped to my feet. They'd been caught!

But before I could speak, Mother continued, "Naked. Their robes stolen."

She sat back and waited for us to quiet.

"They were innocent men—four Dominican friars, murdered on their way back to the abbey after a year of teaching and preaching in the hinterlands. They were not zealots, nor were they hunters of heretics. They were simply friars. The man who tortured Claris and me, and who burned the Pennecks, was not a friar at all. He and his band killed those friars and took their clothes in order to pose as clergy and frighten us into giving up our books." She stopped abruptly and looked at me. "You didn't, did you?"

"Didn't what, Mother?"

"Give up the books. You didn't give him the books, Megge—"

"No, Mother, of course not. They're safe. They're in my pallet, in the lodge."

She actually smiled.

"But that means we are still in danger," I added, seeing myself alone on the slope with my sheep, and those horrible, hooded men coming for me through the grove.

Brighida moved closer to Claris.

"The earl has seen to our safety," Mother said.

Claris spoke up. "He has asked Martyn to protect us."

"Martyn?" I laughed, but my voice, too high, revealed my excitement. "He's a weaver."

"Martyn is more than a weaver, Megge. He told us that, as soon as he was big enough to hold a longbow, Hugh taught him the archer's skills. And have you never noticed his arms?" Claris cupped a hand over her own bicep to mimic a bulging muscle. "He has agreed to protect us. And he has proved his skills to the earl, so he will stay with us until the abbot—the imposter abbot—is found."

"Martyn will live with us?"

"Yes, Megge, he will live with us," Mother said. "We return home in the morning."

CHAPTER 26

Martyn met us outside the gates in his father's cart. Lady Margaret walked us to the great hall, and when Mother and Claris bowed their heads, she kissed their brows. Claris lifted her head, and Lady Margaret touched the silver rose at her throat, her fingers lingering on it for a moment.

Claris inclined her head again. "There are no words to thank you, my lady."

The countess shook herself from her reverie.

"Nonsense, my dear. I am happy to see you, especially here, at Restormel, rather than—" She stopped suddenly. "And I am so delighted to see these girls." She touched our heads, but her smile lingered on Brighida.

Martyn offered his hand to Claris, who bade Lady Margaret good-bye and allowed him to help her into the cart. As Brighida waited for him to help her, I leaned close to her and whispered, "Lady Margaret still visits you in the grove? But she's never had a child."

Brighida closed her eyes for a moment and nodded.

"May she once more conceive."

Martyn offered to help me get in the back with the others, but I asked to sit up on the driver's seat.

"Up you go, then." He lifted me onto the wooden plank then went around to the other side of the cart and hopped up beside me. He clucked once, and the horses pulled away and broke into a trot. I laughed out loud to be moving so fast over that road, the cool air in my face.

I turned around in my seat to wave to the countess and saw Elizabeth standing beside her.

"Goodbye, Elizabeth! Goodbye, Lady Margaret!" Then I remembered my first hot bath, and all that mud. I shouted, "Please thank Polly for me."

Elizabeth touched her fingers to her lips and blew me a kiss.

"And so, you are going to protect us from the abbot," I said looking straight ahead and trying not to notice the bulging muscle Claris had mentioned. I also tried not to think about all the muscles I had felt in his arms when he lifted me onto the cart.

"I'll be keeping watch," he said.

The fields went by, and as we passed a meadow, I thought with longing of my sheep and chickens.

"Is Alfred Gynneys still with the flock?"

"He and Hugh moved the sheep to our pastures to keep them safe."

"And the hens? My rooster?"

"The chickens, too. They'll move them all back today. Alf and I will take over the herding until—"

I had to ask, even though I already knew the answer.

"Are you going to live with us?"

He turned and looked at me. "Do you not want me to?"

I thought about what it would mean to have him always there.

"Will you eat with us?"

"I suppose I will."

"Where will you sleep?"

"Where do you think I should sleep?"

I thought hard. Closing my eyes, I saw a column of black smoke fill the sky. I saw the abbot's cart, full of wailing girls, lumber onto the Penneck's land. I saw the frightened, angry faces of Vivienne and her mother. I watched a rope go around Mother's neck. I heard wolves howl and women whisper. I smelled the fear of a ewe whose lamb had been cut from the flock, and the rage of a black-robed giant who would send innocents to their deaths.

The hairs at the nape of my neck pricked. Would the huge man in the black hood come for us in the night and murder us as we slept? Would he board us up in our own house, as he had likely done to the Bodmin midwife, and burn us all alive?

Even if I vowed to protect the books as Mother had begged me to do, even if I studied Mother's book and learned to wield its power, could I alone ever defeat one such as the imposter abbot?

Then I thought about Morwen and Aleydis's empty bed. How I would feel if a man slept in it? If Martyn slept in it? Would I rest better knowing that anyone who wanted to hurt us would have to get past Martyn?

"There is a bed for you, Martyn."

I returned to my rock that afternoon under a sky gone grey and misty. It was quiet but for the bleating of the sheep. I looked out over the pasture, where the youngest lambs suckled as the ewes grazed. Not even the warm bath had felt this good.

A young man with a thatch of dark-brown hair was sitting on the grass beside my rock, half-asleep, his mouth agape. I looked closely. There was a gap as wide as my little finger in the left side of his upper lip.

A monster . . .

But the cleft reached only to his nostril, and no teeth were missing. Mothers had brought us children with worse.

I tapped his shoulder.

"Alfred."

He jumped to his feet and raised his stick. He was elfin, clean-faced, with a neck as slender and smooth as a girl's; but muscle bulged in the arm that brandished that stick. He lowered it.

"Alfred, I'm Megge. Did Martyn tell you we were coming home today?"

His flashing eyes warmed. "Welcome home, Miss." He pronounced it *niss*. He pointed with his stick. "This is a good flock. A great h–hlea-sure—a great joy, I would think, to shear." His gaze, never resting, scanned the hills, taking in every sheep. This was a herder.

"That they are. How can I ever thank you for keeping watch, Alfred?"

"I am a herder, Miss. And will ye call me Alf? They all do."

"You need some sleep."

"I will stay until Martyn tells me to go."

He was so small. He would be of little help if I were in danger, but he could run for Martyn if the need arose. Now, though, he was falling asleep.

"Alfred," I whispered, "will you guard the sheep tonight so I can sleep inside?"

"Oh, yes, Miss."

"If you go now and sleep, you will be rested."

He didn't even hear me, so attuned was he to the flock and to Martyn, who was coming toward us.

"There," I said. "There's Martyn now. You can sleep in the pen if you want to stay close by while you rest. You will be sure to hear me if I shout."

He lifted his chin and studied the high, silver clouds, as if measuring the height of the sun above the hills.

"All right, Miss. Since Martyn is here."

I lifted a hand to my eyes so I could see Martyn, and Alf pointed to it.

"The guardian's ring," he said.

"It was kind of you to give it back to Morwen, Alfred. It comforted her to see it again. She gave it to me. Would you like it back?"

"It gave me strength. Now it's yours." As he walked slowly down the hill toward the pen, he called over his shoulder, "And I'm called Alf, Miss. Call me Alf."

"Then you'll call me Megge."

He waved without turning back. I could almost feel him smile.

I watched Martyn help Claris bring wood from the hut, the two of them talking as equals, man to woman. It seemed only the sheep had remained the same.

At dusk, fresh from his slumber, straw still clinging to his tunic, Alf arrived to relieve me. I fetched him a bowl of stew from the cottage and went back down for my own supper. We had a hearty evening meal, the five of us. Later, when I joined Martyn at his loom, he gave me his seat and guided my hands through the weaver's motions as though we had done this every day of our lives. As if nothing had changed.

Twilight faded, and voices began to float in through the open door. Women had begun to arrive for moonlight healings. Claris, Brighida, and Mother went out to meet them. When the door closed behind them, I felt my throat swell, and my eyes fill with tears. I looked down at the fabric I had made.

An apprentice weaver, I thought. *But the women of Bury Down are not weavers. They are healers. Seers.*

And I was not one of them.

"Megge?" Martyn put his hand on mine. "Why have you stopped?"

I began to move my feet again, but he shook his head.

"You're tired. Go. We'll finish this tomorrow."

CHAPTER 27

The sun was high and the lodge deserted when I woke the next morning. I dressed quickly and ran up the path and across the field. Smoke rose from the chimney. Claris looked up from the kettle of gruel she was stirring.

"So late," I said.

"You needed your sleep." She ladled porridge into a bowl and set it on the table beside a ball of cheese. "Sit. Eat."

"Where's Mother?"

"She and Brighida are out in her hut. Mistress Trelawney brought her new baby. A cut on his hand, she said."

"And Martyn?"

"Out at the pen with young Alf." Claris smiled. "How I enjoy that boy." She went outside for a moment and returned with a basket of eggs, which she set on the table. "Would you like one?"

She boiled two and wrapped them in a piece of cloth. Thanking her, I finished eating, washed my bowl, and took the eggs with me to the herder's hill.

Sitting on my rock after I had relieved Alf, I picked up one of the eggs and stared at it for a moment. It reminded me of a dream I'd had the night before, a dream of a great white bird. Gentle. A grey-eyed swan. I was at its back, clipping it. Shearing it? It gazed upon me, placid, as I walked around it, surveying it, my finger floating over its silken feathers.

And then I had picked up my shears and clipped off its left wing.

It drew a breath and waited. Would I take off the right as well?

I could not, and I wept at having mutilated so extraordinary a creature. It wept along with me. It wept *for* me.

I shook my head to dispel the image; I could think of it no more. I sat up straight and lifted my face to the sky, savoring the warmth of the sun and the calm air, so unusual on this hill, where a brisk wind usually blew.

The ring of metal on metal shattered the stillness—hammers striking nails, the blows echoing. Was Martyn building something? I scanned the slope, the lawn, the field, the distant hills. No one there. Nothing moved.

And then . . .

Kffff.

Smoke boiled up from the cottage. Flames leapt from the roof.

Claris was in there!

I started to run toward the cottage, but then, from behind me came more hammer blows.

Kffff.

Flames shot up from the backside of the hill, black smoke rolling into the sky.

The healer's hut. *Mother.*

I turned to run to Mother's hut but halted when I heard more pounding. It was coming from the foot of the hill. Down by the creek.

The pen. *The lambs!*

I skidded down the hill and splashed across the stream, my heart pounding with each footfall. That fence—three rails high, braced three strides apart—would not keep marauders out.

From the stream's bank I saw three men carrying torches. They strode quickly around the perimeter with buckets, dousing the ground and the straw. I ran at them. One, tall and slender with a full head of bright-red hair, thrust me aside and set a torch to a pile of straw. The breeze carried the smoke into the barn, where ewes and their newborn lambs rested.

I staggered to my feet, but tree-trunk arms seized me from behind.

"Get the rope!" a man ordered.

I kicked at his legs. I bit his wrists. I screamed as high and loud as I could, but he held tight.

"The rope!" he shouted again.

I could not see him, but I knew that voice, that pungent smell. The abbot!

He dragged me over to the fence.

"This'll do." He heaved me over his shoulder, slammed me up against a post, and held me to it, his pungent scent making me retch.

The man who had pushed me down now dropped his torch, grabbed a coil of rope, and wrapped it around my waist and arms, pinning me to the fencepost. His face, so close to mine, was smooth and fair.

"This is for my father," said Tinker Penneck. "A good man. Your aunt has just paid for her part in making him a cuckold."

A what?

"Get back, Tinker." The "abbot" pushed him aside. "No one cares about your father." The big man came before me, dressed not in robes but in a hooded tunic and leggings. "Where are they?" he demanded. "The books. Where are they?"

The lambs bleated.

Tinker looked toward the barn, and I remembered Claris's words—*He hurts animals for pleasure. Sets them alight, so they say*—and I prayed the lambs would be still.

The post cut into my back, and the rope dug into my stomach. I could not take a deep enough breath to scream.

Another of the men, this one built like a brick, with dark-red hair boiling up from the frayed neck of his ratty hooded tunic, strewed straw at my feet and tossed in the rails Tinker was tearing from the fence. Then they all moved back.

The "abbot" took the torch and slowly brought it nearer and nearer to my face until the heat burned my eyes and sucked away my breath. I heard my hair go up, smelled the stench of it. I spat at him.

"To hell with you, Witch," he growled, lowering the torch to the straw.

It caught. The smoke choked me, but the tight rope cut off even a cough. The lambs and ewes, trapped, coughed and bleated. I struggled to get free so I could release them, but the soles of my boots caught fire, and my feet began to burn.

This was what Mother and Claris had felt, I thought. All because I refused Mother's book. That was why this was happening. This was my fault.

I couldn't breathe. The smoke was suffocating me.

If I live, I promised myself, *I will open that book.*

Heavy boots thudded toward the pen at a run. A man shouted, and cold water hit me in the face.

They're drowning me!

The flames sizzled and went out. I opened my eyes.

Alf's face, fierce, was contorted with rage. Coughing, he dropped his buckets and felt around my waist for the rope. Sliced it away. As I slumped away from the post, he pulled my arm over his shoulder to hold me up. He pulled me away from the post, gasping for breath himself, and lowered me to the ground. Then, like a man possessed, he grabbed a pitchfork and ran bellowing into the barn.

My strength surged back, and I grabbed the other pitchfork from the pile of straw and ran after him.

He searched the barn, pitchfork clenched in his fist, skin black with soot, clothes burnt, hair singed. A ewe took tentative steps toward him, her lamb wobbling behind her, still suckling. Although he never stopped searching for the "abbot" and his men, he opened his hand to stroke the lamb.

Martyn strode into the pen and stamped out the last of the straw fires.

"They're gone," he said. I hoped he had killed them, for part of me still heard the pounding. The crackle and spit of the flames. The last words the abbot had spoken.

To hell with you, Witch.

One of the lambs stumbled into me, and I sat down on the ground and drew it to me. Then I remembered.

Mother!

Chapter 28

"Martyn, the hut!"

He grabbed my arm, and we rushed to the foot of the slope. Smoke rose from the backside of the hill. A cry, and then a moan, drifted down from the summit. We raced into the smoke that shrouded the hilltop, and then down the other side. The smoke hung so thick I had to cover my face with my apron to breathe. Martyn protected his eyes and nose with his sleeves.

We arrived too late. The hut, now just a pile of smoldering ash, must have gone up like parchment, for the fire had already burned itself out. All that remained was the green wood stacked in the drying room at the back.

A moan came from the other side of the high woodpile. We picked our way through the rubble and found Brighida, pinned beneath a charred beam.

Martyn grabbed a green log and shoved it under the beam, using it as a lever. I knelt and put my ear to her lips, which barely moved.

"My arm, Megge. Megge, my arm."

"Megge," Martyn called. He was kneeling near Brighida's feet. "Help me here."

He had raised the beam with the short log, but it was rolling back down toward Brighida's legs.

"Hold this," he said.

I staggered under its weight.

"Hold it still!" Martyn grabbed a longer log, pried up the smoking beam, and thrust it away. Brighida's dress, now naught but char, was seared to her legs.

"Thank you." She exhaled the words through white lips.

"You'll be fine, Brighida," I said, relieved that her legs, though burned, appeared straight. Then I noticed her arm.

The axe that had always hung on that beam had fallen and was embedded in the flesh just above Brighida's left elbow. Blood pooled around it. I took off my apron and wrapped it around the arm just above the blade, tightening the strings until the bleeding slowed.

"Take it out!"

"I can't, Brighida!" I heard Mother's voice. *We leave it in place until we're ready. It stops the bleeding.* I had nothing else to stop the flow of blood with, so I held tight to the apron strings while I thought.

Mother had brought the potter's wife and her infant son here to see about a cut on his hand.

"Brighida, where's Mother?" I asked in as calm a voice as I could muster.

"In there, somewhere." Her voice broke. "She sent me to the lodge for her pouch, and while I was gone, they set fire to her hut." Silence. "She was inside."

"Inside?"

Brighida had to catch her breath to speak. "It must have gone up fast. By the time I returned, only the beams remained. I tried to find her, but one fell on me. I think my legs are burned."

My apron was nearly soaked with blood.

"Do you have it, Brighida? Mother's pouch. Do you have it?"

"I don't know," she said, her eyes closed, her voice weak. "Where is my mother? She can help you."

Claris. What had happened to Aunt Claris?

I searched the ground for Mother's pouch.

I must not think about Mother. I must not think about Claris. Tears fell onto the ground and mixed with the dirt and the char. The pouch was not there.

"Brighida."

Silence.

I put my hand to her chest. Her heartbeat was fast, her breathing shallow. I patted her apron, her dress. I felt beneath her. There. Under her hip.

"Martyn," I called out. "Help me." I rolled Brighida just enough to lift her hip off the pouch. "Pull that out."

He pulled the pouch out from under her and passed it to me.

I knew only the healer's arts I had seen Mother perform, so, mimicking her, I untied the leather thong and unrolled it. There was the rod. Recalling Harold Penneck's bleeding leg, I pointed at the ring of stones just outside what remained of the hut. "Use the embers to heat the end of this rod." I thrust it at him. "Rest the handle on one of the rocks in Mother's fire ring. Tell me when the tip's red."

I looked closely at Brighida's arm. The axe head was wide as four of my fingers. I pulled on it, but it must have been buried in the bone, for it did not budge. Martyn would have to help me pull it out. I took my knife from my pocket, cut a swath from my dress, and folded it into a thick square the size of my hand.

"It's hot," Martyn called from the fire circle.

"Bring it. I need your help." I pointed to a rock. "Set the handle on the ground and rest the rod on that rock. You'll have to pull out the axe."

Martyn looked down at Brighida's arm and retched.

"Oh, Megge . . ." he said.

I pressed on Brighida's upper arm with the heel of my left hand and held the square of cloth balled up in my right.

"Never mind that, Martyn. Pull that axe straight up. I'll press down on her arm. Once the axe head's out, pick up the rod and get ready to hand it to me." I placed my right hand on Brighida's arm. "Go."

Martyn pulled the axe out and threw it aside. I pressed the cloth to the wound.

"Now!" I shouted over Brighida's screams. "The rod."

Martyn picked up the rod by the handle and held it out to me. I lifted my hand, and blood flowed from the wound. Too much blood. I could see nothing but blood. I pressed down again.

The surgeon sewed him last time . . . Needle and thread, like a tailor. I heard the carter's words again. But I did not know how to stitch a wound.

I thought of Dora Tucker's gash and saw Mother hand me her apron. *Tear it in two.*

"Put down the rod, Martyn. We need more cloth." I pointed with my chin to my knife on the ground beside me. "Cut it from my dress."

Martyn cut big squares of cloth, and I wadded them up and pressed them to Brighida's arm, front and back, then loosened the apron around her arm and tightened it over the bandages.

"Tighten the strings," I said.

Martyn pulled them down so hard I gasped.

"Just hold it for now," I said straining to think of something more to do. I did not know how to use Mother's alder stick, so I took the strings from Martyn and held on tight. After several minutes, I loosened them and lifted the cloth just enough to peer underneath. Still pumping. I pressed down hard again.

Martyn was nearly as pale as Brighida.

I lowered my cheek to Brighida's nose. She was still breathing, but faintly.

"We have to get her out of this smoke," Martyn said. "Get her some fresh air," He slipped his arms under Brighida's. Brighida made no sound, not even a whimper. He lifted her shoulders, and we dragged her away from the smoking beams.

Her burned dress still clung to her legs. The swaddling on her arm was soaked. I looked at her chest. It barely moved.

I could not think. Try as I might, I could bring nothing to mind that would help my cousin. I looked back at what remained of the hut, unable to tear my eyes away. Mother's healing room was but embers, heat still rising from the charred wood.

"Megge," Alf called from the other side of the smoking heap that had been the hut. "I've penned the sheep," he said.

He leaned forward, breathing hard, hands planted on bent knees, and coughed until he retched. He picked his way over to me and saw Brighida.

"No," he cried. "Not Brighida!" He knelt beside her and took her hand. Tears fell on it. "Hugh," he shouted, jumping to his feet. "I'll go for Hugh."

"That's too far, Alf. Too far to run."

"He's at your cottage, Megge," Alf said. "With his cart. He helped me get Claris out."

"Please hurry, Alf." *Brighida might not live through this.*

The fingers of her left hand had gone blue. I loosened the apron strings. The blood no longer flowed, but that arm was blue and mottled, the fingertips mulberry. I knew of nothing else to do for her and began to panic.

Martyn, sweaty and soot-covered, his eyes still riveted to Brighida's ghastly wound, said, "I'll ride on horseback to Restormel. The earl must be told what has happened here. Surely, he will send a surgeon."

"It was the abbot, Martyn. Tell him it was the abbot. And Tinker Penneck was with him. Tell the earl."

"Tinker?"

"He's returned," I said. "He's with the abbot. Go!"

"Go, Martyn," Alf agreed. "I'll go for Hugh.

"Quickly," I urged.

Martyn ran down the slope behind Alf, and I looked to the sky. If night fell before the surgeon arrived, Brighida would die.

❦

"Megge!" Hysteria mingled with relief in Lowenna's voice.

"Here, Lowenna," I called and waved.

She appeared from around the stack of green wood, her dress and apron smudged with soot, her hands black with it.

"Megge." She touched my singed hair. "And my dear Brighida." She knelt and put her face next to Brighida's, leaving it wet with her tears. "Hugh is bringing the cart. We just passed Martyn going to Restormel for a surgeon, but we won't wait for one to come. We will take you both to the castle straight away." She put an arm around me. "You're shivering."

"Is Aunt Claris . . .?" I said. "The house. Is it . . . like this?"

"No, child. Only the shingles burned."

"And Aunt Claris?"

"Claris was inside." Lowenna said. "They nailed the door and the window shut, doused the cottage, and set it afire. But your Claris." Lowenna's voice went proud. "She put out the fire in the hearth, climbed into the fireplace with a bucket of water, and closed the metal doors. Then she soaked herself with water and breathed through a wet cloth. The shingles and thatch went up like tinder, but the house still stands. Did you know it is made entirely of stone?"

I heard Morwen recite my father's boast. *No fire made by man has ever brought down a house such as I will build for you.*

"Alf ran through the flames to get Claris out. By the time Hugh and I arrived, the men who had done it were gone."

"Is Claris hurt?" I asked.

Brighida stirred for a moment, moaned once, and lapsed back into stupor.

"She is stunned, but alive," Lowenna said. "She was dazed when Alf brought her out of the house. Alf said she had seemed to be searching for something, but even she did not seem to know what she was looking for." Lowenna looked down the slope. "Hugh has her in our cart and is coming for Brighida. Alf will stay with the flock."

I lowered my cheek to Brighida's. Barely a whisper of breath. We had to get her out of there.

In the distance, a cart pulled by two horses trundled across the field. I waved my arms to Hugh, who sat high above the back of the animals as they strained to climb the long slope.

"She's here, Hugh," I called.

When he reached us, he lifted Brighida out of a pool of blood—more blood than I had seen even in the most horrific of births—and I feared I was about to lose my cousin.

Hugh laid Brighida in the back of his cart, her head cradled in Claris's lap, her arm cradled in mine. Then, he covered us all with one of his hides and whipped the horses toward Restormel.

Polly met us at the gatehouse. Beside her was a skinny boy, all elbows and knees in a torn but clean tunic, and a dignified man with kind eyes, a steady gaze, and straight, light-brown hair parted as perfectly as Brighida's.

"Your friend Martyn's told us what's happened. Mr. Kendall will see to them," Polly said, helping me out of the cart. "A surgeon," she whispered.

Mister Kendall pulled back the hide covering Brighida and looked at her still, white face, those pallid lips, that mottled left arm.

"Take the cart around to my surgery." He clapped a hand on the young boy's shoulder. "William here will guide you."

William hopped onto the driver's seat alongside Hugh; and Mister Kendall ran ahead, disappearing through a high archway.

"This way." William pointed straight ahead along the cobbled road that lay between the castle and the high stone wall surrounding it.

"Come with me, Megge. They will bring your aunt to stay with you once the surgeon's seen to her." Polly took my arm. "It's a wonder you all made it this far, the three of you covered in blood and dirt, and Brighida half-dead. Oh, my poor Brighida."

She took me straight up to the room I had shared with Brighida and filled the bath. As she worked, she muttered about a child near to death and cursed the men who would do such a thing to a household of women.

"And healers, besides." She pulled off my cloak. "What happened, Megge? Can you tell me?"

As she helped me off with my dress, I told her what I could remember from the fragments I patched together as they flashed before me. The last words of the story, "My mother is dead," rang in my ears.

Mother and the potter's wife and son were gone. And I had fled in the cart and left them all behind. I covered my face to hide my horror and shame.

"Here, Megge," Polly said when I had dried off after my bath. She held out a shift and pulled back the coverlet on the bed Brighida and I had shared. "Go to sleep now."

I shook my head. "Have you a frock, Polly? I'd like to go to Brighida."

She walked me down the cobbled road to Mister Kendall's surgery. William slouched against the door, talking to another boy.

"William," Polly said, "is Brighida in there?"

"Aye, Polly. Mister Kendall says she'll live." He pushed open the door, revealing a room little larger than Mother's hut. Inside was a table strewn with instruments and spattered with blood. Brighida, covered up to the neck in a thick blanket, slept quietly on a cot.

"I helped him," William said. "We took it off right about here." He slapped his bicep with his forefinger, and I thought I would faint.

I stayed up with Brighida throughout the night. Each time she moved or whimpered, I went to her so she would not wake up alone. When she stilled, I checked the bandages on her stump. Dry.

Mister Kendall came to see her at dawn and ordered me to go get some rest.

"Go to bed, Megge. Brighida will sleep most of the day."

I went instead to the kitchen to break my fast. There, I found Claris staring into a cup of ale, an untouched piece of barley bread beside her.

"It was him, wasn't it, Megge?" she said. "That false abbot. I didn't see him, but I know it was."

"Yes. It was him. And Tinker Penneck was with him. Tinker said he was doing it for his father. For Mister Penneck."

"For his father . . ." Claris set down her cup.

That bread suddenly looked good. Realizing I was starving, I took a big bite. As I chewed, I asked, "Aunt Claris, what's a cuckold?"

"A *what*?" Claris sat up so suddenly she knocked over her cup. "Where did you hear that word?" She fumbled with her apron, trying to wipe up the spilled ale.

"What's the matter, Aunt?" I found a towel and helped her. "Tinker Penneck said that you had made his father one. What did he mean?"

Claris did not answer. Looking confused, she got up from the table.

"I must speak to the earl about the abbot." Covering her face with her hands, she ran from the room, weeping without restraint.

Hugh came into the kitchen and took a breath to speak; but when Claris ran past him, he leaned down and whispered into my ear, "I'll go back to the cottage and take care of your mother. Your aunt has told me what she wants."

He started to leave, but I had to know why that word *cuckold* had made Claris cry.

"Hugh, what's a cuckold?"

He drew back and looked about as if searching for someone else who might answer me. Then he knelt on one knee beside me and looked at me as if perhaps he hadn't heard correctly.

"A what?"

"A cuckold," I said.

"A cuckold's someone who . . ." Hugh struggled. Finally, his face relaxed. "It's someone somebody has fooled."

Fooled? Aunt Claris had played a trick on Mister Penneck? Impossible.

"He's a surgeon, not a healer," Claris railed that evening as we returned to the kitchen after spending the day at Brighida's side. Mister Kendall had just put us out of Brighida's chamber, refusing the infusion Claris had brought.

"He's trying—" I began.

She stopped and held up a finger to still me. "He's a butcher. This . . ." She held out the cup containing the yellow dock infusion she had brewed. "This is what she needs."

"But he saved her—"

"He chopped off her arm." Claris's eyes filled as they did each time she recalled Brighida's surgery.

"She would have bled to death had he not."

"Wasn't I beside her on the ride to the castle? Yes, she had bled; but the bleeding had stopped by the time we arrived. Her lips were pale, but her pulse, though weak, was little faster than yours or mine. She's young. Strong. With my knowledge and herbs, along with some well-placed surgeon's stitches to repair the muscles and skin, she would have recovered. Without butchery."

Yes, I thought, *you were beside her on that long ride, but you were not yourself. Nor are you yet.*

But explaining Brighida's injury once again—the axe buried in the bone, those mulberry fingers—and why Mister Kendall had

had no choice, would be of no use. Ever since Hugh had left us that morning, she had fretted, pestering Cook, even moving aside Cook's bubbling pots and kettles to brew her own infusion for Brighida. Never before had I seen her so agitated.

It was evening now as we returned to the castle's kitchen, and Brighida had not yet awakened. That afternoon, Mister Kendall had moved her to a bedchamber with a hearth, a window for fresh air, and a servant to tend her; but a few minutes ago, he had lost his patience with us.

"Can't you see she's sleeping?" He tried to make Claris understand. "I've given her a draught. She will sleep until I feel she can stand the pain. Your yellow dock tea—"

Claris looked away from Brighida's still face and stood. She drew a breath and seemed to grow even taller. Her eyes bored into his.

"My infusion—" she corrected.

"Your infusion," he went on, his voice softer, temper no longer tightening his mouth, "will help build her blood. When the time comes." He looked at me, his expression seeming to ask for my help. "You've both been at her side all day. You need a meal. Some rest." He turned back to Claris and extended an arm toward the door. "Come see her in the morning. When she can drink, you can administer your . . . remedy."

"She will recover, Aunt Claris," I said as I pulled open the great wooden door to the kitchen. I took the cup from her and set it on one of the long oaken tables where the scullery maids ate. It was very late, so Cook and her helpers were not there, but she had left plates for us. Bread, cheese, roasted chicken, flagons of ale. I wolfed my food while Claris toyed with hers.

Remembering what Hugh had said that morning and wanting to take my aunt's mind off her worries, I asked, "Aunt Claris, tell me about the trick you played on Mister Penneck."

She looked at me for a long moment, then planted her hands on the table and stood slowly. Taking my hand, she led me out of the kitchen, and in silence we climbed the narrow staircase to the azure-walled room and the high, wide bed we shared.

Two days passed with little change as Claris and I sat in silent vigil at Brighida's side. No sooner would Brighida awaken, moaning, than Mister Kendall's serving woman would give her another sip of the sleeping draught that sent her back into restless slumber.

"You must allow her to awaken," Claris insisted whenever Mister Kendall entered Brighida's room. "She must eat. She must drink something. Look at her: she's wasting away."

On the third day, Mister Kendall finally responded. Pulling back the blanket covering Brighida's chest and shoulders, he revealed the swaddled stump of her left arm.

"Look at it, Claris. It's dry. Clean. Healing." He touched Brighida's rounded cheek. "And she's not wasting away."

"Yet." Claris sounded so like Mother these days.

The surgeon replaced the blanket over Brighida's shoulders, moved to the foot of the bed, and drew back the white sheet covering her legs. "It's here she will face her gravest danger."

Yellowed cloths covered her legs from knee to ankle. "These have been soaked in warm oil."

"Oil? But she needs comfrey—"

"The oil hastens healing," Mister Kendall said, pushing past her to move to Brighida's side. "In a moment, I will remove them, cleanse the skin, and cover it in cold cloths. Cold relieves pain." He sat down on the side of the bed and looked at the bandages. "Now. Are you ready to see the wounds?"

Claris nodded and leaned closer. I stepped back, wincing, and looked over her shoulder.

Mister Kendall peeled back the oily, yellow dressings, glancing often at Brighida's face. Her eyebrows knit together, but she did not awaken.

He spoke to Claris without looking at her. "You'll soon understand why I've given her the draught."

Below my cousin's knees, the angry, crimson flesh was covered with blisters slick with oil and glistening with drops of thin, yellowish liquid. Down the front of each leg were patches of white. "The legs were not broken. But look here." Mister Kendall's finger floated above the gleaming white spots. "Bone. The skin is thinnest over the shin bone, and it is here we must take the greatest care." He glanced up at Claris and shrugged. "Her arm will heal in time. It's this bone—these burns—we must guard."

A young woman wearing a grey shift covered by a white apron, her hair tucked up inside a pristine linen coif, came in carrying a bowl of water and a stack of cloths and set them on a table beside the bed. Mister Kendall dipped the cloths in the clear water, wrung them out, and laid them on Brighida's wounds. Brighida neither stirred nor moaned. Silently, his face revealing no emotion, he then moved to the head of the bed and unwrapped the swaddling around Brighida's stump.

Claris moved to stand behind him. Eyes closed, lips moving, she recited the incantation that summoned the Mentors. It was as if I were watching Mother and Claris at work.

Neither noticed as I touched Brighida's foot and slipped out the door.

The next morning, Claris and I woke up much earlier than the others in the castle—besides Cook and her maids, of course—and were breaking our fast in the kitchen before going to Brighida.

We were finishing our gruel when the great door opened and Hugh looked inside.

Claris looked out the narrow window at the end of the table. "When did you set out, Hugh? It's not yet dawn."

"I arrived last night, just after dark. I didn't want to trouble you so late…" His voice trailed off. "Good morning, Olwen." He nodded at

Cook, who had looked up from her work and watched him come in, and then he came over to sit beside Claris.

Cook's name is Olwen?

Smiling, Cook turned back to the hearth.

"Here you are, then." She came to the table and set before him a huge serving of gruel in a bowl she normally used to serve half a dozen people.

He thanked her but did not touch the food.

Claris did not take her eyes off him. When Cook had returned to her kettles and pots, Claris spoke. "It's done, then?"

I laid down my spoon, wondering *Is* what *done?*

"Martyn and I found little more than ash," he told her gently. "We took it to the clearing in your grove as you asked."

Claris said nothing for a moment. She just nodded, her eyes closed, tears falling onto her apron.

"What's done?" I looked from Claris to Hugh. He looked at Claris.

"Your mother," she whispered. "She's been buried."

"Buried? Hugh buried her?" Morwen and Aleydis had each received all the honors due women of Bury Down. Though they had saved Natalje and the books, they were not heirs as Mother had been. And Mother, a sworn healer of Bury Down, had given her life.

"Mother was buried with none of us there?" My voice sounded small. "With no rites? No words spoken?"

I turned away so Claris would not see me cry, but she took me in her arms and held me.

"I've spoken the words, Megge," she whispered.

I tried to stifle my sobs but could not. I had all but worshiped Claris for her beauty and her gentle ways; meanwhile, my own mother, always busy with her work, brow furrowed in concentration, hands busy, mind and spirit bound by duty, had earned only my scorn. *I do not deserve to grieve*, I thought, yet I could not stop my tears.

"Megge." Hugh's voice was soft. "Nellie Trelawney and the bairn are alive."

Pulling away from Claris, I searched his face.

He nodded. "It's true."

I wiped my nose on my sleeve and looked first at Claris and then back at Hugh.

"But they were with Mother. The child had cut his hand . . ."

Hugh shook his head. "'It's just a scratch,' your mother told her. And the next thing Nellie knew, your mother was pushing her out the door and telling her to go home. No sooner had Nellie crossed Fowey Creek with the babe than she saw the smoke."

Chapter 30

It took weeks of treatment with Aunt Claris's infusion for Brighida's pallid skin and lips to go pink, and even longer for her skin to heal. Every morning, I held Brighida's hand as Mister Kendall cleansed her stump and then opened his vial of pitch, stuck the twisted corner of a piece of cloth into it, and daubed it on the oozing flesh.

When he was through, he removed the moist cloths from Brighida's legs, cleansed the raw skin, and applied unguents and hot oil before wrapping her legs in clean cloths.

Brighida, of course, was the perfect patient—silent, radiant, obedient. Even Mother would not have minded tending such a girl. She merely closed her eyes and suffered the surgeon with the long, delicate fingers, to remove bits of cloth, char, and splintered wood.

Through the summer, Mister Kendall's prediction came true—Brighida's stump gradually healed. By fall, his relentless cleansing, oiling, and bandaging of the burns, coupled with Claris's incantations, comfrey poultices, and healing infusions, had brought the raw, oozing skin back to life.

It healed through the autumn, and by mid-November—and my fourteenth birthday—it had toughened up enough to be massaged.

"We want to keep the skin and muscles supple, so she will be able to walk again," Mister Kendall said. "I will teach you and Polly how to knead the legs without injuring the new skin."

At the winter solstice, we celebrated Brighida's first day without bandages on her legs. The skin—pasty and hairless—resembled bread dough stretched thin, but it was finally whole.

Polly and I worked tirelessly to soften that scarred skin and restore those withered muscles, while Claris plied Brighida with infusions to strengthen her blood. At the castle's Twelfth Night celebration, Brighida took her first step; and on St. Valentine's Day, she took her first walk unaided down the corridor, counting out each step. She had to stop at the eleventh.

As she caught her breath, she said, "Eleven. That's an important number, Megge. It's the number of the spiritual messenger. The day and hour of your birth make the number eleven *your* celestial number."

I did not reply. I did not want to think about spiritual messengers or celestial numbers. We were away from those books, and I wanted nothing to do with them.

By March, I had begun to feel caged. Our walks had lengthened as the days warmed, taking us into more and more distant parts of the castle. The barns and pens were larger than our entire farm, but all I wanted was to return to my sheep and my chickens.

As Polly worked on Brighida, I paced before the windows.

"Megge," Brighida said, "why don't you go out to the sheep pens and see if you can help the herders?"

Polly was rubbing lanolin into Brighida's legs while Brighida exercised her stump, lifting it like a short, fat sausage and waving it up and down and around in a circle.

"Polly . . ." I began.

"You're doing me no good here, girl, with your fretting. Go on outside with the men, where you belong. Get some fresh air."

I tore off my gown and slippers and took my old shift and dress off the peg. I had not worn them since we arrived, but someone had washed them, so they were clean and starched. I pulled them both over my head at one time, and when I jammed my arm into the sleeve, I got stuck. Around and around I went, trying to squeeze my arm through the sleeve and pull the neck of the dress over my head.

"It's shrunk," I cried. "And I'm stuck. Get it off me."

Brighida threw back her head and laughed.

"Finally, Megge, you've grown!"

"My head hasn't grown, Brighida. These things have shrunk."

Polly wiped her hands on her apron and came to me. One of my arms waved in the air and the other was pinned to my side.

"Stop, Megge." She clamped her hands on my shoulders. "Here." She slapped at my hands. "Let me help you." She pulled the strangling garments back over my head, and there I stood, naked.

"Why, Megge, you've become a woman." Brighida's voice was soft and wondering, not harsh or scornful, as I felt toward this new— soft—body I had kept hidden from her all winter.

"Doubtless we can find something you can wear to work with the sheep—some old castoff," Polly said.

I snatched my gown from the floor and pulled it over me.

"I'll stay clean," I said. I picked up my skirts and fled.

I spent the rest of that afternoon in the sheep barn. As I raked up old bedding and shoveled muck into a bucket, I thought about our farm.

Our poor farm. Such violence it had suffered. And my poor Aunt Claris had lost more than a sister, it seemed. She had lost her work. But something more was troubling her, I felt certain, for as each day passed she became less patient, nearly temperamental.

When I was done in the barn, I stored my rake and shovel, then went to my room to wash. I found Brighida resting and Claris walking to and fro.

"We must go back," she fretted. "We must go."

"Mother." Brighida put out her hand to stop her mother's pacing. "I'm not yet fully healed. And the house . . . Hugh will send word when it's ready."

"Bah." Claris seemed to have taken on Mother's scowl and Polly's invectives. "I can tend my own home. I must go."

She continued to pace, appearing lost as she searched beneath the chairs and under the bed, even in the garderobe, for something. I understood her agitation, for I, too, felt lost.

"Aunt Claris," I said, "I know wh—"

"Aunt Claris nothing," she spat. "You know nothing, child." And then, like pus spewing from a lanced boil, it all came out. "You could have learned everything. All the knowledge of healing was there for you. And yet you refused it—the book, the teaching, your apprentice-ship—and now you are left with nothing. We all are left with nothing. Brighida lost her arm, which you might have saved. We all lost your mother. Can you not see that? And the books. We lost the books."

She sat down on the deep velvet chair and looked at her palms, crossed by welts, the once smooth surface puckered and drawn into a short, taut slab of pink.

"Your mother had *The Book of Seasons* with her when she left for the hut that day." Her eyes forced all her anger and frustration onto me. "And *The Book of Time*—he must have taken it, too, for I couldn't find it." And then she began to cry. "He got the books," she wailed. "The Guardian, the Mentors, your mother . . . forever gone. We failed them."

"Is that your fear, Mother?" Brighida asked. "That the books are gone? Have you been suffering under this burden all this time?" She laid her hand on her mother's. "No, Mother. They're not gone. Aunt's book lies alongside yours in the sleeping lodge."

Claris turned slowly to look at her.

"They're safe, Mother."

"Safe?" Claris took a stuttering breath. "Truly safe? I hadn't asked because I was afraid to hear the truth. I feared it would kill me."

"The books are safe, Mother." Brighida took Claris in her good arm and rocked her gently. "Aunt told me to hide her book when she sent me to the lodge to fetch her pouch. Our book was already there. Don't you remember? We were in the grove the night before. So many women came, we were exhausted. When we had finished, we went to the lodge without stopping."

"We brought the books with us . . ." Claris said as if recalling a dream.

Brighida nodded. "Aunt took hers to her hut the next morning, but you left ours in the lodge when you went to the cottage—"

"To make the porridge." Remembering, she smiled.

"Aunt frightened me when she told me to hide her book, so I sewed them both into my pallet." She mimed the quick stitching her mother had taught her. "And piled hides atop them."

"Then they're safe." Claris seemed to melt with relief.

They continued to talk, but their voices faded as Brighida's words sounded over and over in my mind. "Aunt told me to hide her book . . ."

Mother had told Brighida to hide her book before there was any sign of the attackers?

On the first day of April, we were ready to leave Restormel Castle. Claris and Earl Edmund emerged from the gatehouse together, Claris carrying a square bundle under each arm and speaking to him in a low voice.

"No heir yet, my lord. But there is time." She curtseyed. "How can I thank you, my lord, for your kind hospitality?"

Edmund bowed over her hands and smiled.

"I am at your service. And we will find these men."

"Tintagel," Claris whispered. "Look for Tinker Penneck—look for all of them—at Tintagel."

Hugh helped her into the cart, and then they both helped Brighida settle against soft bags of wool. I climbed up onto the driver's seat alongside Hugh. Before I could settle, though, Polly approached carrying a crate. Hugh jumped down to help her with it.

"This is for the ladies," Polly said. She swung it away from him.

I climbed down and went to her.

"Polly, you came to say goodbye."

"Would you leave without your clothes, girl?" She pushed the box at me.

I kissed her cheek. "I saw that tear, Polly. You like me just a little."

"I like that one over there that knows how to be a lady." She jutted her chin toward Brighida. Then she hugged me until I nearly dropped the box. "Next time, you'll present yourself properly, unless you've outgrown these, too. Look at you. You've grown into a wo—" She stopped when she saw my blush, and said in a low voice, "Our Brighida's not the only one who's changed."

Chapter 31

Claris clapped both hands over her mouth when the cart drew into our path and she saw how much the cottage had changed. The shingles were gone, and the stone walls were black. Even the slate roof was black. The lovely chestnut shutters into which Brighida's father had carved sparrows nesting in filigree branches were gone as well, replaced by planks of wood. I thought of Dora Tucker's dark, smoky house and hoped the new shutters could be opened to let in sunlight and fresh air.

But when I looked up at my hill and down at the chicken roost, I was satisfied just to have this farm to come back to. I leaned over and hugged Hugh.

Lowenna helped Claris out of the cart and then reached for Brighida's arm to help her up. When her hand settled on Brighida's stump, she pulled back.

"I'm sorry, Brighida. Did I hurt you?"

"Please don't worry. Lowenna. There is no pain." Brighida squirmed to the edge of the cart, the hem of her dress pulling up as she moved, revealing thin calves smeared with pink and white skin. But Brighida didn't seem to care as she got out the cart without help and stood. Then, leaning on Claris and Lowenna, she began to walk stiff-legged toward the house.

I ran ahead to open the door, but when I pulled on the latch, only the top half opened. Someone had sawed our door in half.

"Hugh?"

"The door and the shutters burned, so we boarded the window and made you a door that would let in even more light to work by. And it will keep you safe. See here?" He opened the other half and pointed. At the bottom of the door was a heavy bolt that moved up and down. He closed that half and fit the bolt into a hole in the stone floor. When he tugged at it, the door remained closed.

"You see? Now you can bolt the door while you are inside, yet still bring in the light. And no one will be able to release the bolt from the outside as they could if it were here," he said. He pointed to the jamb alongside the sill.

I patted his arm. "It's wonderful, Hugh."

Holding my breath for fear of what I would find, I opened both halves of the door and went inside. Turf glowed in the hearth, and hanging over the fire was a kettle of stew. The savory aroma made me realize how long it had been since we had broken our fast.

Lowenna and Claris helped Brighida to a chair, and then Claris hurried out, running down the path toward the sleeping lodge.

I walked slowly through the kitchen, my hand trailing over the table. It was glossy with polish; only its edges had been burned. A new drying rack hung from the ceiling. The curtained shelves were gone. In their place were two deep, wide planks, the lower one holding our bowls, plates, and cups.

There was no curtain. The books would be in plain view.

"Where will we. . .?" I began.

"Hush, Megge," Brighida whispered. Then, louder, she said, "These are just what Mother and I have always wished for. The old ones were far too small. And see here!" Leaning over the table, she ran a finger over the smooth surface of the new sideboard. "As smooth as the loom."

The loom. Holding my breath, I stepped into the workroom.

"How do you like it?" Lowenna asked.

Other than having been singed in places, it was unharmed. And it glowed. Lowenna must have polished every inch of it with beeswax. I threw my arms around her and thanked her.

"You should thank Martyn, " she said, laughing. "It was he who repaired it."

"And you who made it so beautiful." I sat down at the loom and ran my finger over the heddle. "Where *is* he?"

"Out on the hill with Alf." She pointed.

Martyn sat on the ground next to my rock, and Alf was perched on top, legs crossed. I could not see the hut—or, where the hut had been—but I could almost feel its presence, and Mother's along with it.

Claris and Brighida—and, now, the Caerlins and Alf—were all I had left.

"You have done all of this for us, Lowenna," I said. "How can we ever thank you?"

"There is no need, Megge. Your mother and aunt gave me back my life." She smiled. "And we're friends. Now, let's see to your supper."

Claris returned to the cottage, her step almost as light as a girl's. Though she hadn't brought the books with her, I knew she had found them.

"Lowenna." Embracing her, she looked around the cookroom. "How lovely. How can we ever thank you?" She looked into the workroom. "It's all still there, and better than before."

"A little beeswax is all." Lowenna stepped outside, returning a moment later with a bulging sack. "Now let's eat." She took out a jug and a loaf of bread and set them on the table.

Brighida stretched out her legs, wincing, and Claris looked under the table

"Oh, your foot." She turned Brighida's left foot from side to side. "It's swollen again."

"It doesn't hurt," Brighida protested. "Please don't fuss—"

Claris reached for a stool and propped Brighida's leg on it while Lowenna slid her knife from her pocket and and sliced the bread. Its scent, mingled with the smell of meat and broth, made my stomach grind.

I took four bowls down from the new shelves. My hands shaking from hunger, I filled them from the kettle and carried the bowls to the table, setting one before Brighida then searching the sideboard. "Do you know where the spoons might be, Lowenna?"

"On the shelf . . . perhaps behind the plates? But we have this . . ." She nodded toward the bread.

I shook my head. "Brighida needs a spoon. It's hard for her to steady a bowl and use a piece of bread—especially fresh bread like this—to scoop her food."

Brighida picked up one of the bowls. "Ours are heavier than the ones at Restormel. And the bread looks delicious. Let me try."

She reached for a piece of bread and dipped it, carrying broth and meat easily to her lips. Looking up, she smiled broadly at each of us as she did every time she overcame an obstacle. While the others savored their meal, I gobbled two bowls of stew and then wiped the bowl clean with a thick piece of brown bread, ate the bread, and guzzled a cup of ale.

"Thank you, Lowenna," I said on an exhalation, sitting back in my chair, finally sated. After a moment, I glanced at Claris.

"Go, Megge," Claris said. "You needn't sit here with us. We've news to share, and I know you've other things to do. We'll see to the rest later."

Wrapping my cloak around me, I climbed the slope, noticing that the hawthorn bushes had already sent out buds and that the grass was scattered with bluebells. Ribbons of warm air laced Bury Down's wind. I would have taken off my cloak, but when I started to untie the laces, I remembered what it covered and pulled it tighter around me. Beneath it, I still wore the castoff dress Polly had given to me the day she saw I was becoming a woman.

The gowns she had sent were a lovely gift, but how could I wear them here? They were far too fine. I would have to make new clothes quickly.

Hearing men's voices, I looked up.

"Megge!" Alf jumped off my rock.

"Alf!" I ran into his arms. He, too, had grown over the winter. Although still slender, he was nearly as tall as Martyn. "How can I thank you for taking such good care of my sheep?" My flock. So many lambs! "What's happened here?" I laughed. "How many new lambs do we have?"

"Eight," he said, his chest out.

"Then we'll have a great deal of work to do this spring," I said, feeling like myself again.

"Megge." Martyn had changed over the long winter, his eyes losing some of their youthful eagerness, his face its boyish grin. His gaze rested on me for a moment, and he smiled. "Are you ready to resume your apprenticeship?"

I laughed and opened my cloak.

"I shall have to if I wish to wear clothes that fit."

"That dress suits you," he said, his eyes rising from my hem to my sash, and from sash to bodice. He was not laughing. He was studying me. "Perhaps you're ready to exchange your pen for a kitchen, your rock for a cradle."

"Nonsense," I said. "I'll have plenty of babies—out in my pen— come June." I laughed to dispel his serious mood. "Alf, you'll be here for shearing season?"

"Aye. Have you seen the pen, Megge? We replaced the broken rails." Alf took my hand and began to pull me toward it.

"I came out here to see you first."

"And your sheep," he said with a grin.

"Do you mind if I spend a moment here before I come down to see the pen?" I once again felt Mother behind me. I felt all the seers of Bury Down, all the Mentors who rested in the grove; they seemed to be waiting for me to say or do something.

But it was not yet time. Looking at the remains of Mother's hut, and then past it into the stone ring—into Bury Down—I felt a chill. Something still eluded me. Something important.

I heard Natalje's soft voice. . . . *a truth more terrible than death itself.*

Despite everything that had happened, it was not yet time for me to take up Mother's book.

Chapter 32

It was a hot morning in the middle of August when Brighida stepped into her dress and, for the first time since her injury, tied her own sash. She left the lodge leaning not on me but on her own walking stick as she climbed the steep path to the cottage.

When we reached the well, Claris stopped to draw a bucket of fresh water. Brighida reached into the grain barrel and scattered a handful for the chickens. I went to the roost and rooted around beneath the hens for eggs.

This is how it should be, I thought. *All of us working.*

We had just finished the morning meal when Lowenna knocked on the door.

"Hugh is taking me into the village to see an old friend. Would any of you care to come? We can carry you and your wool."

Claris laughed. "Thank you, Lowenna. We've so much wool, and it's so warm these days, it would take us three trips on foot to deliver it all."

I jumped up from the table. "Have you room in the cart for a dozen bags?"

Hugh helped me load the wool into the cart; and after we delivered it to Mister Tucker's shop, he drove us to the other side of the village green.

"Here, Hugh. Stop here." Lowenna pointed to a cottage with one small window.

"I'll wait with Hugh," I told her as she descended from the cart. The day was too warm to venture inside one of those smoky huts.

As Lowenna entered her friend's cottage, a mule cart drew up across the road from us. The driver helped an old woman out and drove slowly away as she crossed the road and sidled up to Hugh's cart. The crone looked at me, her sly smile showing a gap where an eyetooth should have been. She was so close I could smell her foul breath when she rasped, "I know that *aunt* of yours."

Her coarse hair was grey, and the skin around her mouth and eyes as thin and crinkled as old parchment; but ever since the day I had seen her on those church steps, stalking my family with her vile gaze, I had heard that gravelly voice and seen those silvery eyes in my dreams.

She tilted her head and lifted one eyebrow, and her gap-toothed smile went scornful.

"*Claris*," she growled, drawing out the name. "Sorceress. She has something that should have been mine."

"Horrid old witch—" I started to jump down from the cart.

"That's enough." Hugh reached over and pulled me back up beside him.

Lowenna came out of her friend's cottage and looked from me to the brazen old woman. She hurried to the cart and pulled herself up.

"Hugh," she said, "let's go." She looked down at the old harridan. "Go back to Tintagel, Aggie, or wherever it is you've been hiding."

Hugh tore his eyes from the old woman and shook the reins.

Lowenna dropped her hand to my knee and whispered, "Aggie Gough. A bitter old woman."

I looked back at the old woman, and she was smiling.

"Your aunt Claris," she sneered. "Whore."

When the cart stopped in front of our cottage, I jumped out and ran into the cookroom, dropping my empty woolsacks on the floor.

"Aunt Claris, who is Aggie Gough, and what is she to you?"

Brighida, sitting at the table, looked up from *The Book of Time*. Claris's knife stalled for a moment over the onion she was chopping. Her eyes stayed tight on it, though, and I couldn't tell if her tears were from the onions or from hearing that name.

After a moment, she put down her trembling knife and wiped her hands on her apron.

"She's no one, child. She has no power over us." Just what she had said that long-ago day on the church steps.

"Does she mean to do us harm?" I asked.

Claris slowly sat down at the table beside Brighida and motioned to me.

"Sit," she said, her voice quiet. "Agnes Gough." She tipped her head back, and her eyes roved back and forth over the drying racks as if reading the story of Agnes Gough from the hanging herbs. "Agnes. Gough."

"She hates you, Aunt Claris."

"Hush, Megge. Let her tell it." Brighida's eyes remained fixed on her mother's face.

"She says you have something that is hers."

"Megge," Brighida warned.

Claris laid her palms on the table and just breathed quietly for a moment.

"Megge," she finally said, "will you please fetch me a cup of spring water?"

I poured some ale instead and handed it to her. She took a sip.

"When I was growing up, here at Bury Down, Agnes and her family lived in one of the huts in the bailey outside Restormel castle. Her first husband, Robert, was a blacksmith, and they had two children. Their son, Michael, followed his father into the trade.

"But Robert was a cruel man; he beat Michael until the boy was big enough to fight back, and then he beat Agnes. Only once, but he nearly broke her neck. Her voice was never the same afterward. Always rasping, always rough.

"A terrible fire in the smithy took Robert's life the very next day." Claris raised an eyebrow. "Agnes and her children stayed on at Restormel castle, Michael working at an anvil, and Agnes dabbling in charms."

Brighida nodded, and I kept quiet.

"I never knew Agnes or Michael until I was about your age, but they knew of our family, of course. Gytha was the great seer, counselor to the Earl of Cornwall, and we lived on all this land—land many believed was a boon from the earl, though it has been ours since Bury Down was a hillfort. Though it was truly our land—known throughout Cornwall as The Land of the Second Sight—every ruler seemed to think it was his to deed it to us anew. And so, for a thousand years, every ruler has done just that in exchange for our sight and our counsel.

"Earl Richard was no different, nor is his son, the pious Edmund. They both gained from our skills, and we have been safe, thanks to their protection. Even now, though we farm and shear and weave and heal, the villagers believe we live off the earl's bounty.

"So, can you understand why Agnes Gough, a blacksmith's widow raising two children, might have coveted Gytha's power? And why she might resent us even now?"

She looked at Brighida and me until we nodded.

"But why does she *hate* you?" I asked. "And why does she call you a whore?"

"Megge!" Brighida drew back her hand.

Claris took Brighida's hand and held it for a long time. She frowned and shook her head as she thought. Then she leaned back and looked at both of us.

"It is no simple matter. You see, when I was sixteen, I visited the castle with Gytha. There, I met and fell in love with Michael Gough. So handsome. Those eyes . . ." Claris said. "Amethyst . . ."

She said nothing more for a moment, but then went on. "When my grandmother learned of this love, she forbade the union and warned me that Michael was no ordinary blacksmith. 'He's something of an alchemist,' Gytha said, 'and he wants you only for your book.'"

Claris looked down at her hands. "He only wanted *The Book of Time*."

She still grieved, I realized.

"And Agnes wanted me to marry him so that our firstborn child would inherit it."

I recalled Agnes's claim: *She has something that should have been mine.*

"So that's what she—" I began.

"But you married my father," Brighida interrupted.

"Yes." Claris paused. "My grandmother quickly betrothed me to Gregory Carver, the son of the earl's master carpenter. A handsome young man. Golden hair, blue eyes. Gytha had chosen him for me long before, just as she had chosen a master mason for Megge's mother."

I waited while she took another sip of ale.

"The betrothal wasn't a simple matter, though, because although Gregory wanted to marry me, someone else already loved him and wanted to marry him." Claris looked down and shook her head, and then looked back at me. "Agnes's daughter."

In a flash of memory, I saw Agnes lock eyes with Jenifer Penneck, and then I saw Jenifer whirl away, warning, "Stay away from me, Mother."

"Mistress Penneck?" I cried. "The man Gytha had chosen for you was already in love with Jenifer Penneck?"

Astonishment gave way to something like pride. Claris lifted her forefinger to silence me and looked at me out of the corner of her eye.

"Penneck was not her surname then. And I did not say Gregory loved her." She wagged her finger. "I said that Jenifer wanted him." She sat back again. "Well, the day Gregory and I were wed, Agnes stood outside Bury Down and shouted into the grove the very words Beatrix had spoken over your mother and me when we were born. How she knew that curse I have never learned. But she swore vengeance, as did Michael.

"They both soon left Lostwithiel and went to Tintagel, where the earl was building his castle. I never saw Michael again."

Brighida and I nodded, waiting for more.

"Jenifer married Francis Penneck," Claris went on. "An older man, widowed, with a twelve-year-old son—Tinker—by his first wife. Not the man Agnes wanted for her daughter." Her expression changed, consternation giving way to tenderness. "But Jenifer was soon blessed with a daughter. As was I."

This is for my father, a cuckold—

As if in a vision, I saw a young Jenifer Penneck gaze with love at the handsome Gregory Carver, then turn away from him in tears, her hand upon her belly, and cast a provocative smile upon Francis Penneck and walk away with him.

"She tricked him," I said. "Jenifer tricked Mister Penneck so he would marry her, even though she was already going to have a baby. She was going to have Gregory Carver's baby."

Claris closed her eyes and turned her face away.

"Let us not speak of trickery."

It was all coming together.

"Is this why Tinker Penneck called his father a cuckold?"

"Come, Mother." Brighida stood and tapped Claris's elbow. She looked at me—hard—and shook her head as if ashamed of me as her mother rose. "Mother and I will be out in the herb garden. Would you please finish chopping that onion?" She pointed at it. "We will be back once Mother has had some fresh air."

Pulling in the corners of her mouth just like Mother used to do, she shook her head again and followed Claris out the door.

I slept that night on that notion—trickery—and awoke thinking about Vivienne Penneck, who also had needed a husband, and for the very same reason. The next morning, as Martyn examined the broadcloth I had woven, I took a deep breath and asked, "Martyn, were you especially good friends with Vivienne Penneck?"

"Not especially," he said, still measuring by handbreadths the length of fabric.

"Did you know her well?"

"I knew her brother, Harold, with the limp."

That Harold walked at all was thanks to my mother's work.

"But how well did you know Vivienne?"

He stopped measuring. "Megge, what do you want to know about Vivienne?"

"Were you and Vivienne betrothed?"

"Betrothed?" He put down the broadcloth. "Betrothed? Megge. I was her brother's friend. I could have been Vivienne's older brother. We were . . . We were like . . . like brother and sister."

"Like you and me," I said quickly.

He pulled his lips shut and rocked back and forth for a moment, studying me.

"Megge," he finally said, "you are no longer a child. And I am no longer a boy." He looked hard into my face. A moment passed. "You and I . . . Why are you asking me this?"

"Because I saw her. She was standing behind you at the loom. I saw her touch you. I saw how she looked at you."

Martyn put up a hand to silence me. "Vivienne looked at me the same way she looked at every other man in the village. To me, she was a neighbor, Harold's sister. Nothing more. To other men she was . . . something else. Why are you asking about Vivienne?"

He was telling the truth.

"No reason."

CHAPTER 33

That afternoon, I waited for Aunt Claris and Brighida to stop working so I could ask Claris more questions about Agnes Gough and Tinker Penneck, because I had remembered that both Agnes and Tinker had lived in Tintagel. And now, here was Agnes Gough getting out of the same kind of cart Tinker Penneck had been driving the day the "abbot" arrived.

Was Tinker back? Was the "abbot"?

I tried to catch Claris's eye, but she and Brighida were deaf and blind to me as they worked, heads together, murmuring incantations and grinding herbs under the pestle.

Claris scooped some of the herb dust from the mortar and scattered it on the table. She swept a hand over it, smoothing it, and then, with her finger, drew a symbol in the dust.

"You see, Brighida, this symbol looks much like the one on that page, but see here . . ."

I got up from the loom and watched them. Absorbed in their book and its cryptic symbols, they would be at this for hours.

It was still early, but I left them and went to the lodge, closed the door, and felt my way to my pallet. I wanted to lie down and think, to try to understand. I threw my arm over Mother's book, which, for reasons even I did not understand, I kept hidden in my bed, wrapped in a thick blanket.

I fell asleep and dreamed of Claris. Of her soft grey eyes. Of those dreamy eyes gazing into violet eyes. Of those violet eyes going black with rage.

I awoke breathing fast, my heart pounding, and reached for Mother's fire kit. I lit the candle and patted the blanket that covered Mother's book.

There. Square and solid and heavy, its very heft comforted me. I inhaled, and its musty scent brought back my mother's demand. *Look at it, Megge. You must look.*

I could almost hear her voice and feel her fingers trying to guide mine, trying to make them trace the symbols. *Just touch it, Daughter. Why won't you touch it? What do you fear?*

I sat up, and the book fell to the floor. Its swaddling fell away, and a page of fresh vellum slipped out of the book. On the page was a coarsely drawn image of a woman and two girls standing close together. Apart from them, all alone, stood another woman, but she was cast into shadow. It made me think of the four of us—now three living and one gone.

Mother had known what was to come.

I looked at it closely. This drawing, though coarse, had taken time. It was not the work of a moment, not a hasty message written in distress. How long had she known?

Our time here is so brief, Daughter. Soon, dark days will be upon us.

Mother could have begun it the very day she spoke those words. The day Morwen made herself my master. And then, the day she was to die, knowing her time was near, Mother must have put it into the book and sent Brighida back to the lodge with it. To protect Brighida. To safeguard the book. Then she had sent Mistress Trelawney away, and only she had burned.

The door to the lodge opened, and Brighida and Claris entered quietly. I wrapped the book in its blanket and set it aside.

"How long did Mother know, Claris?"

"Megge, you're awake."

"Mother knew," I said. "Before it happened, she knew we would be divided. She saw it. As her notation in her book, knowing that I cannot read her symbols, she drew a picture. A picture of the three of us standing together, apart from her." I held out the sheet of vellum. "She knew, Aunt Claris. And yet she did nothing to stop it."

Brighida and Claris remained silent.

"How long did Mother know?"

"She knew—we both knew what might happen—the day we saw the man who said he was the new abbot on the church steps."

"You knew as well? If you both knew, then why did you do nothing to stop him?"

She let out her breath and shook her head. "Because your mother believed she still had time to . . ." She stopped. "Who can change destiny, Megge, their own or another's? Some can foresee what is to come and do what is in their power to stay the hand of suffering, but to defy fate? It cannot be done."

"'Stay the hand of suffering?'" I shouted. How dared she make such a claim? "For whom did you 'stay the hand of suffering,' Claris? Do you think Mother did not suffer out there in that hut as they burned her alive?"

"Megge . . ." Brighida's voice held a warning.

I pointed to her empty sleeve. "And you, missing an arm and walking on stiff legs. Do you not suffer?" My eyes flashed back and forth between them. "What is the purpose of knowing, of seeing, of learning? What is the purpose of these books? Of their so-called knowledge and wisdom? If they teach us only to blindly follow fate, then I spit on them."

"Megge, calm yourself." Brighida touched my arm.

I drew back my fist, but let it fall.

"You. Standing there beside your mother. You dare tell me to calm myself? It was *my* mother who died, not yours. All of this happened because your mother loved Michael Gough yet married Gregory Carver. She stole the man Jenifer Penneck—Jenifer Gough—loved. The man who fathered Jenifer's child. And that child—your own half-sister—became a vessel for three generations of festering hatred."

"Megge, stop," Brighida warned.

"What, Brighida? You never guessed you and Vivienne were half-sisters? Why, Vivienne looked more like you than I ever did."

Brighida drew her arm back, her hand open as if to slap me.

Claris touched her sleeve. "It's all right, Brighida."

Brighida's eyes had turned to steel. "I know who she was to me, Megge. I've known since I was six years old."

I realized at that moment I had been in the dark all my life.

I had to get away from them and out of that cave. Where was my stick? It was dark outside, and the dark was dangerous without a stick. There were wolves—and who knew what else—out there. Hooded men. They were out there in the fields and the hills and the village and the churches, all of them waiting to hurt us because the wise and powerful Gytha had wanted the handsome Gregory Carver for Claris.

If this was wisdom, give me my rock. My sheep. My ignorance. Give me my solitude and my eventual lonely death. For Brighida might as well have said it: "You're not one of us."

Where was my stick? I had to leave that cave.

But I could not leave. Not yet. I turned again to Claris.

"And what about Vivienne, whose fate, as you call it, was to repeat her mother's folly? You and Mother could have helped her. She came to you. But did you? Did Mother's knowledge of healing help Vivienne? Did your knowledge of herbs, did your wisdom, save her? Did either of you 'stay the hand of suffering' for Vivienne? Or for Gwyneth, an innocent? Her confession freed you, but it sent her to the stake alongside her sister and her mother."

I picked up my book and held it under my arm.

"Your grandmother's curse has come to pass. But death by fire is nothing compared to the degradation you and Mother have brought upon us through fear. 'Never open the books in the same place at the same time,' you always said. But in separating the books—in separating knowledge from wisdom—you robbed us of their power. Power which, Mother taught me, is courage. 'What power do knowledge and wisdom give us,' she said, 'after all, but courage?' Shame on you both for succumbing to fear."

Claris turned on me then, returning my rage. "Do you know nothing, Megge? You saw those hooded men ransack the cottage. Do you think they were seeking courage? Do you really believe they murdered Clarissa Gloyn over a litter of pigs? *Think, Megge.* Clarissa. The one who killed her mistook her for me. But she did not possess *The Book of Time*, and so he returns, again and again, seeking me. Seeking *us*. And, why?"

She did not wait for me to speak. "Because we hold the books. And the one who masquerades as an abbot covets their power— power you cannot yet begin to comprehend. The books have been kept apart for centuries, Megge, not out of fear but to preserve their combined power from one who would use it to sate his own greed, his own lusts, his own ambition."

"But in keeping them apart, Claris, you robbed us all of the courage that comes when the two are joined. You and Mother could have been two powerful women, and yet you chose instead to be two halves of one weak one, and for what? For the sake of fate?"

"You misunderstand both the nature of the books and our role in their keeping." Claris's voice was weary now, defeated. She spoke each word slowly, clearly. "It was not for your mother and me to bring them together, Megge. Did you never listen to Morwen's tales?

"It was not for your mother and me to unite the books. Only one person might do that—the one chosen by the Guardian. And the power they offer, Megge, is not courage. Your mother told you it was courage simply so you would not fear what you said you felt 'writhing' within *The Book of Seasons*. So you would accept your birthright.

"For what you felt was power. Power intended to sustain those who have entrusted their lives to—"

"Entrusted their lives to what?" I cried. "To fate? As you and Mother did? To something that would consign innocents to the flames? Well, I shall learn about what you call fate, Aunt. You may wink at it, and steel yourself for it, and stand by like a goddess as it claims those . . . those . . . those lesser mortals not schooled to see it coming and step handily aside. But I shall defy it, for fear is the only true curse, and fear is born of ignorance. I shall bring knowledge and wisdom together if you will not. Courage is all the *power* I need."

I picked up Mother's book and left the lodge with it, closing the door on Claris's reply.

Once outside, I breathed deeply of the damp night air. The sliver of moon, so bright against the night sky, did nothing to light my path, and I made my way blindly to my place on the hill.

Sitting on the ground with his back against my rock was Alf, covered in a mantle I had made for him. I had taken the fabric off the loom just the week before. I had finished it, pounded it, soaked it, dried it, and stitched that cloak to keep him warm on a cool night such as this. And Alf had borne that garment away like a treasure, thanking me with his crooked smile. Tonight, it covered him as he slept, his back against my rock.

As I watched him doze, the tenderness of a mother overtook me. Could I ever stand by and allow fate to take Alf? Could I allow it to burn him as it had burned Mother, to nail his limbs to the ground? To maim him, as it had maimed Brighida?

Fate be damned. I would not.

CHAPTER 34

I climbed atop my rock and watched the sheep for the rest of the night. In the morning, I awoke overcome with shame.

I tried to remember all the cruel things I had said the night before, all that I had accused my aunt of doing out of fear and weakness; and I realized I, too, was guilty of cowardice. Fear had dogged me all my life.

My eye drifted toward Mother's book, the book she had begged me to protect, still wrapped in its blanket and lying on the ground beside my rock. How would I ever fulfill that rash vow to unite knowledge with wisdom? What had I even meant by those words? And what would happen to me if I did?"

I got up and paced, but my eye was drawn again and again to that book. Unable to stop myself, I unwrapped it and looked. The symbols at the center of the cover, so familiar—only five—filled me with longing. I stared at them, yearning to understand them, and began to feel as though a sudden thirst had come over me and I had to quench it.

And only Claris could help me.

I would have to go back. I would have to swallow my pride and ask her to teach me.

But how could I go back after having raged at her? What could I possibly say to make her forgive me?

From my rock on the herder's hill, I watched the cottage until Claris came outside to draw a bucket of water from the well. She would let me come back. She was too kind to do otherwise. But could I? I cringed at the thought of asking.

I paced the summit.

The morning sun revealed a shaggy ewe. Had Alf and I somehow missed her when we sheared? She would be too hot on a day like this. I had to find Alf.

I grabbed my book and ran down the hill to the cottage. As I reached for the latch, the top half of the door opened.

"Aunt Claris, where is Alf? There's a ewe—"

Claris smiled as she welcomed me inside.

"You need no excuse for returning, Megge."

Hoping to make amends with my cousin, I looked from the cookroom into the empty workroom.

"Where is Brighida?"

"She is preparing a bag of fleece for market." Claris tipped her head toward two full sacks lying by the hearth. "We'll soon leave for the village."

Claris was leaving! My heart pounding, I thrust my book toward her.

"Aunt Claris, before you go, would you please tell me about the symbols on the cover of *The Book of Seasons*?"

"You looked, Megge." Not taking her eyes from mine, Claris inclined her head toward the table, pulled out two chairs, and sat down.

I placed my book on the table beside *The Book of Time*, which she must have been studying. Wasting not a moment, Claris unwrapped *The Book of Seasons* and pointed to the first symbol in the short line at the center of the cover.

"This single line represents *Isa,* the runic symbol for the number eleven."

"Eleven," I repeated. "What is this one?" I pointed to the next symbol. "It looks like a sickle, or a scythe. It must mean that something must be cut. But how am I to know what is meant to be cut or sliced?"

Claris reached up to the drying rack and pulled down a handful of dried herbs. She crumbled them and scattered them over the tabletop, then drew a sickle in the herb dust with her fingertip.

"This 'sickle,' as you call it, is called *Quartus*—the quarter moon, waxing and waning. The direction the moon faces denotes the phase of the moon under which the incantation—these five symbols— must be spoken." She pointed to the left-facing moon. "This is the waning quarter moon."

It would take a lifetime to understand. This, I finally realized, was why heirs were given their books at the age of six.

I'm too old to embark on this now, I thought.

"And yet," Claris said, her eyes still on the herb dust strewn on the table, "you just have. Call on the Mentors," she said gently, "and they will teach you."

The door opened, and Brighida came in with a full woolsack slung across her torso and a basket of eggs and herbs in her right hand. Saying nothing to me, she turned and went back outside. Unable to speak for my shame, I looked down at the tabletop and pretended to study the symbols Claris had drawn in the herb dust.

Claris picked up the two full sacks lying by the hearth and slung them over her shoulders.

"But, Aunt Claris, the other symbols—"

"Everything you need to know is at your fingertips." She kissed the top of my head. "Courage, child." And she was gone.

The Book of Seasons lay in a shaft of late-afternoon sunlight that drew my eye to those five figures etched into the center of the cover: *Isa, Quartus*, a bent hammer, a bird, and a woman holding out her arm.

The first time I saw *The Book of Seasons*, at dawn on the day I turned six, I seemed to know those symbols. They had seemed to speak to me. But that was long ago. Now, there was but one thing to do if I wanted to understand them. I had to summon the Mentors.

As I had seen Mother, Claris, and Brighida do countless times, I closed my eyes and murmured, "*Scientia nupta sapientia potestas est.*"

I waited, but no voices spoke to me as they seemed to speak to Mother whenever she had called on them. I opened my eyes and looked at the first symbol: *Isa*, the runic symbol for the number eleven. And I heard Brighida's voice as clearly as I had heard it that day in Restormel castle, when she had just taken her eleventh step.

"Eleven is the master number of the spiritual messenger. The day and hour of your birth make the number eleven your celestial number."

The second symbol I already knew: *Quartus*, the waning quarter moon.

I let my finger float above the third symbol. It looked like a hammer with a long, crooked handle and called to mind the one Hugh had been using to fix his cart the first time I saw him.

"It looks like he's wielding the *Was*," Brighida had said. "It's a scepter. The ancient gods were said to have carried it as evidence of their power."

The next symbol was a bird with a wide wingspan and a prominent beak and tail. An eagle. I remembered Claris often pointing out the stars that made up *Aquila*, the eagle's constellation, and I recalled her patient voice saying, "The work must be carried out under the proper celestial constellation."

The final symbol was a rough etching of a gowned woman holding out a string in one hand and gripping shears in the other.

"Atropos is one of the Fates," Mister Gynneys had once said. "She clips the string of life."

I sat at the table for a very long time, unable to take my eyes off those symbols. When finally I pulled my gaze away, I noticed that the sky had gone dark. Realizing how late it was and that Brighida and Aunt Claris had not returned, I went outside to look for them.

It was too dark to see into the woods. I looked into the sky to see if the moon would be full, and I saw Altair, the brightest star in the constellation *Aquila*. It shone just off the tip of the waning quarter moon.

Isa, I thought. My celestial number. *Quartus*, the phase of tonight's moon. *Was*, a symbol of power. *Aquila*, the constellation hanging above me. *Atropos*, who clips the string of life.

This incantation is meant for me, I thought. *And it is meant to be spoken this very night.*

I went back inside the cottage, wrapped *The Book of Seasons* in its blanket, lit Morwen's lantern, and, with the book under my arm, began the long walk up the herder's hill to Bury Down. When I reached the clearing, I set the lantern and the book at the foot of the granite headstone shaped like a tall clover with a cross engraved at its center.

Morwen's resting place.

I closed my eyes and spoke the incantation. "*Isa. Quartus. Was. Aquila. Atropos.*"

Chapter 35

egge."

I opened my eyes. Standing before me was Morwen. Radiant, smiling, she held her hands out to me.

"Morwen." I could hardly speak. "Is this a dream?"

"What are dreams, Megge, but moments in spirit? Are dreams not more real than life itself?" Morwen closed her eyes. "It's radiant you were in your own dreams, my Megge. Do you remember, lass? I can see you now, spinning with Adaem, 'round and 'round, head thrown back, eyes shining with mirth, a child with but a child's heart. You had laid all your fears at slumber's door for a moment, only to gather them back into your heart upon returning to the waking world."

She opened her eyes and looked at me, her smile gone but her eyes gentle.

"Do you not yet know who you are, lass?" She dropped her gaze to *The Book of Seasons*. "You've become the strong young woman I knew you would one day be. You heeded your mother's message—mine, through her—that knowledge and wisdom bring courage. But as the kindest of us, your gentle Aunt Claris, taught you, knowledge wedded to wisdom also brings power. And today, you've found and spoken the incantation that was meant for you."

Her image faded, giving way to that of a woman with a regal countenance.

"You spurned your mother's teachings," said the great seer Gytha, "yet you heeded those of Morwen. Eschewing the rigors of healing, you embraced the solitude of herding. The land stilled you. The sheep taught you courage and selflessness. Time matured you. And your mother's death impelled you to take up your inheritance. It is time. Look at your book, Megge, and *remember*."

Gytha's image gradually became that of Mother, her expression and her voice, for the first time ever, as soft and loving as Claris's. At Mother's side were Vivienne, Gwyneth, and Jenifer Penneck.

"We have all returned to the living world many times," Mother said, "to guide your books back to you."

Gwyneth, her skin smooth, her face fair, smiled. "The four of us followed our destinies—into fire—that you might find yours."

"You walk a path walked by but one other," Mother said. "The time has come, Daughter. *Remember*."

Mother's face then faded into the ether, leaving me alone again with Morwen, whose soft brown eyes held mine. She looked at the cross that marked her resting place, and her voice lost some of its lilt.

"For a thousand years, I have guarded and guided the books."

Morwen is the Guardian. Of course.

"Aye," she said.

My heart lightened. If Morwen was the Guardian, then she would once more return to the living world. She would—

She shook her head. Her eyes held mine, and I held my breath. Was she never to return? Who would protect the books? Who would preserve the Mentors?

"Long ago," she said, not waiting for me to speak, "though you recall neither the time nor the name by which you knew me, I was your pupil and you were taken from me. It's *your* books I have guarded. Your power I've wielded while awaiting your return. With that power, I've brought forth healers, thinkers, seers, and kings to bring us through the darkest days Britain has ever known, all now Mentors who will serve at your command in the hard times to come."

At *my* command?

"As Guardian, Morwen? Is that what you're saying? That I am to succeed you as Guardian?"

Morwen shook her head slowly. "Can you truly tell me, lass, that you don't know who you are? Who you once were? Why, 'tis your own inscription carved into the cover of *The Book of Seasons*. Those five symbols—you carved them there yourself. You knew them when first you saw them, just as you knew that the book had once been yours.

"You've a vow to speak this night, Megge. If you've the wisdom to know what it is and the courage to speak it, the Mentors and I will help you keep it. Will you do what you've come to do? Have you the courage to do what you must?"

I picked at my fingers and thought hard. What was Morwen asking of me? My fingertips touched my ring, and the words she had spoken the day she put it on my finger came rushing back. *The circles of life, of death, of transition, of rebirth.*

Rebirth.

"Think, child," Morwen urged. "Think back to my tales. To the stories of Natalje . . ."

I remembered every tale Morwen had made me commit to memory—the stories of Natalje, of Adaem, of Gytha, of Murga . . .

Of Murga. Bury Down's first seer. Murga.

I closed my eyes and rolled the name over and over in my mouth. I formed it with my lips. *Mur-ga.* And then I remembered very clearly the first time I had heard that name, but it was not in one of Morwen's tales.

It was the night I turned six. Morwen and I had stepped over the low wall and into Bury Down.

"This, once, was Murga's grove," she had said. And my gaze had fallen upon that frightening rowan tree, its branches all blown to one side as if it were fleeing for its life. The sight had set my heart to pounding.

"Morwen," I had whispered. "This tree . . ."

And at dawn the next morning, during my vowtaking ceremony, I had gazed upon the symbols carved into the cover of *The Book of Seasons*, and they had silently called to me. A thought, a sigh, nothing more. *Murga*. And I had known that name as my own.

My eyes shot open as I recalled with utter clarity what had happened next. *For so long*, the book had whispered, *we have been lost to one another.* A surge of tenderness had flowed through me, and I had wanted only to touch my book.

But when I laid my hands upon it, my fingertips began to burn, and a voice had called me a murderer.

All my life that coarse whisper had accused me. *Murderer*. I had always believed it had come from Mother's book. But, harsh and hateful, that voice was not the loving murmur of *The Book of Seasons*.

"Morwen!" The words came rushing out. "It was not *The Book of Seasons* that burned me, was it?"

She shook her head.

"Nor the curse, nor the power of the book, as Mother and Claris said."

"No, Megge."

"What was it that burned me that night, Morwen? Tell me, for the Mentors are asking me to remember, but I cannot."

"The life you've chosen to forget was a hard one, Megge. And another time of great need soon will be upon this land, a famine such as the world has never known, and only you can marshal the power to stem the tide of suffering for Cornwall.

"The night you were born, we feared you would learn too soon who you once were, and that when you heard the name *Murga* you would flee. And so we—your mother, Claris, Aleydis, and I—named you Margaret, a name so like Murga—and so like Morwen—that you would not fear Murga's name when you heard it."

Margaret. Morwen. Mar— I stared at her. "Martyn?"

Morwen said nothing, but a wry smile played upon her lips.

Martyn. I struggled to comprehend.

But Morwen went on. "When you were a child we gave you glimpses, nothing more, of the past. We told you tales of your ancestors, stories to make you love the ones who would perish if you fled. We gave you fears a child could summon the courage to vanquish—a giant, a witch, a conjuror's curse.

"But still you feared. And so, I begged your mother to allow you an apprenticeship to an old bard and a young weaver . . . to give you time. Time to grow up. Time to learn that the Mentors would come to your aid when you called upon them. As Gwyneth did the night you begged the Mentors to save your mother and Claris. Time to find the courage to look upon a life long past."

I recalled the words Brighida had spoken the day I nearly fainted at the grain bin. *A memory, perhaps, of another time . . . a former life that wants to be recalled . . .*

And then I heard Natalje's words. *Soon you shall face a truth more terrible than death itself . . .*

Morwen's voice was flat. "That time has come, child."

Chapter 36

ut I was not a child. I was a woman. And if this was the night the Mentors had chosen to reveal my forgotten past, so be it. I would look.

I picked up my lantern, nodded to Morwen, and followed her to the edge of the grove. She waved her arm in a wide arc, and the gnarled old rowan with the outflung branches was suddenly afire, an old woman bound to its trunk, her feet and legs engulfed in flames. Gaunt men and women stood around the pyre, their dirty hands gripping shovels and picks, their voices echoing the curses of a leather-aproned man heaping wood upon the flames.

Witch. Murderer.

"Morwen." I struggled to understand. "What has this woman done? Why are they burning her?"

"Watch, Megge," Morwen said. "And remember."

Bury Down Circle, that low stone ring, seemed to grow before my eyes into a great high wall encircling a thriving village. Lively children came and went from low huts shaped like beehives. Robust men and women filled woven baskets from overflowing granaries. It was a time of great bounty and merriment—a harvest festival, it seemed.

But in the midst of the revelers stood an old woman, head cocked to one side, looking up at the sky and mumbling to herself. As the villagers neared her, she urged, "Set aside a portion of your bounty against lean days, lest hunger take you."

Shaking off the seer's warning, the villagers went on their way, burdened with full baskets of grain.

Seasons passed in the blink of an eye—leaves fell from the trees; the winter rains came; and when the rains had ceased, soft grasses pushed up through tilled earth. A blazing sun then appeared, its relentless heat withering the shoots and scorching the fields. The next summer brought ceaseless rains that washed away the fallow earth. The third summer, another blistering sun. Under its glare, tilled earth turned to stone. And as autumn approached, the cooling air began to ring with the clash of shovels and the thud of picks as men dug shallow trenches and slipped swaddled corpses into them— no rites, no cists—and covered them with dirt.

Morning breezes lifted mothers' wails from over their babies' still faces. Night winds carried the groans of desperate men digging up those swaddled remains and dragging them back to their fires and spits. The place reeked of despair.

Every granary save one was now empty, and before that bin stood the elderly seer and a gaunt young mother with a withered babe in her arms. Both women gripped with one hand the same half-full cup of grain. A shadow fell over them. Behind the wasted mother loomed a giant of a man wearing a leather apron and clutching the handle of a hammer. He stared down at the old seer . . .

I recoiled from the vision. "Morwen," I begged, for I knew that stare. "I'll not—"

"You'll look," Morwen said. And she forced still more upon me.

Steeling myself, I met that hateful gaze. I had to blink, for my vision had gone cloudy and rheumy. It was as if I were struggling to see through the eyes of someone very old.

"Aye," Morwen said. "Through Murga's good eye."

Resisting the urge to pull away, I followed the blacksmith's gaze as it moved steadily downward and settled upon an old woman's knotted hand. Murga's hand. *My* hand. A hand, I now saw, that was not offering the starving woman that half-full cup. It was trying to pry it from her hands.

I wrenched myself from the vision and opened my eyes. Mother's voice cried out from the ether, *Megge, no!*

I whirled about and shouted into the night, "What more would you have me see? That hand was Murga's. And it was taking the cup from that starving mother, not giving it to her. Murga fed herself from that bin while the villagers starved. It was her hoarding—*my* hoarding—that had starved that village."

Scientia nupta sapientia, I heard the Mentors whisper.

"'Knowledge wedded to wisdom?' Do you mock me? Murga showed no wisdom. It was the man in the apron who served justice. The blacksmith. He was right to have burned her." I corrected myself. "To have burned me."

It struck me then that Murga's crimes had followed her into this life. Into my life.

"When Murga returned to the living world," I shouted, "the blacksmith followed her. Disguised as an abbot, he burned Mother. He would have burned Claris and Brighida. Without Alf's help, I, too, would have perished at his hands."

If only I had.

"The blacksmith seeks more than the books and their power," I shouted. "He seeks a reckoning. He could have found those books Brighida had hidden in the sleeping lodge when we fled to Restormel. But he will be satisfied only when I and those I love are dead."

Weak with remorse at what I had done to that young mother a thousand years before, and at what had been done to my family because of me, I closed my mind to the cries of the Mentors.

A thousand years, I thought. *I have been fleeing this knowledge for a thousand years.*

But now I knew. Morwen had made certain I would learn what I had done. Finally, I knew who I once was and I saw the path I had once walked.

Picking up my book and Morwen's lantern, I turned to leave the grove but looked back first at that lone rowan.

Such a vile crime. I must have made myself forget. And yet, the blacksmith remembers. So do the Mentors. So does Morwen.

On my long walk down the hill to the cottage, I thought back on Morwen's words.

You've a vow to make this night, Megge. If you've the wisdom to know what it is and the courage to speak it, the Mentors and I will help you keep it.

I must have come back to end the evildoer's life, I reasoned. Only then would Brighida and Claris be safe.

There could be but one vow Morwen would have me make. But would such a vow halt the blacksmith's murderous rage? Would it settle accounts? Would it quiet his unstill spirit?

There was but one thing to do. I spoke my vow quietly.

"If it will preserve the lives of Claris and Brighida, the only family remaining to me, then I will take my own life tonight and never again return to the living world."

CHAPTER 37

I pushed open the cottage door and looked into the cookroom. Untouched. Claris and Brighida must have gone straight to the sleeping lodge.

Setting my book on the table next to *The Book of Time*, I took Claris's soft leather pouch from the sideboard, unrolled it, and pulled out one of her lovely, cloudy-green candles. Even death, I felt, was sacred. It merited ritual. Crossing to the hearth, I brought up the fire and touched the candlewick to it.

But how does one take her own life?

I looked up at the herbs on the drying racks above my head and then down at the books in my arms. Surely, there was a potion.

If you've the courage to make that vow, the Mentors and I will help you keep it.

The Mentors would help me—Morwen would help me—if I asked. Removing the spent candle from the lantern, I put Claris's glowing taper in its place.

"*Scientia nupta sapientia potestas est*," I said, my voice resolute but my sweat stinking of fear.

The ether was silent.

I waited.

Taking a ragged breath, I was just about to repeat the words when a gust of wind swept in and blew back the cover of *The Book of Time*. Etched in the leather by a skilled hand were fine hatch marks depicting in exquisite detail an old woman standing at a granary beside a low, round hut. Her outstretched hand held a cup piled high with small specks.

Grain.

Facing the old woman, one arm reaching out as if to take the cup, was a young woman with sunken eyes and saw-blade collarbones, who held in her other arm a sleeping child. There were no words beneath the image, no symbols, nothing to guide me.

I stared at that heaping cup. At the gnarled hand that held it out. At the wasted hand that reached for it. Heart pounding, I turned the book over and searched the back cover for another picture. There was none. I looked again at the image of the women with that heaping cup, staring until my eyelids drooped and my vision blurred.

I knew then that the old woman—that Murga, that *I*—had dipped that cup into the grain barrel, scooped out a heaping portion, and offered it to the young mother with the haggard face. I watched now, as if in a dream.

She leaned close and whispered in my ear, "I've gone dry. I've no milk for him."

As she took the cup from me, her baby released a long final sigh, and she lowered her gaze to look at him. Seeing his dusky face, she let out a cry and tipped her hand, spilling the grain. I reached for the cup and tried to take it from her so that I might fill it again, and as we grappled for that now half-empty cup, a shadow fell over us.

A huge man reeking of smoke stood behind the grieving mother, his great bulk blocking out the sun. He held my eye for a long time and then dropped his gaze slowly to my hands, which were still trying to pry the cup from the hand of the sickly young mother.

The blacksmith's eye moved to the child, its face still and its skin the blue-white of a mother's first milk, and he smiled. Leaning in close to me, his foul breath warm on my ear, he whispered, "The books, Master. Give me the books, and I will spare you."

I turned and spat in his face.

He looked back at the dead child.

"Murderer," he said quietly, slowly, as if savoring the word. Then, wiping the spittle off his face with the back of his hand, his eyes never leaving mine, he growled, "Witch. Murderer."

Over and over he repeated those words, his voice growing louder each time. Catching the eye of a passing villager returning home from the burial grounds with his pick, he shouted, "She has killed our youngest."

Soon, the whole village had gathered. Taking up the chant— "Witch! Murderer!"—they seized me and dragged me away, tied me to the trunk of my rowan, and set me alight . . .

"Enough." Morwen's voice shattered the vision. I swam up as if from the pit of a black well, hungry for air. My eyes opened, and I gasped for breath.

Morwen spoke gently. "You were not the evildoer. Surely, you see that now."

Still struggling to catch my breath, I could not reply.

"You saw the coming drought and warned the village of the lean days to come, but they spurned your counsel. When the blazing sun scorched their fields, the blacksmith—the pupil you had once spurned for his greed—turned them against you, blaming you for the drought. Doling out scraps of his own reserve, he told them you would let them starve.

"But the young mother," I protested. "I fed the young mother. Why . . . ?"

"Because she asked, Megge. You would have fed them all had they but come to you. The blacksmith—"

"Colluen," I said, remembering my former pupil's name.

"Aye, Megge. Colluen." Her voice carried her satisfaction. "Colluen knew you would share what you had and then starve alongside them, so he fed their fears and planted suspicion. When the last infant died and they put you to the stake, he returned to our round-house and stole your writings."

"For their power," I said.

Morwen nodded. "Aye. When he was your apprentice, he gleaned enough from your teachings to make his way back to the living world. But before he could learn how to craft his own destiny, you dismissed him. And when he killed you and stole your writings, Anwen—you knew her in this life as Aleydis—hunted him down and lodged an arrow in his heart.

"When she returned with the plank and the hide, I brought to mind every word I had ever heard at your knee, taught her your symbols, and she inscribed them on vellum. Two books we created—one that held the wisdom of the celestial world, *The Book of Time*, and one that held the knowledge of the physical plane."

"*The Book of Seasons*," I said.

"One with the plank for its cover, and the other with the hide.

"As Anwen and I worked, we were guided. Each line we wrote, we soon realized, was an incantation that summoned a spirit possessed of great knowledge or wisdom. When we came to understand the power the books had amassed—the power to sustain life and call forth the Mentors—we spoke the very first incantation you had taught me—*Scientia nupta sapientia potestas est*—and summoned Murga herself.

"The great seer told Anwen, 'Etch in the cover of *The Book of Time* an image of what you saw the day I died.' Then to both of us she said, 'Protect the power that sustains the Mentors and guide the books into the hands of those destined to increase the knowledge and wisdom of the world until the time comes for me to return. You'll know when that day comes, for it is you who shall call me back.'

"Knowing that the writings must never again come together in the hands of one such as the blacksmith, Anwen and I separated them. She returning to the western cliffs with *The Book of Seasons*, and I remaining at Bury Down with *The Book of Time*.

"The wise Anwen became the wife of a man of the sea and passed the book to her own daughter, charging her to pass it to her own heirs until Anwen herself would carry it back to Bury Down.

"Anwen returned to Bury Down when we were very old, and we passed together into eternity. For a thousand years, we have guided the books from apprentice to apprentice, and heir to heir, until we could place them in your hands."

I saw the young Bryluen and the intrepid Anwen—my aunts Morwen and Aleydis, companions to the very end—and I heard Claris weep when Aleydis died. *We owe her everything, Megge. One day, you'll come to know who your great-aunt truly was.*

"But Colluen the Blacksmith, who murdered Murga, still craves her power," I said, still unable to call myself by the name of the ancient seer. "It is his whisper that taunts me."

"Aye. The blacksmith's spirit still abides in the ether, though through the centuries he has found many a kindred soul in the living world. Even now, he—"

I held up a hand to silence Morwen so I could think. *Kindred soul in the living world.* The words brought back both Claris's story of her ill-fated love—*He was no ordinary blacksmith . . . he only wanted my book*—and the last words I heard Jenifer Penneck speak. *This man is no abbot! He is not even a friar. I know him. He is my—*

He was her brother. The imposter abbot—Jenifer Penneck's brother, Agnes Gough's son—was Michael Gough, Claris's first love.

Colluen the Blacksmith—and his kindred—were still at large.

I looked down at *The Book of Time* and *The Book of Seasons* lying side-by-side on the table and recalled that day in Restormel's kitchen when Claris had wept with torment at the thought the abbot had taken the books.

I stretched my hands over *The Book of Seasons*. The room suddenly became very warm, then stifling, until it felt as if the air were being sucked from it. I struggled to breathe.

Show me my path, I silently asked the Mentors.

— *Isa*, came a cracking voice. *Quartus. Was. Aquila.*

I held my breath. Already I had spoken the incantation. The words had lifted the veil between the ether and the living world, the past and the present. But what would happen—what would I become—when Murga herself spoke the final word?

Mister Gynneys had said that Atropos cuts the string of life. Was that what I would then do? Would I become a murderer? Would I murder Michael Gough?

Heat began to rise from the book. I lifted my hands, drawing them slowly away. Why had Murga gone silent? Why would she not speak the final word?

Murderer. The growl carried the acrid reek of the abbot. I covered my mouth to muffle a scream and looked around. The room was silent, and I was alone. The Mentors had gone.

Murga was waiting for *me* to speak the final word, I realized.

Atropos, I thought. *She cuts the string.*

Another famine was coming. Morwen had said so. With it, I realized, would come the chance to make amends. To stand alongside Claris and Brighida as a woman of Bury Down and stem the tide of suffering for the people of this land. There was but one thing to do.

Taking a breath, I closed my eyes and lowered my hand to *The Book of Seasons.*

"Atropos."

As the word left my lips, I felt my spirit clip the string that had given life to the blacksmith's whisper, the string of fear that for so long had bound me to a ghost. Resolve pounded through my veins like molten iron. Recalling my rash vow to Claris—*I will unite knowledge and wisdom*—I called out to the Mentors.

"I swear to protect *The Book of Time* and *The Book of Seasons* and preserve for the Mentors the power that sustains their spirits forever in the books."

Chapter 38

I listened for Morwen's voice—or for Mother's or Gytha's—to welcome me into the company of the Mentors, finally a woman of Bury Down, and set me on my new path as protector of the books, as protector of the people of this land. But the ether was silent.

Had I misunderstood? Was there another vow I was meant to speak? Had I not been accepted into their company? Had I been found wanting?

"Morwen?" I called out. "Mother?"

Silence.

Claris. I had to go to Claris. She could tell me what had happened, what had robbed me of my moment of communion with the Mentors. I opened the cottage door and looked outside. It was still dark, the moon so high in the sky she looked little larger than the head of a pin.

Picking up Morwen's lantern, I left the books on the table and made my way to the lodge. Claris and Brighida, tired from their long walk to the village, would surely be sleeping, but I was certain they would want to learn that I had spoken my vow and chosen the path of protector.

They would want to learn?

What was I thinking? They were seers. Even before they left for the village that morning, they had known what was meant to happen this night. If nothing had befallen them, they would have been at my side as I spoke my vow. Claris would have draped me in the seer's crimson cape and welcomed me as a woman of Bury Down.

Suddenly chilled to the marrow, I ran down the hill, tripping over rocks and sliding on wet grass, my heart pounding, my throat tight.

The door to the lodge was closed. Out of breath, I leaned hard on it until it opened, and I looked inside. All the pallets were still neat, the blankets and hides untouched. The candle in my lantern was now just a stub, but its faltering flame showed me I was utterly alone.

Perhaps they had met a traveler, I told myself. Someone ill, someone who needed their help. Perhaps they had stayed with Dora Tucker. But hope failed me, and it was too dark to search for them now. They had traveled through the forest; I would never find them in this black night.

My breath caught. Natalje had spoken of darkness, of peril. What was it she said?

"Natalje." I closed my eyes tightly and begged. "Help me to remember your words so that I might find Claris and Brighida, for I fear for them."

My breathing slowed, and my pounding heart quieted as a voice filled me, a voice as soft as a dream and gentle as a caress.

As you take your first steps into a new life, remember this. You are not alone—never alone—child. The path we take to fulfill our vow often leads us into darkness and peril, but when yours does, you may trust in the kinship of the Mentors.

As Natalje's words faded, I basked for a moment in the comfort of her voice. Then my heart began to pound again and my breath to quicken. That had not been Natalje's voice. That had been Claris's.

Claris—

Claris was amongst the Mentors.

I called on the sight.

"*Scientia nupta sapientia potestas est.*"

In the candle's dying flame I saw Brighida standing in a moonlit copse, stunned, her mother sprawled at her feet.

"Aunt Claris!"

The flame went out.

I opened the lantern and huffed as softly as I could upon the tip of the wick, but the ember had died. Stretching out my arms, I searched the blackness of the cave and through gritted teeth demanded, "Show me more."

Murderer, came a whisper, and in my mind's eye I saw a hooded figure slip away into the woods, leaving Brighida weeping over her mother's body.

The molten iron pulsing through my veins went cold, and I called into the night, "Darkness and peril is it to be, then?"

I patted the floor alongside my pallet, rage soaking into my bones as I searched blindly for a candle and for Mother's fire kit. Finding a fresh taper, I set it into the lantern and lit it, hands trembling, then tried to slow my breathing and force myself to remember the path I had chosen. Protector, not murderer. Protector. *Protector.*

I repeated the word until I felt I could trust my voice, and then I spoke quietly to the Mentors, whose silence told me they were welcoming my aunt into their midst.

"I shall find Claris's body," I promised. "I shall bring her home and give her the honors due a woman of Bury Down." My voice shook again with fury and grief as I thought of my murdered aunt. *I will not allow rage to consume me. I will not allow it to alter my path.*

I gritted my teeth, calming myself by speaking only to my aunt. "And then, Aunt Claris, I shall take the path—"

Before I could finish, a face began to take shape in the shadows—a man's face, contorted with fury—and I locked gazes with Murga's onetime apprentice.

"Murderer," whispered Colluen the Blacksmith. And then he smiled.

Lust for vengeance thickened my blood. Fists clenched as if to strike a blow, I shouted, "You seek a reckoning, Blacksmith?"

Scientia nupta sapientia—

Morwen's voice, tinged with warning, stopped me. A host of Mentors joined their voices to hers until I could hardly hear my own thoughts.

Scientia nupta sapientia . . . Over and over they chanted as the power of Bury Down rose from the ether, settled over me, and took root within me. I thought of Morwen and Aleydis, who had protected the books in order to pass their power to me. So I could use it to protect—

"To hell with you, Witch," came the voice at my ear. "Give me the books and I will spare you."

"Spare me?"

Scientia nupta sapientia . . . The chant rose to a crescendo.

"I am Megge of Bury Down," I called out. "Who are you to spare me?"

The chant went silent.

"The books are mine, Blacksmith. And you have no power over me."

Potestas est, came one brittle voice.

Murga's words hung in the air for a very long time. When they had faded, I realized that both the blacksmith and the Mentors had gone. I was alone.

And I had work to do.

I went to the door and looked out. The air was still, the night sky clear. I picked up my lantern and left the lodge. In this last hour before dawn, I would prepare the workroom to receive the body of my beloved aunt. I would give Alf the dreadful news and ask him to send Hugh and Martyn to the copse with the cart. I would find and comfort my cousin.

And I will protect her.

My rage hardened into resolve that grew stronger with each step across the pasture on my way to the cottage.

There was no time to take the newly woven cloth from the loom, so I took a length of soft fabric from the basket beside the loom, folded it, and laid it on the long workroom table. I looked out the door. The sky was going pink. It was time.

She's been out there all night, I thought. *Frightened. Suffering. Grieving.* Picking up a loaf of bread and a jug of ale, I closed the door behind me and set out for the copse.

"Yes," I affirmed as I neared the woods. "I will see to Claris and Brighida."

And then, Blacksmith, I will see to you.

Characters

Adaem: (*Ah-dehm´*): Captain of *The Navigator*. From Aldestowe.
> Husband of Gytha of Bury Down
> Father of Natalje
> Grandfather of Claris and "Mother"
> Great-grandfather of Megge and Brighida

Agnes Gough: (Agnes *Goff*): Conjurer
> Mother of Michael and Jenifer
> Grandmother of Harold, Vivienne, and Gwyneth Penneck

Aleydis: (*Ah-lee´-dis*): huntress. From Aldestowe.
> Daughter of Beatrix Couper. Sister of Arjen
> Aunt of Claris and "Mother"
> Great-aunt of Brighida and Megge

Alf: Shepherd and shearer

Anwen: Huntress. From Tintagel
> Scribe and protector of the writings of Murga

Arjen: Stonemason, builder, artist. From Aldestowe
> Former holder of *The Book of Seasons*
> Son of Beatrix Couper. Brother of Aleydis
> Husband of Natalje
> Father of Claris and "Mother"
> Grandfather of Megge and Brighida

Beatrix Couper: Midwife and conjurer
> Mother of Arjen and Aleydis
> Grandmother of Megge and Brighida
> Sister of Egbert Couper ("Roon")

Brighida: (*Bri-gee´-dah*): Apprentice seer
> Heir to *The Book of Time*
> Daughter of Claris, cousin of Megge

Bryluen: (*Bree-loo´-en*)
> Apprentice to Murga

Gregory Carver: Master carpenter
Husband of Claris

Claris: Seer of Bury Down, Holder of *The Book of Time*
Mother of Brighida
Twin sister of "Mother"
Aunt of Megge
Widow of Gregory Carver

Colluen: (*Cah-loo´-en*): Blacksmith.
Rejected apprentice to Murga, the Seer of Bury Down

Dora Tucker: Shopkeeper
Wife of Gus

Edmund, Second Earl of Cornwall (reign: 1272-1300)
Husband of Margaret de Clare, Countess of Cornwall

Egbert Couper ("Rudh"):
Brother of Beatrix
Uncle of Arjen and Aleydis

Elizabeth: Lady-in-waiting to Lady Margaret

Francis Penneck: Carter
Husband of Jenifer Gough
Father of Tinker, Harold, and Gwyneth

Gregory Carver: Master carpenter
Deceased husband of Claris

Gus Tucker: Weaver, tucker, wool merchant
Husband of Dora
Gwyneth Penneck:
Daughter of Francis and Jenifer Penneck
Sister of Harold and Vivienne
Half-sister of Tinker

Gytha: Seer of Bury Down, former holder of *The Book of Time*
Wife of Adaem
Mother of Natalje
Grandmother of Claris and "Mother"
Great-grandmother of Megge and Brighida

Harold Penneck: Assistant carter
    Son of Francis and Jenifer Gough Penneck
    Brother of Vivienne and Gwyneth
    Half-brother of Tinker

Hugh Caerlin: Herder
    Son of Lowenna
    Brother of Martyn

Jenifer Gough Penneck:
    Daughter of Agnes Gough, sister of Michael Gough
    Second wife of Francis Penneck
    Mother of Harold, Vivienne, and Gwyneth Penneck
    Step-mother of Tinker Penneck

Mister Kendall: Surgeon at Restormel Castle

Mister Gynneys: Herder, shearer
    Father of Alf

Lowenna Caerlin: Homemaker
    Mother of Hugh and Martyn

Margaret, Countess of Cornwall: Wife of Edmund,
    Second Earl of Cornwall

Martyn Caerlin: Weaver
    Son of Lowenna
    Brother of Hugh

Megge: (*Meggie*): herder, shearer, apprentice weaver
    Heir to *The Book of Seasons*
    Daughter of "Mother"
    Niece of Claris, Cousin of Brighida

Michael Gough: (Michael *Goff):* Blacksmith
    Son of Agnes and Robert Gough
    Brother of Jenifer Gough Penneck

Morwen: Bard and shearer

"Mother": Healer of Bury Down, Holder of *The Book of Seasons*
    Mother of Megge
    Sister of Claris, aunt of Brighida

No first name. Called *Mistress, Mother, Sister, Aunt, Niece*

Widow of stone mason

Murga: First Seer of Bury Down

Natalje: (*Nă-tal´-ee*)

Former holder of *The Book of Time*

Wife of Arjen

Mother of Claris and her unnamed twin sister ("Mother")

Grandmother of Megge and Brighida

Trelawney, Nellie: shopkeeper, wife of the village potter

Polly Pounfrect: Governess at Restormel Castle

Richard, First Earl of Cornwall (reign: 1257-1272)

Son of John, King of England

Father of Edmund, Second Earl of Cornwall

Robert Angwin: Stone mason

Robert Gough (*Goff*): Blacksmith

Deceased husband of Agnes Gough

Father of Michael Gough

Tinker Penneck:

Son of Francis Penneck and Francis's first wife (deceased)

Half-brother of Harold and Gwyneth Penneck

Vivienne Penneck:

Daughter of Jenifer Penneck

Vitale Magor: artist (deceased). Former holder of *The Book of Seasons*

Father of Arjen

Husband of Beatrix Couper

Acknowledgments

Julie, Richard, and Tia Tamblyn provided gracious hospitality during my research visits and taught me about the ancient Bury Down hillfort and the history of Botelet, the manor in its shadow, present in Megge's day and listed in the Domesday Survey of 1086.

Mary Jones—historian, writer, Chair of the Old Cornwall Society, and docent for the town of Lostwithiel—provided illuminating details on Restormel Castle and life in thirteenth-century Cornwall, and held my feet to the fire when my early drafts went awry.

Church historian Carole Vivian took me to churches and sacred sites throughout Cornwall, teaching me about pre-Christian Cornwall and the role of the Church in medieval life.

Beta readers Peggy DiPastina, Jacqui Doran, Cindy Duda, and Mary Jones read the early drafts and offered the suggestions and questions that moved the story along to the next draft. Author Boman Desai and editor Vinnie Kinsella helped me polish the manuscript for submission, and Zumaya editor Elizabeth Burton provided additional edits that enriched the story.

Tamian Wood created this gorgeous cover art and interior design and was infinitely patient and kind.

To all of you, my deepest appreciation.

And to David, Buster, Cassie, Princess, Samantha, Grace, Annie, Kate, and Marigold ~ my thanks and love for this charmed life we share.

— Rebecca

About the Author

Rebecca Kightlinger holds an MFA in creative writing from the University of Southern Maine's Stonecoast MFA program. The full-time writer of the *Bury Down Chronicles* series, she studies medieval medicine, Anglo Saxon wortcraft, the arts and manuscripts of the mystical healers, and the history of Cornwall. She travels to Cornwall, England to carry out on-site research for each new book.

About the Editor

Vinnie Kinsella is an editor and book publishing specialist from the Pacific Northwest. His work with books began when he and his second-grade classmates wrote and illustrated a story about the adventures of an ice-cream-loving giraffe. Years later, he earned his master's degree in writing and publishing from Portland State University. He has since helped hundreds of authors and publishers release quality books into the world. For more information about Vinnie's work, visit vinniekinsella.com.

About the Poet

Award-winning feminist poet **Annie Finch** is known for mesmerizing performances and deep, holistic expertise in poetic craft. Annie's most recent books include *The Poetry Witch Little Book of Spells* and *A Poet's Craft: A Comprehensive Guide to Making and Sharing Your Poetry*. Based in Washington DC, she travels to perform her work and offers online classes for poets & seekers. She can be found on line at www.anniefinch.com.

About the Designer

Tamian Wood, born near Oxford England, is currently living and working in her cozy lake front office in North Florida. Using art, photography, typography and digital collage techniques, she creates book covers that sell, in a variety of genres. She works with several publishers and a growing number of indie authors. Her most famous client to date is Pope Francis, whose Encyclical Letter, won first place for cover design. She holds degrees in Computer Science and Graphic Design Technology, and is a proud member of Phi Theta Kappa National Honour Society. She can be reached at Tamian@BeyondDesignBooks.com, www.BeyondDesignBooks.com

About the Audiobook Narrator

Jan Cramer is a London born actress trained at The Central School of Speech and Drama and has worked in Theatre, TV, Film, and Radio. Now a very busy voice over artist and award winning Audiobook Narrator, Jan is proud to have narrated over 100 audiobooks. She has enjoyed every single one of them. Find her online at:
www.voiceannouncements.com

Excerpt from
THE LADY OF THE CLIFFS
Book two in the Goddess Trilogy

CHAPTER 1

AUGUST 1285
BURY DOWN, CORNWALL

First light had yet to find its way through the dense alder canopy when I stepped into the copse to search for Brighida. I wanted to call out, but this little wood, now a place of death, felt sacred, so I whispered her name as I picked my way along its winding path.

"Here, Megge." My cousin's voice came to me from just around the next turn. I found her sitting on the ground shivering in her thin summer tunic. Mud caked her hair, dotted her face, and appeared to have been splashed over her arm, her hand, her nails. The still form of her mother lay on the ground beside her covered by Brighida's cloak. My cousin leaned over and tucked a loose edge of it under her mother's hip.

"Brighida . . ." I dropped my stick and the bundle I carried, took off my cloak, and wrapped it around her.

"What happened here?" I wrapped my arms around her to stop her trembling, then touched her cheek to brush away a speck of mud.

I rubbed it between my finger and thumb. That wasn't mud. I touched the hood that covered Claris's face. Black and sticky, it felt as if someone had soaked it in tar.

"Brighida." A chill crawled up my spine. "What happened here?"

She stared into the trees, her eyes dull. "We were on our way home. We had sold all the fleece and were talking about the things we could buy. 'A horse,' Mother had said. 'Perhaps a cart.' And then he—" She looked at me now with the eyes of a child awakening from a nightmare.

"The imposter abbot—" she lifted her arm as if pulling a great cowl over her head. "The blacksmith, Michael Gough. He stepped out from between the trees, put an arm around her neck and jerked it, then dropped her to the ground.

"He said something to me . . ." She seemed to search my eyes for the memory, but then gave up. "I just stood there staring. I, a seer of Bury Down, had seen—could see—nothing."

She still hadn't blinked.

"Brighida?"

"It was dark when it happened. We had stayed in the village too long." She looked with sorrow at her mother. Then, as if seeking comfort, looked back up at me. "Tell me, Megge, did you feel it when her spirit left her? Did you know? Is that how you knew to come for me?"

I shook my head. "I knew only after the Mentors had welcomed her into the ether." *After I had spoken my vow,* I thought but did not say. We would talk of that later. "A vision came to me. Of you . . . here . . . with her."

I reached out to touch bluish fingertips visible at the edge of that sodden cloak.

"Leave her, Megge." She tucked them under the cloak.

"But why? Why can I not see her?"

"Go." Though her voice was firm, her heavy-lidded eyes, pink-rimmed and shot with red, betrayed her fatigue. "I will tend to my mother." She wiped her nose on her sleeve. "You'll help me . . . later . . .

put her to rest in the grove. But for now, I must be the one to care for her. You couldn't possibly understand. But you must go."

"Already I've sent Alf for Martyn and Hugh. They'll be here soon with the cart. Can't I wait with you?"

She shook her head. "You'll be tired, Megge. A vowtaking is a serious matter. You'll not have slept."

"You knew?"

She smiled as gently as her mother might have. "Of course I knew. I was with you in spirit."

"Why, then, will you not let me see her?"

I too am now a woman of Bury Down, I thought, wanting to pull out my hair. Why can I still not see my cousin's heart or read her thoughts as she can mine?

"They'll be here soon, Megge. Please. Go back to the cottage. Prepare a place for her in the workroom. That long table—"

"The table is ready."

"Please, Megge." She was weeping now, the sound so strange that I realized I had rarely heard her cry. Not when her legs had been burned and her arm destroyed, nor when Morwen and Aleydis had died, nor even when my mother had been killed. Had she wept alone? Had my own grief kept me from noticing hers?

But I saw it now. And I knew that, at that moment, Brighida was not the seer of Bury Down. She was just a girl who had lost her mother. She was seeing only the horror that had befallen them both, something so awful she had to hide it even from me. But who else could help her now? She had no one left but me.